P9-DDD-453

4 Years Trapped in My Mind Palace

Johan Twiss

Twiss Publishing, Copyright © 2016
by Johan Twiss
All rights reserved.

Editor: Heather Monson
Cover Design: Johan Twiss & Micah Wardell
Proofreader: Kent Meyers

No part of this book may be reproduced in any format or in any medium without the written permission of the author. This is a work of fiction. The characters, names, incidents, places, and dialogue are products of the author's imagination, and are not to be construed as real, or are used fictitiously. Any resemblance to actual persons, living or dead, or actual events is purely coincidental.

ISBN-10: 1520110529

ISBN-13: 978-1520110523

DEDICATION

To Aaron Grant, for listening to me ramble about this story when it was only an idea trapped in my mind palace.

4/24/2021

for Charlotte
Happy 14th birthday
♡
Bubbe

CHAPTER 1
STRIKE OUT

It's been two years since I received my life sentence of imprisonment. I only know it's been two years because Mom and Dad came to wish me happy birthday.

My mom brushed back my red hair—which was desperately in need of a haircut and approaching the length of long girly hair—and squeezed my hand. She smelled like the flowery lavender laundry detergent she always used, making me miss home even more.

"Happy fourteenth birthday, son," she said softly, still squeezing my hand.

I wanted to squeeze back, but couldn't. I saw the shiny beginnings of a tear form in her blue eyes, but she quickly pulled them back with a blink.

"Yeah, happy birthday, Aaron," Dad said solemnly. The man smelled like chlorine and stood off to the side where I couldn't see him. He avoided eye contact with me as if I were Medusa and would turn him to stone. In reality, I felt like one of Medusa's statues— trapped.

I learned about Medusa in sixth grade English class. That was over two years ago, and I've never been back to school since. I will probably never go back. It's strange to admit, but I miss school...a lot. I miss having friends, playing sports and reading books.

3

But you know what I miss the most? I miss playing trombone in the jazz band. Now, that was freedom. I didn't even know what jazz was when the Ygnacio Valley Elementary band director assigned me to play trombone.

He handed me the bright brass instrument with the long U-shaped slide and said, "Sorry, the saxophones are all taken. I need you to learn to play this." And learn I did. Playing the trombone just seemed natural, like the slide was an extension of my arm and the bell was a megaphone to the melodies playing in my head. At eleven, I was invited to join the Glenbrook Middle School Jazz Band, even though I was still in elementary school. We placed second in the state competition at Disneyland. But that was my last year in the band. Those were the days. *Freedom.*

My mom stroked my red hair again, pulling me out of my thoughts and back to reality.

"Sorry, we can't stay long," she said, bending over me to position her face a foot away from mine. Her long gray hair was pulled up in a tight bun, and the creases around her deep blue eyes had grown larger over the last two years.

Dad walked into view and flipped through the five channels available on the old black and white television in my room. The man looked like an aging Latino movie star, with broad shoulders, regal patches of gray on the sides of his jet black hair, and a perfect bronze complexion. Somehow I missed those genes, with my red hair, freckles, and skin that burned within five minutes of exposure to the sun. But I'll probably never sunburn again. At least that's a plus.

The reception *was* horrible on the old television. I didn't care though, since I could never change the channels or do anything about it.

"We're going to a work party tonight," Mom said, trying to keep up the one-way conversation. "Your father made pool salesman of the year! They're going to award him a nice bonus and a free trip to Hawaii. Isn't that exciting!?"

So that's why he's so tan. Spending all summer outside selling pools in California would do it. His success didn't surprise me. Dad had always been a smooth talker and a driven worker. Before my imprisonment, we would spend hours doing projects together, like building my old tree house, and he would tell me funny stories about growing up on the family farm in Colorado. According to my mom, Dad really threw himself into his work over the last year, ever since my incarceration began.

Dad continued fiddling with the TV antenna, slapping the side of it as he swore under his breath. He pushed and prodded the V-shaped rods, attempting to get a clearer picture of the Giants baseball game, and turned up the volume to compensate for the poor picture. The voice of the announcer boomed from the TV.

It's the bottom of the ninth and Will Clark is up to bat for the San Francisco Giants on this warm and breezy Saturday here at Candlestick Park. The Dodgers lead the Giants 3-to-1 with runners on second and third with two outs. The Giants' all-star, Will the Thrill, has a chance to tie up the game with a base hit.

"Linda, he doesn't care," my dad called to her. "The boy can't even hear you."

"You don't know that!" my mom shot back with a piercing glare. "I wish you would talk to him more. It's his birthday for heaven's sake! You can't even talk to your own son on his birthday, can you, Robert? You're paying more attention to that old TV and a stupid baseball game than to your own flesh and blood!"

Low outside fastball on the corner of the plate. Strike 1, the announcer called.

My dad stopped playing with the antenna and looked up from the TV. "Linda, don't start this again!"

His gaze met mine for a moment before he turned his head away and broke the eye contact. Dad bowed his head toward the ground, his body frozen. *Maybe I am Medusa.*

A hard line drive down the third base line…and it's landed foul. Foul ball. Strike 2.

"I…I," Dad stuttered. "Oh, Linda, I can't do this."

Throwing his hands in the air, I watched him turn away, shoulders slumped, and stomp out of view. His footsteps echoed in the long hallway outside my room.

My mom harrumphed. "That man drives me crazy! Crazy I tell you! Oh, Aaron. Don't let him get to you. I want you to know he loves you. We both do. This…change…it's just hard on him."

Hard on him! What about me?

"We love you, Aaron. We are going to be gone the next two weeks in Hawaii as part of the vacation Dad's company is giving us. Your father needs a vacation, and this will be good for him. We will come back and see you when we return. Happy birthday, son."

As their footsteps left my room, so did the smells of chlorine and lavender. The clock was in my line of sight and I quickly calculated how long my parents had stayed this time. Eight minutes, thirty-two seconds. I sighed in my mind. Not only were they visiting less, but their visits were getting shorter and shorter.

Will Clark takes his time entering the batter's box. The count is 0 balls and 2 strikes. Here's the windup, and the pitch. Swing and a miss on a hard slider, low and away. Strike 3 and that's the ballgame, folks.

I wonder if eventually they will just stop visiting.

***

My cruel incarceration is due to the cursed rope swing in the murky waters of Dingleberry Creek. You'd think, with a name like Dingleberry, I would have known better. That's where I sealed my fate two years ago.

It was a scorching July afternoon in Bradley, California. Never heard of Bradley? Well, you wouldn't be the first. It was also my last day in Bradley before my family moved from the farmland of central Cal to a city in the Bay Area called Concord. My dad got a new sales job with a pool company, and despite my constant protests, we were moving.

My best friends, Mike and Leon, planned to give me one last adventure around our small town. We rode our bikes off the massive dirt ramps we built in an abandoned field and then played basketball in the park. To cool down, we stopped at the corner store for a slushy and finished the day flying from the rope swing into the old swimming hole at Dingleberry Creek.

Good times.

Three days later I was in a new city, with zero friends, celebrating my twelfth birthday while lying on a hospital gurney, unable to move a muscle.

The docs did everything they could to help and transferred me to San Francisco General Hospital to see a specialist. They stuck me with needle after needle, ran test after test, and scanned my brain. Nothing they did made me any better.

"We believe your son has a rare form of Cryptococcal Meningitis," Dr. McPhearson, the specialist, had told my parents. Doc McPhearson was young, with a short pig nose and a bushy brown mustache that attempted to hide his prominent nostrils.

"Has Aaron spent significant time at the base of eucalyptus trees, or does he regularly ingest dirt heavily soiled with bird droppings?" he asked my parents.

Seriously? I mean, what kind of questions are those?

Why, yes, doctor! Our son's favorite snack is bird poo mixed with a little dirt and he loves to swing like a koala bear from the forest of eucalyptus trees in our backyard.

This is why I like to call him Dr. Idiot.

Confused by Dr. Idiot's odd questions, my parents simply answered, "No."

But the doc's question told me exactly where I picked up my meningitis. It was Dingleberry Creek. Some genius had planted a bunch of eucalyptus trees around the swimming hole and the trees attracted a lot of birds. My guess is I ingested something in the water and got whammied. But I had no way to tell them this.

I remember thinking, "Maybe Dr. Idiot isn't so stupid after all. He was smart enough to diagnose me correctly." But then he continued to speak and shot that theory out the window.

"Mr. and Mrs. Greenburg. I must be honest," Dr. Idiot continued. "I am obligated to tell you that your son is as good as dead. He is completely unresponsive and in a vegetative state. We highly doubt he can hear or even recognize you and that the meningitis has caused severe and irreparable brain damage."

Wait. What did he say?

NOOOOOOO!!!!

I'M HERE!

I CAN HEAR YOU!

MOM.

DAD.

DON'T LISTEN TO DR. IDIOT!

But it was no use. What could I do? They couldn't hear me and I couldn't even control my eyes or eyelids to get their attention. They moved involuntarily, as did my bowels. Gross, I know. All I could do was listen and stare straight ahead, trapped for life.

My parents tried to care for me at home, but after three months, they couldn't handle it anymore. They were too old and too busy to provide the full-time care I required. Plus, the stress of the situation led to arguments between the two, and I heard every single shouting match. It made me sick to know I was causing their fights. I know it's not my fault, but it still makes me sick. It's really Dingleberry Creek's fault. Did I mention I hate Dingleberry Creek? If not, then know that I do—a lot.

Moving on...

I mentioned that my parents are old, and they really are. I'm an only child, "a surprise gift from God," my mom would say. They tried for years to have children of their own and resigned themselves to the fact it would never happen, until my mom miraculously became pregnant at the age of forty-six. That makes her sixty now, and my dad is sixty-one. I wasn't lying when I said they were ancient.

But now their 'surprise gift from God,' me, had turned their life upside down a second time. I could hardly blame them when they agreed to move me out of the house to live in the Restwood Suites Senior Care Center a few miles away in the neighboring city of Walnut Creek. The manager at Restwood agreed to admit me, even though I was still a minor. Plus, their rates were reasonable, or so I heard as my parents discussed it.

The food and entertainment, on the other hand, are highly suspect. I get fed through a tube in my stomach, but whatever they are putting through that tube makes my stomach turn like Benedict Arnold. I learned about him in school, too.

The food gives me awful gas pains, and when my body pushes out the gas, I can't even move to get away from it or blame it on anyone else. Awful, I know.

During the first few weeks at Restwood, there was no entertainment whatsoever. All day I just faced the wall in front of my bed and stared at this painting of a bowl of fruit on a table. After hours upon hours of endless boredom, I felt myself edging to the brink of insanity.

Then one day, it all changed. Somehow, I pulled the painting with the fruit into this new world created in my head—a place I like to call my mind palace.

It was a giant castle surrounded by green rolling fields, bordered by a dense, dark forest. Here in the palace, the fruit would come to life and we would embark on wild adventures, fighting off human-sized attacking ants, saving the world from spider robots, and racing Corvettes through the dirt roads of the palace grounds.

I explored every inch of the palace with the help of the fruit—at least as much of it as possible. Though most of the castle stayed the same, with a throne room, banquet hall, kitchen and armory, other parts were always changing, like the north clock tower. No matter what we tried, we could never find a passageway that led to the tallest tower of the palace.

But after one particularly long adventure trying to make our way to the north tower while simultaneously fighting off an invading force of purple alien cows, I was absolutely starving and could not help but eat my friends—Mr. Apple, Orange, and Banana. I ate the fruit slowly, savoring each juicy bite and remembering the sweet tastes of these fruits I could no longer eat. After finishing the snack, I couldn't bring the painting back into my mind palace again. I felt too guilty for eating my friends.

Luckily, a well-meaning nurse, Nurse Penny, donated an old black and white TV for my room. All the other rooms had regular color TV's, or so Nurse Penny told me, but the Restwood manager decided to save money and not put one in my room since I was supposedly brain dead.

Cheapskate.

Since the reception was bad on the old TV, Nurse Penny brought a movie from home and hooked up a VHS player so I could watch something without static.

Unfortunately, she only brought one video with two home recorded episodes of *Sesame Street* from 1976. C'mon Nurse Penny, it's 1987! *Top Gun*, *Short Circuit* and *Karate Kid 2* all came out on video last year. If you could bring me one of those that would be totally awesome! And I keep seeing grainy commercials for a movie called the *Princess Bride*.

Sigh. Well, sigh in my mind since I can't sigh out loud.

I'll never see any of those movies. Instead I will be subjected to the same episodes of *Sesame Street*, every morning, for the rest of my life.

I tell you what. If I hear another thunderclap, and The Count says, "*fourteen potato chips, AH-AH-AH,*" one more time, I may have to pull him into my mind palace and punch him in the face fourteen times, *AH-AH-AH.*

CHAPTER 2
SOLOMON THE GREAT

I heard Barry Jackson humming a tune down the hallway and smelled the scent of pine cleaner as he entered my room. Barry was the janitor and one of the few African-American employees at Restwood. I always heard him whistling or humming a tune as he walked the hallway, and the man was quick with a friendly smile. Plus, he actually talked to me like I was a human being. His visits and our pseudo conversations were one of the few highlights of my week.

"Guess what, Aaron old-buddy old-pal?" Barry asked in his husky voice as he moved in and out of my view, mopping the floor.

What, Barry? I said to myself.

As if he could read my mind, he answered back.

"You're getting a roomie today. A new man is moving in by the name of Solomon Felsher. He's a little…" Barry leaned his head back into my view, let out a whistle, and waved his finger in a circle around his ear. "But he used to be a famous jazz musician. I actually have one of his records from back in the day. Man almighty, that cat can play the sax. I wonder if he'll sign my record for me?"

Great, I'm going to have a crazy old guy next to me now. That's kinda cool he's a jazz musician, but I hope he doesn't snore.

"Hopefully he doesn't snore," Barry said.

Yeah, that's what I just said.

"My wife snores like a freight train. Drives me nuts." Barry stopped mopping the floor and paused in front of me. His bright smile faded as he knitted his brow, causing deep wrinkles to form along the dark chocolate forehead below his bald scalp.

"I honestly don't know if I can take it anymore. My wife and her snoring, that is. I may start sleeping on the couch, but if I do, I know it's going to upset her. I told her she was snoring, but she don't believe me. She just thinks I want to sleep on the couch so I can sneak away at night. Lord knows why? We been married twenty-eight long years! I love the woman, don't get me wrong, but sometimes she's straight-up crazy…and bossy. Sometimes I wonder why I stay with her, now that all our kids are grown and out of the house."

Barry paused and looked me in the eye. "What do you think, Aaron?"

People do this to me all the time. For some reason they feel compelled to share their life problems and hidden secrets with me. Probably because I'm like a pet dog that can't talk back. All I can do is sit and listen, even if I don't want to.

Barry, quit complaining, I said in my head. *Life could be much worse. Trust me.*

Barry nodded and continued mopping, exiting from my line of sight as he mopped the corner of the room. "You know. That's a good idea. I'll buy me some ear plugs on the way home, and I should get her a nice bouquet of flowers. They got a lot of wildflowers growin' out back in the garden. Maybe I'll sneak back there after my shift and snag her some. You won't tell nobody, will you Aaron?" Barry said with a wink.

Ha, very funny.

Barry moved his mop back and forth across the room, coming in and out of my view. He finished mopping the last corner and headed for the door.

"Thanks again for listening," he said before exiting. "And don't go surprising us by getting up and walking just yet, the floor's mighty slippery. See you next week, Aaron."

Check you later, Barry.

After Barry left, the smell of pine cleaner lingered in the room as I waited for Nurse Penny to arrive, check my vitals, and turn on *Sesame Street*. But, for some reason, she was late, which never happened.

Bored, I played one of my favorite pastimes that I like to call, "Clock Watch." Basically I stare at the clock and let it put me into a trance.

Tick, Tock, Tick, Tock, Tick, Tock, Tick, Tock, Tick, Tock, Tick, Tock...

Sometimes I will pull the clock into my mind palace where it's mounted half-way up the side of the north tower of the castle, kind of like Big Ben in London. Then I ride the minute hand around in circles like a Ferris wheel. And if I'm feeling really crazy I will jump onto the second hand and hold on tight as it blasts around in a circle. Now, that's an adrenaline rush.

The clock finally reached 9 a.m., which meant Nurse Penny was officially thirty minutes late. I pulled my mind out of "Clock Watch," wondering if anyone was going to check on me today, when I was greeted by the sounds of a man yelling down the hallway.

"I don't need a wheelchair. I know how to walk. Who is this kibitzer anyways?" the male voice yelled. He had a distinct accent. East Coast? New York, maybe?

"Relax, Dad. This is the manager, Mr. Wilson, and the charge nurse, Ms. Penny. You're going to be staying here for a while, and Mr. Wilson and his staff will take good care of you," answered a female voice that I didn't recognize.

"Oy vey, my own daughter is putting me away like an old shoe. Why don't you just leave me alone at home and let me grow old and die like an honest Jew?"

"Dad, you're not well. We've talked about this. Your dementia is getting worse, and you need constant supervision to keep you safe."

"Dementia? What dementia? I don't even know what that means. Ouch! Watch it, you schmuck! That's my foot you crashed into the doorframe. Who taught you how to drive this thing?"

"Sorry, Mr. Felsher," a nasal voice replied. "If you could just keep your feet on the wheelchair footrests, that would be helpful."

Oh, great, I thought, recognizing the nasally voice and the stale cigarette smell of Mr. Wilson, the cheapskate manager of Restwood Suites.

Luckily, the smell of peppermint, which was Nurse Penny, and two new smells of baked bread and aftershave covered the scent of Mr. Wilson as they entered my room.

"Oy! My foot hasn't been smashed that bad since Buddy Rich dropped a bass drum on it back in '63—may the man rest in peace. You know he died earlier this year. Brain tumor they said. Maybe I have a brain tumor. Maybe it's causing this *dementia* you claim I have."

"Dad, you don't have a brain tumor. They checked for that already. Remember, we've talked about this a dozen times. It's not safe for you to stay by yourself anymore. Like last week, when we found you in nothing but your bathrobe, playing saxophone in the middle of an intersection. You thought you were with Stan Getz playing at the Savoy."

Still out of my line of sight, I heard the grumpy Mr. Felsher harrumph. "That's crazy, Talia. I never played with Stan at the Savoy. But I did play with Charlie Yardbird there. We played until 4 a.m. Speaking of which, where is Betty? Don't tell me I can't bring Betty with me into this prison."

"Who's Betty?" asked Nurse Penny, puzzled.

"It's his saxophone," answered Talia. "Dad, we are going to bring your sax after you get situated. Mr. Wilson said you can play it during rec hours each day."

"Yes," answered Mr. Wilson. "I'm sure the other residents of Restwood Suites would love to hear you play in the rec hall. It's not often we get live entertainment."

I heard scuffling noises, and Mr. Felsher, who I assumed was the one who smelled like aftershave, gave a grunt and grumbled under his breath in a language I didn't recognize.

"Here, let me help you up, Mr. Felsher," Mr. Wilson offered.

I heard a quick slap of a hand. "Get your hands off me you klots! I can get up myself."

After a few prolonged grunts, Mr. Felsher seemed to give up with a sigh.

"Oy, my back is stiffer than Benny Goodman in a tuxedo. Maybe if the beautiful Nurse Penny would be willing to lend me a hand that would be okay. I could never turn down help from such a charming woman," Mr. Felsher said in a friendly voice.

"Daaad," Talia chastised through clenched teeth.

"What, I'm just complimenting a beautiful woman. Every woman deserves to be complimented. Since when did that become illegal?"

I heard Nurse Penny giggle softly, her peppermint aroma filling the air.

"I would be happy to help you, Mr. Felsher," Nurse Penny replied.

It sounded like Mr. Felsher was helped to his bed and a few seconds later, Nurse Penny came into my view to check my vitals.

"Oh, good morning, Aaron," she spoke to me softly as the rest of the intruders continued talking to each other. "You're going to have a new roommate. Oh, won't that be nice, dontcha know."

Nurse Penny smiled, creating big dimples in her plump, rosy red cheeks. I estimated she was in her late 50's, since she was always telling me about her two grandbabies—and the fact she continually dyed her graying hair a bright blond color. When I first came to Restwood Suites, it took me a while to get used to her strong Wisconsin accent. But after a few months of all the "Oh's," and "dontcha knows," it started to grow on me.

I hoped Mr. Felsher's rough accent would grow on me as well, but I had little hope.

"Leaving me already, I see," Mr. Felsher cried.

"Dad, I've got to go to work now," Talia answered. I heard the faint sound of a kiss on a cheek. "I'll come back to visit in a few weeks and bring the kids with me. We're going to see Richard in South Carolina before school starts again."

"How are you and Richard?" Mr. Felsher asked, his tone changing to a soft and caring voice.

Talia was quiet for a few seconds and ignored the question. "Love you, Dad, and behave yourself."

Mr. Felsher sighed. "Oy, you sound like my mother. Who's the parent here?"

"Goodbye, Dad."

"Goodbye, child. Be good. And I still love you, even though you've locked me up like a puppy at the pound."

"It's a pleasure to have you staying with us," Mr. Wilson's nasally voice echoed in the room. "I'll accompany your daughter to the front. There's a little more paperwork we need signed. Nurse Penny will help you get settled and she will check back on you throughout the day."

"Wonderful. You'll be my ray of sunshine, Nurse Penny."

Nurse Penny stifled another giggle and I listened as Mr. Wilson and Talia's footsteps exited down the hallway, taking the contrasting scents of baked bread and stale cigarettes with them.

"Oh, Mr. Felsher, let me introduce you to your roommate, Aaron," Nurse Penny said as she gently patted me on the head. "Oh, he's quiet as a mouse and a darling little boy, dontcha know."

First, I'm not a little boy! I'm fourteen. Second, I totally object to having a crazy old guy sleeping next to me. What if he goes all psycho and suffocates me in my sleep? This is a horrible idea.

"What's wrong with the kid?" Mr. Felsher asked Nurse Penny. "Besides his smart mouth."

Smart mouth? I can't even talk! Plus, that's rich coming from a loud-mouth like yourself. I could hear your complaining from the other end of the hallway.

Nurse Penny patted my head again, like a little puppy dog. "Oh, Aaron has a rare form of meningitis. He's basically paralyzed from head to toe. The doctors believe he's brain dead, but I'm not so sure. If you ask me, he still has that light in his eyes."

"Oy, he's not brain dead," Mr. Felsher said matter-of-factly. "He might be a smart aleck teenage punk with long girly hair and no brains—I just met him so I'm not so sure yet—but he's definitely not brain dead."

Thanks for the vote of confidence, weirdo.

"Now, now Mr. Felsher. That's not very nice to say. Aaron is a good boy and he won't bother you at all. 'N so, Aaron."

"Is that true, Aaron. Are you a good boy? If so, I apologize."

You can take your apology and blow it out your saxophone.

Mr. Felsher broke into scratchy laughter.

"I change my mind. I like the kid. He's funny."

Nurse Penny raised her eyebrow and gave Mr. Felsher a disconcerted look. I didn't blame her. Who makes fun of a paralyzed kid that can't defend himself and then calls that kid funny?

"Well, Mr. Felsher, I will be back in a few hours. There is an emergency button on the side of your bed. You just push it if you need any help."

I heard Nurse Penny leave and realized she forgot to turn on my daily dose of *Sesame Street.*

No Sesame Street today. Hooray! My prayers have been answered. There is a God!

From my side, I heard the shuffling steps of Mr. Felsher and eventually the man came into my view, bringing a stronger scent of aftershave with him. He was tall and thin, but not sickly thin, and he wore a red, flowered Hawaiian shirt and a pair of blue jeans. His hair was a mass of curly gray locks and his dark brown eyes seemed to rest upon his wide crooked nose, which had a few stray nose hairs sticking out of it like a creeping vine.

He stood straight in front of me and squinted his eyes, looking me up and down as if surveying a wrecked car.

"So, kid, since it looks like we're going to be roomies for a while, let me formally introduce myself. My name is Solomon Felsher. You can call me Solomon the Great or Solomon the Amazing. All my friends do."

I think I'll stick with Solomon the Loud or Solomon King of the Aftershave. I wish you weren't here and I hope you don't snore, or kill me in my sleep.

"It's a pleasure to meet you, Aaron. And may I ask, what is your surname?"

Surname? What's a surname? I have no idea what you're talking about.

"Or rather, what is your last name?"

My last name is Greenburg, not that you can hear what I'm thinking. So call me whatever you want, 'cause there's nothing I can do about it.

"Well, Aaron Greenburg, I have two things to share with you. One, I do not snore—or at least my late wife, Dolores, may she rest in peace, never told me I did, though she snored like an elephant playing a bassoon. And two, there is a God, and for some reason he's seen fit to pair our two sorry selves together in this miserable place. So I guess we better make the most of it."

CHAPTER 3
GOODBYE COUNT

WAIT. YOU CAN HEAR ME!

"Oy, no need to shout, kid. Of course I can hear you. I already have a headache from listening to that Mr. Wilson and his weaselly voice. His nose is stuffed up more than a teddy bear."

I laughed at the joke in my mind.

"Good. So you have a sense of humor."

And you're a mind reader. This is crazy. Who are you? How did you learn to read minds? What am I thinking now?

Solomon shook his head, causing his gray curly hair to bounce and bobble around like springs. "I'm no mind reader, kid. You sound like a dreykop, you know, a little cuckoo."

Solomon spun his finger in a circle around his ear. "I can hear you speak and I speak back. It's called having a conversation. You should try it sometime."

But I can't speak. I'm frozen stiff, like a dead person. I'm talking in my mind, and you're hearing me. So logically that makes you a mind reader. I read about a mutant like you in one of my comic books before I got sick. You're like Professor Xavier. You're a telepath.

"Kid, you're speaking gibberish. I think those comic books have turned your brain into oatmeal mush."

I didn't know what to think, worried Solomon could tell what I was thinking, but I felt a mixture of fear and excitement. Finally, after two years of solitude, I had someone to talk to! Or at least think to. But what if Solomon *was* a mutant or an alien? What if he not only heard the thoughts in my brain, but he wanted to eat it too?

I'm a sitting duck, I thought. *Maybe that's why he chose to come here. There's nothing I can do to stop him.*

I heard the heavy footsteps of Nurse Penny as she rushed back into the room.

"Oh, silly me. Wouldn't ya know, I forgot to turn on Aaron's television show," the plump nurse said as she turned on the VHS player and TV.

A black and white image of Big Bird walking in a park came to life, followed by the dreaded theme song about sunny days and clouds, which was really annoying since it had been two years since I saw a sunny day or a cloud.

NO! Sesame Street is back, I groaned in my mind. *The Count wins again.*

"My dear sweet Nurse Penny. May I ask you a question?" Solomon spoke up over the *Sesame Street* theme song.

Nurse Penny nodded and smiled her kindly smile. She really was the nicest nurse in the facility. "Certainly Mr. Felsher. What's your question?"

Solomon ran his hand through his gray-haired curls and scratched the top of his head.

"Do you think I'm a mind reader or an alien or a mutant? They say I'm crazy, but the kid," Solomon said with a wink, pointing at me with his thumb, "the kid is worried I am a mutant and can read his mind. If you could assure him I'm no mutant or an alien, I think that would put him at ease."

Nurse Penny's smile faltered and she silently mouthed the word, "what?"

"Just tell the kid I'm not an alien who's here to eat his brains. I think he needs the reassurance."

Nurse Penny wrinkled her brow and gave a single nod. "Uhm…right. It's been a long day Mr. Felsher. Perhaps you would like to rest and take an early nap before dinner. How does that sound?"

If you are an alien who's here to eat my brain, just do me a favor and leave Nurse Penny alone. She's a nice person.

Solomon turned his gaze from Nurse Penny to myself. "Kid, you have class, looking out for Penny over yourself. I give you that. But don't worry. I'm no alien and I'm not going to hurt anyone. What can I do to prove it to you?"

Nurse Penny arched an eyebrow as she watched Solomon talking out loud to me.

First thing you can do is turn off this show and never allow it to be played again. Ever.

Solomon walked over to the television and turned off *Sesame Street*. The opening skit with Grover and Big Bird disappeared.

Nurse Penny was about to object when Solomon held up his hand. "The kid is way too old for this. It bores him stiff," he said to Nurse Penny, holding a straight face before breaking into a chuckle.

"Bored stiff," he laughed. "Get it?"

Funny.

"I thought so," Solomon answered. "Anything else I can do for you kid—before Nurse Penny forces me to take a nap?"

Nurse Penny's second eyebrow arched. She stood speechless, probably assessing if Solomon was sane enough to leave alone by himself, let alone with a paralyzed kid.

I'm pretty sure Nurse Penny thinks you're crazy. You might want to stop talking out loud to me.

"Kid, people have called me crazy my whole life. When I was eight, my mom called me crazy for sliding down the rain gutter on the side of our ten story apartment building in the Bronx. My dad called me crazy for quitting my job with the railroad to travel with my band and play saxophone for a living. Louis Armstrong once called me crazy for playing drums and sax, at the same time, while sipping a virgin mojito between breaths. And my wife, well she called herself crazy for marrying me, may my sweet Dolores rest in peace."

Solomon bowed his head and paused for a moment.

"I think I can handle dear Nurse Penny calling me crazy as well, but she's too beautiful and kind to say it out loud," Solomon continued and winked at Nurse Penny.

Nurse Penny looked like a deer in the headlights. She slowly nodded. "I really think you should lie down and take a rest now. I'll come bring you a snack. Would you like some Jell-O?"

Nurse Penny gently held Solomon's elbow and pulled him back toward his bed. Solomon rolled his eyes and winked at me. Apparently the man liked to wink.

"Oy, you must be the one who's a mind reader, my dear Penny. I've been craving green Jell-O since the moment I arrived at this prison. If you could add some whipped cream on top, that would make my day complete."

Nurse Penny and Solomon moved out of my line of sight as he lay back on his bed.

"You just rest Mr. Felsher. I'll be back with some ice water and your Jell-O shortly."

"Thank you, Penny. You truly are my guardian angel."

I listened as Nurse Penny's footsteps echoed down the hallway. Once she was out of earshot, Solomon grunted, pulled himself out of bed, and shuffled back into my view.

"She is a nice lady, that Penny," Solomon said, nodding toward the door where Nurse Penny had exited. "I really was craving green Jell-O."

You're lucky, I thought to Solomon. *I wish I could eat Jell-O. I wish I could eat anything. All I get is this liquid stuff fed through a tube. I haven't tasted any food in two years.*

Solomon pawed at his scruffy chin, releasing a stronger scent of aftershave, and he nodded sympathetically. "I tell you what. I'll give you a taste. Just a sliver of Jell-O on the tongue. How does that sound?"

If it were possible for my eyes to light up with excitement, they would have been brighter than a Christmas tree. The taste of food, real food, unearthed an animal instinct in me. I wanted to roar and cheer and dance at the same time—all of which was impossible.

That would be totally awesome! Really? You would do that for me?

"Of course I will. But on one condition," Solomon said with another wink. "As long as we're roommates, no talking to me before eight in the morning. I need my beauty sleep."

CHAPTER 4
DEMENTIA DREAMS

Over the next few weeks, I pushed and prodded my mental connection to Solomon. We shared conversations, jokes and watched TV together. I learned that Solomon could only hear what I like to call my "conversational thoughts." These were thoughts that I direct toward others, observations, or questions I asked in my mind, as if I were speaking out loud. But when I kept my thoughts non-conversational, fluid and open, I could keep those thoughts private.

Not only was this a relief to me, but I think Solomon appreciated it as well. Otherwise, he would be stuck listening to the non-stop jabbering of my mind, like a three-year-old who couldn't stop talking.

At first, it was difficult for me to turn off my conversational thoughts, but after some practice, I got the hang of it, and I was thankful to have a little personal space I could control.

I also learned that Solomon could not hear my thoughts while he slept, which was nice, because the old man took a lot of naps. He didn't snore, thank goodness, but he did gently wheeze while he slept, which my super hearing picked up clearly. Luckily, it didn't wake me up, once I was asleep.

Since I can't voluntarily control my eyes or eyelids, I often fall asleep with them wide open. It makes for some really weird dreams, but you get used to it. Most of the time my eyes close on their own, and sometimes they stay closed when I wake up—which is really annoying. Once, my eyes stayed closed for three days straight. Then, instead of watching *Sesame Street*, I only had to listen to it.

But thanks to Solomon, I would never have to endure *Sesame Street* again! And after one week of getting to know the old man, I decided he wasn't half-bad. Besides being able to read my thoughts, and being overly eccentric, he seemed pretty normal. I kept waiting for one of his dementia episodes to occur, but nothing happened. That is, until one night when I fell asleep with my eyes open, awakened to the sound of Solomon mumbling to himself.

"I gotta get to the fight," Solomon muttered in his sleep. "Waxer said he can get me in. I *gotta* get to the fight."

What is going on? I thought, my groggy mind coming to life. My eyes were still open, even though I had been asleep, and I heard Solomon shuffling along the floor, mumbling about a fight. The room was dim, lit by a sliver of light that passed between the window curtains from the streetlamp outside. The clock read three in the morning.

Solomon shuffled into view. His hands were grabbing at something imaginary in the air while his head looked side-to-side and he squinted his eyes with a devious look.

"Papa is still at work and momma's taking care of the baby. Now's my chance," Solomon whispered.

Solomon. Wake up, I called to him in my mind.

Solomon turned his head toward me and his eyes stared straight through me.

Solomon. You're sleepwalking. Wake up, I called again.

Solomon knit his brow and he continued staring. "Who...are...you?"

What are you talking about? I'm Aaron. You know who I am.

"Who...are...you?" Solomon asked more forcefully.

A sharp, piercing blow hit my mind. The world spun around in a blur of colors, and I felt myself falling backward before all went black.

When I came to, I was in a large dining hall that looked like the inside of a castle.

"Am I in my mind palace?" I thought out loud, but no one responded.

What am I doing here? I thought. *This is weird. I never told myself to come here. Solomon's sleepwalking in our room asking 'Who are you?' and I need to wake him up before he hurts himself—or me.*

The place looked like my mind palace, but I had never seen this room before and something…something was different.

The walls and floor were made of stone and a giant fireplace, with a fire roaring inside, was built into the wall. The reddish glow of the fire lit the room, casting light onto an enormous wooden table lined with ornately carved wooden chairs, and filled with more food than I had ever seen in my life.

Mounds of fresh-cut carrots, cucumbers, watermelon, oranges, apples and dozens of fruits and vegetables filled silver bowls and platters. Golden dinner rolls, the size of my fist, were piled two feet high in the center of the table with trays of sizzling steaks and chicken sitting next to it.

And then there were the desserts. Dozens of tiered silver trays were stacked with different cakes, pies, and donuts.

The smells were intoxicating, and my mouth watered as I stared at the feast. Fine china dishes and silverware were set at each chair, with crystal glasses full of bubbling root beer. Ignoring the neatly placed settings of fine china and crystal glasses, I dove into the delicious piles of food like a wild man, gorging myself on everything in sight. The scents and the tastes sent my body into a sensory overload of pure joy. I ate until my stomach felt like it would explode, and then I ate some more, shoving handfuls of cake and pie into mouth until I felt like I was going to throw up.

"This is so good!" I exclaimed with a full mouth of chocolate cake, crumbs and icing flying from my mouth as I sat on the table next to a mountain of buttered rolls.

I swallowed my food and pinched myself to see if I was dreaming.

"Ouch!" I yelped in pain. "That felt real."

I had done stuff like this before, pulling things into my mind, like the painting of fruit and the clock. I always knew they were fake and that I was imagining them. But this felt…different. It felt real.

I wiped my face and hands with a golden napkin from one of the table settings and looked around the strange, new room. The fireplace suddenly glowed twice as bright, literally roaring as if it was a dragon coming to life. I turned my back to the fireplace to avoid the light and saw a new door become visible from the shadows in the corner of the room.

The heat from the fireplace intensified as the light continued to grow brighter and brighter. Beads of sweat rolled down my face and it felt like the light was pushing me toward the door. Though the fire stayed in the fireplace, I was sure the room would burst into flames at any minute. I ran for the door, snagging an apple and a roll along the way. My back felt like it was on fire as I pushed my way through the heavy door and collapsed to the floor of another room.

The burning heat immediately ceased. I turned around and the door was gone. Instead, I found myself on the floor of the tiniest kitchen I had ever seen. It was dark and moonlight streamed through a window above a small table with two chairs. Jammed next to a miniscule sink was a short refrigerator with rounded corners.

The faint sound of a music playing on a radio echoed from another room. It sounded like an old big band jazz ballad.

Life is grand, now that I have you
Life is grand, when you are near
Know that I will never leave you
I pray you never leave me, my dear.

Someone tapped me on the shoulder and I spun around in a fast circle. A little boy sat cross legged on a makeshift bed in the corner behind me. He wore dark trousers, a tan long sleeve shirt buttoned up to the neck, and black curly hair that stuck out from an old, brown driving cap. The cap reminded me of the one my grandpa used to wear before he died.

"*Who* are you?" the kid asked with a frown. "And whatcha doing in my apartment? If you're here to steal momma's new refrigerator, you should know I'm a trained boxer and I will knock your *lights out!*"

The kid stood and held his two fists up, ready to fight.

"Whoa, kid. I'm not here to fight you. My name's Aaron. And who are you?"

The kid eyed me suspiciously until he saw the bright, red apple and fluffy dinner roll in each of my hands.

He licked his lips and slowly lowered his fists. "You gonna eat those?" he asked.

Still stuffed, I shook my head and handed them to the kid. "They're all yours."

The kid grabbed them and took a small bite from the apple, savoring it, before he took an equally small bite from the roll.

"Mmmm, this is good," the kid moaned. He took one more bite of each before restraining himself and setting them on the table. "Thanks for the food, but I better save the rest for Mama, Papa and my baby sister. It's been a long while since we had any fruit or fresh bread in the house," he whispered and gave me a wink.

I felt a twinge of guilt as I watched the kid savor his last bite, remembering how I had gorged myself like a wild pig only minutes ago.

"My name is Solomon Felsher," the kid said, sticking out his hand to shake mine. "But you can call me Solomon the Great or Solomon the Amazing. All my friends do."

CHAPTER 5
TEN STORIES DOWN

My jaw dropped. *What is going on?* I thought. *Did Solomon pull me into his mind? Is he having a dementia dream and somehow I'm in it?*

"Solomon," I said slowly. "I need you to wake up now?"

The kid looked at me like I was crazy. "Wake up? I've never been more awake in my life," he said in a high-pitched whisper. "Tonight's the big fight! The fight of the century! And I'm stuck here like a piece of gum to a shoe. My mom says no eight-year-old is going to a fight by himself. Well, I'll show her."

I looked at him blankly, shrugging my shoulders. *What is little Solomon talking about?* I thought.

"Are you kiddin' me? You don't know about *the* fight? The heavy-weight championship of the world! It's Jack Dempsey v. The Wild Bull Luis Firpo. The fight's happening tonight just across the Harlem River at the Polo Grounds."

"Okay," I said with a nod. "Are we in Harlem, then? Is this New York City?"

Solomon arched an eyebrow, shaking his head in disbelief. "Oy, kid. You don't know bupkis, do you? No, this isn't Harlem! This is the South Bronx. You're in the middle of the Jewish Borough. Say, you're not Jewish, are you?"

I shook my head. "Not really," I answered. My grandparents on my mom's side had been Jewish, but they died before I was born, and my mom had never really practiced it.

"You must be from out of town, then. What, are you from Boston?"

"California," I answered.

Solomon lowered his eyebrow and nodded in understanding. "That explains it. Well, stick with me and I'll show you around."

He unlatched the kitchen window and used the table to climb out onto a small ledge.

"We'd better get goin' if we're gonna catch the fight. Waxer said he can get me in. I bet he can get you in too. C'mon, follow me."

Solomon beckoned me over with his small hand. He scooted over on the ledge to make room for me. I stuck my head out the window and my eyes went wide.

"I'm not going out there," I protested. "That must be a hundred foot drop to the ground and that ledge is only two feet wide!"

"Oy vey, quit being a baby. It's only ten stories up. I do this all the time. Momma's the one you gotta worry about. If she catches you in our place..." Solomon let out a low whistle, "then you'll really be dead. So hurry up. We gotta get to the fight."

Although I was older and a foot taller, I found myself following little Solomon's commands as if I was the child. I shakily climbed my way out onto the ledge and Solomon shot me a grin.

"Good job. Now follow me."

I slowly scooted my feet side-to-side across the ledge of the old brick building struggling to keep up with Solomon as he zoomed along the ledge, waving at the other tenants as he passed their kitchen windows.

We followed the ledge around the corner of the building until we reached a thick metal pipe running from the top of the building all the way down to a dark alley below us.

"Okay. Now for the fun part," Solomon said, patting his hand against the blackened metal pipe. "The pipes are bolted to the building at each floor so use your feet to stop yourself and scoot down past the bolts."

"No way. Are you serious?" I asked.

Solomon nodded with excitement. "It's easy. Just wrap your hands around the pipe like this and—"

But as Solomon reached over to grab the pipe, his back foot slipped off the edge and he started to fall backwards into the night sky. My natural instincts and reflexes kicked in, sending me diving toward Solomon as he fell. Reaching out, I grabbed one of his flailing arms as he disappeared over the ledge. The jerk of his body's weight nearly pulled me over the edge myself, but I anchored my body by holding the pole with my other hand.

"You okay?" I called to Solomon.

"Phew, thanks. That was close. But yeah, I'm okay," Solomon called back. The kid did not seem nearly as rattled as he should have after almost plummeting to his death.

I tried to pull Solomon back up, but I didn't have the leverage, the room, or the arm strength to do so. "Can you reach the pole?" I asked.

Solomon nodded. "Yeah, just swing me a bit closer and I can reach it."

"Are you sure? Because last time you tried to grab the pole, you nearly died."

"Of course I can reach it," Solomon retorted. "I've slid down this pole dozens of times. That fall was just an accident."

Yeah, a deadly accident, I thought to myself.

I swung Solomon toward the pole and the kid reached out and grabbed it like a monkey swinging on a vine. I immediately felt the weight come off my shoulder and I looked over the edge at the kid.

"Thanks, Aaron. See you at the bottom," he called and then proceeded to slide down the pole like a fireman.

Adrenaline mixed with my nerves as I clenched the pole in a death grip deciding whether I could really follow Solomon down the pole.

What if I slipped and fell? I thought. *Would I just wake up from Solomon's dream?*

Reluctantly, I slowly inched my way down the pole, using my shoes, which I realized for the first time were made of old leather, to squeeze the sides of the pole until felt my feet catch against the U-bolts securing the pole at the next floor down.

"Oy, c'mon Captain Slow!" Solomon called from the ground. "We still have another two miles to get to the Polo Grounds. Waxer's not goin' to wait for us forever!"

Refusing to be shown up by an eight-year-old kid, I loosened my grip on the next floor and slid down a bit faster. After two more floors, my nerves eased and I couldn't help but smile as I flew down the remainder of the way.

"That was awesome!" I shouted as my feet hit the ground.

"Attaboy, Aaron. And thanks for savin' my life. I woulda hated to have gone out before seeing Jack Dempsey fight. Now follow me. We gotta get cookin'."

Little Solomon took off walking at a quicker pace than I thought possible for a kid with his short legs, and I felt like an Olympic speed walker as I tried to keep up with him. A few dim streetlamps lit the road, and I was amazed to see a handful of old-style, Model-T-looking cars drive by, with a few more parked on the road. We reached an intersection where the street signs read 151st and Courtlandt Ave.

"This way," Solomon said, pointing right.

We turned the corner, up Courtlandt Ave., and ran smack into a tall, heavyset man with thick jowls like a walrus, a blue uniform, and a round Bobby police hat.

CHAPTER 6
THE FITZGERALDS

"*Woomph*," gasped the officer. "Why, you little hooliga—Oh, it's only you, Sol. What are you doing out at this time of night? Your mum has a right mind to whip you silly for running away again."

"Hey George," Solomon replied, unfazed. "I ain't runnin' away. This is my cousin, Aaron, from California. I'm just givin' him a tour of the neighborhood, ya know."

"Uh-huh. A night tour? This tour doesn't happen to cross the river over to the Polo Grounds does it?"

Solomon shrugged his shoulders and shook his head. "I ain't tellin'."

Officer George let out a curt chuckle, causing his thick jowls to jiggle. "Go on, get out of here. Waxer warned me his little Rabbit's Foot might be wandering the streets tonight. He even gave me a silver dollar to make sure I told you to hurry along if I saw you. And from what I hear, ol' Jacky Boy is going to need all the luck he can get to win tonight's fight. I only wish I could see it in person."

"Don't worry George, I'll tell ya all about it tomorrow."

"Uh-huh. Now off with you two. You'd better hurry so you're not late. But if your mum comes complaining to me about you running away again, I'll tell her to whip you something fierce, you hear?"

"Yeah, yeah," Solomon said with a wave. "See you tomorrow, George, and tell Lily 'hi' for me."

Officer George tipped his hat and gave us a wink as we hurried off down the road.

"Who's Lily?" I asked.

"Oh, she's George's wife. She sells flowers at the corner every morning. Whenever a fella buys a paper from me, I tell 'em to make their lady happy and go buy a flower from Lily's to take home. I probably make George and Lily an extra five dollars a month. That's why George gives me a pass whenever I'm out at night."

We passed street after street, the numbers getting higher as we went—152nd, 153rd, 154th…

"There's Waxer's Gym," Solomon said, pointing to an old brick building with a sign above it that read, *Wachsmuth Pugilist Academy.* "That's where I take my boxing lessons. Waxer teaches me personally. He's training me to be the next Heavyweight Champion of the World!"

"And that's the same Waxer that's sneaking us into this fight?" I asked incredulously.

Solomon nodded his head matter-of-factly.

"No offense, Solomon. But why would someone like Waxer sneak *you* into a fight?"

"Simple," Solomon replied, as if the answer was obvious. "I saved his life and now he thinks I'm his good luck charm. You see that corner up ahead?"

Solomon pointed to 161st Street.

"I was sellin' my morning papers on that very corner when I convinced old Chester Wachsmuth to stop and buy one. Ten seconds after he stopped, these two cars crashed right where Waxer would've been crossing the road. He said I was his good luck charm and started calling me his Rabbit's Foot. He gave me a job cleaning up around the gym, and he gives me lessons after I finish each day," Solomon said, raising his two fists and releasing quick jabs into the night air.

We turned at the corner of 161st and walked a few more blocks before my jaw dropped.

"Is that what I think it is?" I said, pointing to a massive white building with flags along the top. It stuck out in the night sky, high above the surrounding buildings.

"That," said little Solomon proudly, "is the brand new Yankee Stadium. Ain't it the cat's pajamas? They just opened it this year."

"You mean I'm seeing Yankees Stadium the first year it opened?"

Solomon nodded. "Finally, the Yanks got their own stadium here in the Bronx instead of sharing it with the Giants at the Polo Grounds."

"I didn't know they used to share a stadium with the football team."

"Football? That crazy leatherhead sport? No way. The Giants baseball team plays at the Polo Grounds. Now they're all jealous and tryin' to make the Polo Grounds bigger to match Yankee Stadium."

"But it's the San Francisco Giants, not the New York Giants," I said, thoroughly confused. I'd watched plenty of San Francisco Giants baseball games with my dad—that is, before my paralysis.

Little Solomon laughed. "In your dreams, California kid. The Giants will never leave New York. That'll be the day."

I decided not to argue the point further. We passed the magnificent Yankees Stadium, and the crowds of people and cars began to grow in the street. We reached a bridge at Harlem River, and I read a sign, *Macomb's Dam Bridge*.

Squeezing in between grown-ups, I followed Solomon onto the bridge as we zipped and weaved through the crowd. It appeared that the whole of New York was coming to watch the Jack Dempsey fight. As we crossed the bridge, the stadium known as the Polo Grounds was lit up like noonday. The growing crowds squeezed in tighter, with thousands of people flocking to the stadium.

"This way," Solomon called over the buzz of the crowd. "Waxer said to meet him at the west gate near the telephone booths."

We passed by men wearing suits with fedora hats and women in long sleek dresses with short hair, fur coats, and colorful hats that reminded me of snow beanies.

"Those are flappers. Aren't they?" I asked Solomon, remembering them from my history class.

"Oy, you better believe they are. My mama's always saying I gotta watch out for those flapper dames, but I'm not sure what she means. They seem nice enough. Hey, there's Waxer over there, c'mon!"

We approached a large man standing next to a red telephone booth. The only way I can describe Waxer is used and abused.

The man had no neck, a squat face covered with deep pock marks, and a flattened nose that looked like it had taken one too many punches. He was balding, with a bad comb-over of greasy gray hair, and wore suspenders with a white button-up shirt and a blue bow tie. The sleeves were rolled up on his shirt, showing surprisingly muscled forearms for someone so old, and he had a thick cigar hanging out of his mouth.

"There you are, kid," Waxer called, seeming agitated. He released a puff of smoke and the tip of his cigar burned bright orange. "I was worried you weren't going to make it. I put a lot of money on this fight, and I need my Rabbit's Foot here by my side."

Waxer hunched over slightly, noticing me for the first time.

"And who's this?" he asked Solomon. "You didn't mention bringing a friend. I'm not sure I can get the both of youse in. The place is already sold out of 80,000 tickets, and they say there's at least another 20,000 yahoos trying to gets in."

"Ah, sure you can get us in, Waxer," little Solomon responded, shooting me a quick wink. "If you think I'm lucky, my cousin Aaron here is twice as lucky. They call him the *Four-Leaf Clover of California*. Honest truth. In fact, he's so lucky he just saved my life on the way here. That's why I brought him along."

Waxer knit his brow, deep in thought, and pulled his cigar out of his mouth to tap the ashes to the ground.

"You say they call him the *Four-Leaf Clover*, eh?" Waxer asked, nodding his head slowly. "Yeah, okay. I can get youse both in. Lord knows we need all the luck we can get tonight. Jacky Boy is up against his toughest opponent yet—*The Wild Bull Firpo*. That crazy Argentinean might just be the one to take down old Jacky, and I've got too much money ridin' on this fight for that to happen."

"Don't you worry, Waxer. Between Aaron and me, that klutz won't stand a chance. Nothin' and nobody's gonna beat the champ tonight. Just you wait and see."

Waxer nodded and gave little Solomon a pat on the head. "Alright youse twos. Follow my lead. One of the fellas workin' security owes me a favor. Just stay on my coattail and we'll be five rows from ringside in a jiff."

True to his word, we followed Waxer to an entrance gate where a police officer stood watching over the crowd.

"Freddy," Waxer said to the officer, gripping the officer in a firm handshake.

"Waxer," the officer said, with a tip of his hat. "I was only expecting two of you. The boys will have to share a seat. Is that okay?" the officer asked

Solomon beamed. "That would be swell, officer."

"Sounds good to me," I added, finding myself smiling as well. I had never followed boxing, except for the latest news on Iron Mike Tyson and watching the movie *Rocky*, but the buzz of the crowd and the excitement in the air was contagious. Even though I had no idea who Jack Dempsey was, I had the overwhelming desire to root for the guy. He *had* to beat The Wild Bull.

Officer Freddy led us into the stadium and down rows of seats until we were nearly at the ring itself.

"Here you go, Waxer. These are the best seats I could get you. I need to get back to my post, so you fellas enjoy the fight."

After offering our thanks, Officer Fred tipped his hat and left us sitting five rows up, with a perfect view of the ring.

"Ladies and Gentleman," an announcer boomed over the loudspeaker. "Welcome to the New York Polo Grounds for the fight of the century—the reigning Heavyweight Champion of the World, Jack Dempsey v. the challenger, The Wild Bull, Luis Firpo. The Wild Bull Firpo sits in his corner and into the other corner enters the champ, Jack Dempsey!"

The crowd went wild as Dempsey entered the ring at his corner.

As the announcer continued his introductions, Waxer leaned over and blew a puff of smoke from his cigar. The rank smell, mixing with that of thousands of other cigars and cigarettes, made me light-headed.

"This is the toughest fight of Jacky boy's career," Waxer said, his eyes fixed on the two fighters. "Firpo is strong as an ox and can take a beating, but Jacky's quick as lightning. He can throw a punch and hit you in the kisser before you see it coming. If Jacky Boy protects himself and keeps landing his punches, he should win. He's just gotta protect himself from Firpo's big right hook, or he'll be in trouble."

"Say!" Solomon exclaimed, pointing a finger to a man a few rows down and to our right. "Is that Babe Ruth?"

"Yeah, I believe it is," said Waxer, squinting his eyes for a better look.

"And do you know who's only sitting a few seats in front of him?" spoke a stranger from the row behind us.

We all turned to face the stranger, who wore a friendly smile. He had tight yellowish skin and slick, blonde hair parted down the middle. Sitting next to him was a gorgeous woman who looked like a movie star. She had short, strawberry-blonde hair, and wore a white dress encrusted with jewels that matched her long white gloves.

"That's J. Edgar Hoover. To think, we're sitting only a few paces away from the most powerful man in the world," the stranger continued before lighting his own cigarette.

"Oh darling," the woman at his side spoke, "be a dear and light mine as well."

She held up a long black stick with a cigarette lodged at the end of it for the man to light.

It seemed everyone in New York smoked, and the smell was seriously making me nauseated. I imagined my own lungs turning black as I inhaled the fumes and coughed.

"And who might you three fine gentlemen be?" the beautiful woman asked, offering a gloved hand.

"The name's Chester Wachsmuth, miss" Waxer said, holding the woman's hand delicately before gripping the man's in a solid handshake.

"I'm Solomon Felsher, but you can call me Solomon the Great or Solomon the Amazing," Solomon replied confidently, much to the delight of the strangers.

"My name is Aaron Greenburg," I said, shaking their hands next.

"It's a pleasure to meet you all. Allow me to introduce myself. My name is Francis Scott Fitzgerald and this is my wife Zelda."

"Charmed," said the woman with a smile.

"And what do you do? Mr. Fitzgerald," Waxer asked.

"Oh, he's an author," answered Zelda, brightening with excitement as she spoke. "Perhaps you've heard of his last novel, *This Side of Paradise*, or read some of his short stories in the Evening Post?"

Waxer gave her a blank look. "Er, yeah…I think I may have heard about those before. I don't get the chance to read much, though. I run a boxing gym in the Bronx off 161st and Cortlandt. If you ever want some lessons, Mr. Fitzgerald, feel free to stop by anytime."

Zelda squealed in delight. "Oh, my Scotty in a boxing ring. Now that's something I would pay to see."

"Hey," Mr. Fitzgerald protested. "I trained in the Army. I bet I would be a great fighter in the ring."

"Training was all you did in the army, my dear. Lest you forget, the war ended before you deployed."

Mr. Fitzgerald rolled his eyes. "Ah well, it looks like the real fight is about to begin. I'd be happy to hear your expert opinion on it afterwards, Mr. Wachsmuth. It would help me seem the smarter man when I discuss it with my friends and colleagues this next week."

"I'd be happy to," replied Waxer with a wide smile that showcased his yellow-stained teeth.

We turned our attention back toward the ring and watched as Firpo removed his gold and black checkered boxing robe. Dempsey removed his white robe and the two fighters met in the center of the ring, knocking gloves.

Next to the reporters, a man in a dark suit with a circular straw hat rang the opening bell.

DING!

The fight began.

CHAPTER 7
THE CHAMP

Dempsey came out of his corner swinging, throwing a big right hook and then a quick left.

"Good," Waxer said, "he's going right at him, trying to make this a short fight."

The two giants-of-men wrapped each other up with their left arms, exchanging hard blows to the head with their right. Firpo backed away, seeming a little dazed when Dempsey hit him with a lightning fast right to the body. Firpo went down. The crowd went wild, but by the time the referee counted to three, Firpo was back up and ready to continue.

"Firpo's hanging on, but it looks like Jacky Boy's too fast for him," Waxer's commentary continued.

Just then, Firpo showed his power and dropped Dempsey with a right, causing Dempsey to fall to one knee.

"C'mon Jacky Boy!" Waxer shouted. "Get back up!"

Dempsey recovered quickly and went on the attack, knocking Firpo down again, but The Wild Bull popped right back up.

The slugfest continued and Dempsey knocked Firpo down five more times, one of them taking him seven counts to get up. But no matter how many times Dempsey knocked him over, Firpo would not stay down.

Firpo attacked wildly, throwing hard right hooks. The sound of his glove connecting with Dempsey's head echoed over the roaring crowd. But Dempsey held on and Firpo backed him up against the ropes.

He struck another right to Dempsey's chin, sending the champ over the ropes, out of the ring and onto the reporter's table right in front of us.

The crowd gasped as Dempsey flailed his arms, his feet pointed in the air, and his head hit the table. As he struggled to get up, I saw a nasty gash on the back of his head where he had hit one of the reporters' giant, metal typewriter.

Old Waxer was standing up from his chair, wringing his hands together and muttering prayers under his breath. Solomon stood up on our shared chair, his face full of dismay as we watch the fallen Dempsey.

It seemed like an eternity, but Dempsey crawled back into the ring by the count of nine from the referee. I was sure it had been longer than nine seconds, but Dempsey made it back in and stood up on his own power ready to continue the fight. He held off Firpo, landing a few more punches of his own, until the bell rang, ending round one, and the fighters retreated to their corners.

"My, my," Mr. Fitzgerald said from behind. "That was some action, wouldn't you say, boys?"

"Did you see how fast Jack landed those rights, and then a left and then an uppercut?" Solomon said, acting out each swing to the amusement of the Fitzgerald's.

"Why, Solomon, I do believe you could give those two brutes a run for their money someday," Zelda said with a wink.

Solomon brightened at the compliment. "That's right, miss. Old Waxer here is already trainin' me to be the next champ. Ain't that right, Waxer?"

Waxer shook his head dismissively, showing a toothy yellow grin. "You keep training, my little Rabbit Foot, and you never know what big things youse can do in life."

"Amen to that," Mr. Fitzgerald offered. "And what about you, Sir Aaron? What would you like to do when you grow up?"

I wanted to answer that I just wanted to walk and talk again, but I knew that would make no sense to the rest of them. In honesty, I had no idea what I wanted to be since there was nothing I could be. But before I could respond, the bell rang and the fighters were back at it in round two.

The fighters came out slower than they had in round one, both clearly worn down with the beatings they had administered to each other. They wrapped each other up in what looked like a hug/headlock and exchanged hits to the head. Then Dempsey knocked Firpo to the ropes, landing a series of blows.

"*Yes!*" Waxer shouted. "Attaboy Jacky. Don't take any more chances. Don't let him get you with his wild hooks."

Firpo wrapped up Dempsey again, trying to slow down the onslaught, but Dempsey pushed him away, sending Firpo down with a left to the body and a right to the chin.

"I can't believe he's still getting up," I said, amazed. "That's the eighth time Dempsey has knocked Firpo down."

Waxer nodded his head in agreement. "I knew this would be Jacky Boy's toughest fight yet. Firpo is strong as a bull, but he's wearing down. He won't be able to take much more."

Firpo rose again, but much slower this time. He looked worn and dazed as he wrapped up Dempsey and moved the champ against the ropes. He landed another combo, hitting Dempsey with punches to the head and body. But Dempsey shrugged off the blows and went after Firpo with two quick punches to the head. Firpo fell down to the mat like a giant tree in the forest.

"*ONE....TWO...THREE,*" called the referee, holding up his fingers as he counted out loud.

Firpo didn't move.

"That's it! That's Jacky Boy's favorite combination—a sharp left hook to the chin followed by a right cross. Look at him. Firpo's done I tell you!" Waxer exclaimed.

"FOUR...FIVE...SIX," the referee continued.

Firpo laid flat on his back with his gloves over his face. He rolled over to his side, desperate to get up as the referee counted, *"SEVEN...EIGHT."*

"C'mon, stay down, Firpo. C'mon. I have $500 riding on this fight. Stay down," Waxer pleaded. He was wringing his hands together like a python trying to squeeze itself to death.

"NINE," the referee counted, holding up nine fingers.

I waited breathless with Solomon hanging on my arm and the crowd hanging on the referee's final words.

"TEN," the ref shouted.

The crowd erupted into celebration. The fight was over. The champ had won again.

"YES!" Waxer cheered. He wrapped Solomon and me in a bear hug with his meaty hands and lifted us high into the air. "My two lucky charms came through!"

As Waxer crushed us with his hug, my heart beat with exhilaration. Here I was, in 1920's New York, moving around, talking like a normal person, and experiencing one of the greatest boxing matches in history. It all felt so real and tangible. I felt truly alive here, but I knew it couldn't be true. Still, that didn't stop me from enjoying the moment and the excitement flooding through the stadium.

As the crowd continue to cheer, we watched Dempsey run over to Firpo, who was still hunched over on his hands and knees. Dempsey wrapped up Firpo in a hug and pulled The Wild Bull to his feet.

"Now that's a true champion," Waxer said, pointing to the ring. "Did youse guys see what he did there? Even though he won, he didn't leave Firpo down. Youse never hit a man when he's down. Never. Always remember that."

Solomon and I nodded in understanding.

A wave of flashing bulbs from old cameras exploded around the ring. The bright white flashes filled my eyes, blinding me. I squinted rapidly, feeling myself fall backward into my seat, but I never hit my chair and felt myself continuing to fall into what seemed like a never-ending hole.

I blinked again and suddenly, I was back in my room at Restwood Suites, frozen in my body, staring at the wall in front of me. The morning light crept into the room from the slit between the curtains and the clock read 6:35am.

Solomon! Solomon, can you hear me?! I shouted in my head. *Where are you?!*

The old man was not in my line of sight and I worried he had left the room during his episode.

Solomon. Where are you? I called.

"Oy, why the shouting kid? I thought we had a deal. No waking me up before eight a.m. I'm sleeping here. Don't you know an old man needs his rest?"

But...but don't you remember? I was just in your head. We were at the fight, you know, Dempsey v. Firpo.

Solomon went silent and I heard him slowly get out of bed and shuffle into my view. He wore a white V-neck T-shirt with blue pajama pants and his curly gray hair was matted on the back, making it stick out to the sides like a crazy person.

Solomon gave me a serious stare. "You want to run that by me again, kid. You say you were in my head. You saw the Dempsey v. Firpo fight?"

I quickly retold the whole story from the beginning, starting with how Solomon woke me up at 3 in the morning with his mumbling. The details were still fresh in my mind as I mentioned everything from his mom's new refrigerator, to sliding down the pole, Yankee stadium, meeting the Fitzgeralds, and of course, Waxer getting us into the fight.

"Huh," Solomon said, scratching his head.

Seriously, I thought. *I just told you I went into your memories while you were having a dementia dream, living the memory like I was there with you, and all you can say is, 'huh.'*

"Oy, what else do you want me to say? You're the one with the crazy mind palace and I'm the one with this crazy dementia disease. Seems like we're both a little crazy so why should any of it make sense."

I shook my head in my mind, amazed at how easily Solomon disregarded the event. It was the same way he disregarded his ability to read my thoughts. To him, it was just part of life and it needed no explanation.

"But thanks for bringing back those memories, kid. Like good ol' Waxer. That man was like a second father to me. He died when I was sixteen. Lung cancer. Not surprising since he smoked cigars all day every day."

No kidding. It seemed like everyone smoked back then, I thought, deciding to carry on the conversation with Solomon, though I was still somewhat annoyed by his lack of desire to understand what had just happened.

"Nasty habit," Solomon continued. "Don't you ever smoke, Aaron. I've never met a smoker who doesn't wish they could quit. Easier to never start than to quit. As my mother used to warn me, if you smoke you'll die young and look old like Waxer—and as you saw, Waxer was not what you would call a good lookin' guy, though, I think that had more to do with his early days as a fighter."

I chuckled in my mind, picturing Waxer. The dude was definitely not going to win a beauty contest. But behind his rough, crusty exterior, he was a genuinely nice and caring guy. I felt bad that Solomon lost him so young.

So, Waxer died when you were sixteen?

Solomon simply nodded.

Sorry to hear that. He was nice—a little superstitious, but I liked him.

Solomon shrugged. "That's just part of life, kid. We all have to go sometime. The important thing is doing something good with your life while you can. Waxer had a big heart. He helped out a lot of kids, like myself, over the years. That's the true measure of one's life. As Waxer would say, 'youse remember that.'"

CHAPTER 8
SOLOMON HAS A GRANDAUGHTER

"*GRANDPA!*" a tiny voice squealed. The owner of the little voice smelled like freshly cut grass.

I heard Solomon sit up in bed as the little voice entered our room.

"Jesse, my boy. Come over here and give Grandpa a hug." I heard the running of feet and a soft *whoomp*.

"Oy, now that's a hug," Solomon said.

A pair of new footsteps entered the room and another voice spoke—a girl this time.

"Hi, Grandpa," said the girl, her sweet scent of oranges filling the room.

"Sarah, my darling. You look so grown up. I hardly recognized you. And Talia, my loving daughter and the ruthless judge who sentenced me to this prison—if your children were not so beautiful I would disown you."

"Hey, Dad," Talia said nonchalantly, ignoring the jab. "Jesse just finished his baseball game, and we wanted to stop by to say hi."

"We won eight to four," Jesse announced excitedly. "I had a double and a triple, but I struck out once."

"Attaboy, Jesse. And don't worry about the strikeout. We all strike out sometimes. Keep practicing and you'll be playing in the majors in no time."

51

"I just wish Dad was here to watch me," Jesse said in a dejected voice.

"I know, I know," Solomon responded, followed by a short silence.

It sounded like Jesse was about to cry, when Talia spoke up. "Jesse, why don't you and I go see if we can get you and Grandpa some Jell-O," Talia said.

"Now there's the best idea I've heard all day," Solomon pronounced loudly. "And if you can swing it like Benny Goodman, see if you can make it green Jell-O with whip cream. It's my favorite. Think you can do that for your ol' grandpa?"

I heard Jesse sniff, before saying, "Okay. I can do that."

"Attaboy. And if you get lost, just ask for Nurse Penny."

Talia and Jesse left the room, taking with them the smells of fresh-cut grass and baked bread.

"So, who's your roommate?" the girl, named Sarah, asked.

She walked into my view and my eyes went wide, well actually they didn't since I can't move them, but my brain was telling my eyes to go wide.

"His name is Aaron Greenburg," Solomon said, "and I think he likes you."

I sighed in my mind. *Solomon, I hate you.*

Solomon let out a chuckle.

"He's not much of a talker," Solomon continued. "But the boy does have a beautiful mind—like a palace that's full of imagination. He keeps it clean like a palace too, don't you Aaron?" his voice full of warning.

Quit being ridiculous, Solomon.

"Yes, his mind may be a palace, but that doesn't cover up the fact that he does need a haircut, don't you think? Oy, his hair is almost longer than yours, Sarah."

SOLOMON!

Sarah smiled at me, dimples forming on her freckled cheeks as she revealed a row of hot pink braces along her white teeth.

I felt my heart beating faster and wished I could smile back.

Her bright blue eyes were magnified behind a pair of pink glasses that sat atop a tiny nose covered in freckles. Her sandy-brown hair, which for the record was way longer than mine and went at least five inches past her shoulders, was frizzy with big bangs. But above everything else, there was her scent. Sarah smelled like oranges. The smell was so intoxicating that I almost didn't even notice the sweet Star Trek T-shirt she was wearing with a picture of Data, from the brand new *Star Trek the Next Generation* show.

Since Solomon could change the channels for me, I was finally getting to see all the new TV shows on our grainy black and white television. Though Solomon wasn't a big fan of the new *Star Trek*—he preferred the original.

Sarah was definitely an original, and she was very pretty.

Wonderful, I thought. *There's a beautiful girl standing in front of me and I'm wearing hospital pajamas with a blue flower print, my red hair is down to my shoulders, there are tubes and IV's sticking in all over me, and wait a minute…is that drool I feel running down my chin. Someone, please, kill me now!*

"So what's wrong with him?" Sarah asked, concern crossing her face as she looked at me like I was a wounded bird.

"Oh, he's got some sort of Crocodile Meningitis thing."

It's Cryptococcal, I corrected him in my mind.

"Yeah, yeah, Cryptococoa Meningitis," Solomon said as he shuffled over next to his granddaughter and into my view

It's coccal. Cryptococcal. Not cocoa. How are you getting this wrong? It's not that hard to say. Here, I'll spell it for you. C-R-Y-P-T…

"Anyways," Solomon continued, ignoring my spelling. "He's paralyzed from head to toe. Can't even talk or control his eyes. But he's a good kid, even if his hair is long."

"That's so sad," Sarah said. "He looks like he's only twelve, just a few years older than Jesse."

I'm fourteen, I groaned in my mid. *My birthday was last month.*

"Oh, he's fourteen, the same age as you," Solomon told Sarah. "He's just thin. You should see the liquid they feed him through that tube."

Thanks for pointing out the giant tubes going into my body. I appreciate that. Why don't you point out the drool on my face while you're at it?

"So why doesn't the rest home give him a haircut?" Sarah asked.

Solomon shrugged.

My mom usually gives me haircuts, but she and my dad haven't been by in a while, I said. *In fact, I'm not sure where they are. Dad's trip ended weeks ago. Maybe they decided to stay in Hawaii and leave me behind.*

Solomon sighed. "Chin up kid. I'm sure they will come visit soon."

Sarah wrinkled her brow. "What did you say Grandpa?"

"Oh, nothing sweetie. Say I have an idea. You still want to be a hairdresser, right?"

Sarah nodded enthusiastically.

"Why don't *you* give our friend, Aaron, a haircut?"

I froze with fear. Well, I mentally froze, since I was already physically frozen. The idea of Sarah, pretty Sarah who smelled like oranges and wore a Star Trek T-shirt, being so close to me as to cut my hair, was terrifying.

"Well, Mom let me practice on Jesse the last few times. Boys' hair is so much easier than girls' hair. Maybe I can come by after school starts on Monday and give it a try. Do you think he will mind?" Sarah said, raising her eyebrows hopefully.

Solomon chuckled and gave me a wink. "Nah, I'm sure Aaron would love to have you cut his hair. It would be a special treat."

Mind still frozen.

"Maybe you can give old Grandpa a little trim off the top as well," Solomon said, pulling one of his gray curls straight up and letting it bounce back into its normal curly spring shape.

I heard footsteps coming our way, accompanied by the scents of fresh-cut grass and baked bread.

"Grandpa, I got you green Jell-O with whipped cream, just like you asked."

"Wonderful, my boy. You are the man of the hour," Solomon replied.

"Oh, and Dad," Talia spoke up, "I almost forgot. Here you go."

Talia and Jesse were still out of my sight, but I heard something swipe against a leg and Solomon let out a tiny gasp. "O Talia, I take it back. You're no longer disowned."

From my limited view, I saw Solomon reach out and grab a large maroon leather case and give it a hug. There was a name engraved in fancy cursive on the side. In bright gold lettering it read, *Betty*.

CHAPTER 9
SARAH BELIEVES

Solomon looked twenty years younger, his body gently swaying as he played the glistening brass saxophone known as Betty. The rich melodies he pulled through the instrument were hypnotic—some making me want to dance while others made me want to cry. Solomon had been giving me a daily crash course in jazz appreciation since Betty arrived, playing classic jazz standards along with songs he had written himself. As he shared each new song and told me stories of playing with great jazz legends, I realized just how little I knew about the history of jazz, even though I considered myself a jazz fan after my jazz band days.

The particular song he was playing made me want to cry and smile at the same time, though I couldn't do either in my paralyzed state.

Solomon finished the song with a long string of notes that started high and ended low, holding the last note for an impossible length of time as he slowly decrescendoed to a close.

All was silent as the residual feeling of the song resonated through the room. Neither of us wanted to speak and ruin the moment. But after another five minutes or so, Solomon sat down in a chair in front of my bed and spoke softly.

"Now *that's* a song."

Yes, it was, I said in my mind.

"How did it make you feel, Aaron?"

I hesitated for a moment, embarrassed as I tried to assemble the words for my feelings.

I felt...sad...the whole song, but at the same time I was relaxed.

"Go on," Solomon encouraged.

Well, it was like...like I understood the sadness and was okay with it. I knew it would never fully go away, but I remembered that there had been good times before. I know it sounds stupid, but when the song ended, I wanted to smile and cry at the same time. Yeah, that sounds dumb when I say it out loud.

Solomon shook his head, "Not at all. You spoke beautifully, my boy. I couldn't have said it better myself. We'll make a jazz connoisseur of you yet."

What was the name of that song? I asked.

"That," said Solomon, "was *Blue in Green*. It was originally done by Miles Davis on trumpet and John Coltrane on saxophone. John Coltrane is one of the best, but don't tell him I said so."

You sounded great. Did you perform that song a lot before you retired?

Solomon gave me a sad smile. "I haven't performed that song for anyone, except you, in six years," Solomon said and then harrumphed. "And I'm *not* retired. A true musician never retires. Kinda like an old quarterback never dies. He just fades back and passes away."

What? I thought.

Solomon shook his head and sighed. "It's a joke kid. Old quarterback...fades back...passes away. Get it?"

I groaned in my mind as understanding dawned on me for the bad football joke.

"Never mind. We'll work on that humor of yours, kid. Say, are you excited to get your haircut today?"

My heart thumped in my chest at the thought of Sarah trimming my hair. I had tried to not think about it all day, but that only made me think about it more. Even though I did my best to keep those thoughts fluid and non-conversational, I was sure

Solomon knew exactly how excited I was, but I did my best to contain it.

Uhm, yeah. It'll be nice to finally get my hair cut. But can you do me a favor? Can you just make sure I don't have any drool on my face this time?

Solomon nodded and used a paper towel to dab my chin. "There you go. Now you won't be drooling over my granddaughter," Solomon said with a chuckle.

Not funny.

That made Solomon chuckle more.

I do have a question about Sarah, I said, trying to change the subject away from my drool. *What's wrong with her dad? I know Jesse misses him, and I remember Talia saying she took the kids to go see a man named Frank in South Carolina. Is that their dad? Or is their dad dead?*

Solomon's chuckling faded to a smile. "You know. For someone who can't figure out a joke, you sure are observant. Maybe you ought to ask Sarah about her father yourself."

Before I could respond, reminding Solomon that I can't speak to anyone, except him, our door opened and the scent of oranges glided into the room.

"Hi Grandpa," Sarah said in her sweet voice. She was wearing a red 49ers T-shirt and faded blue jeans this time, as she came into my view and gave Solomon a hug.

A Trekkie and a Niners fan! This girl is something else! I thought.

"Oy, where are your manners, Sarah?" Solomon said, nodding his head toward me. He winked. "Don't forget to tell Aaron hello as well. You don't want your first client to feel ignored."

Sarah's face went a shade pinker as she turned to face me. "Sorry about that, Aaron. It's good to see you again. I brought my bag of supplies with me," she said excitedly, holding up a black bag. "I'll have your hair cut and styled in no time. I hope you don't mind hair gel."

I hate hair gel, I thought, but then Sarah flashed her pretty smile with pink braces. *On second thought, maybe hair gel would be a nice change.*

Sarah pulled out a barber's bib from her bag and Solomon raised my bed to help me sit up higher. A trail of goose bumps lined my neck where she brushed my hair aside to attach the barber bib. She ran her hands through my hair, rubbing it between her fingers.

"He has a thick head of hair," she announced, nodding her head approvingly. "The gel will work nicely."

"I'm sure it will, sweetie. I'm going to go ahead and leave you to your work and grab myself some Jell-O and a soda. I'll be back in a few minutes."

Wait, what? You're leaving me alone?

Solomon chuckled. "Of all the boys in the world I would trust to leave my dear granddaughter alone with, you're the safest kid on the planet. And don't worry, Aaron. She won't bite. She might snip your ear by accident, but she definitely doesn't bite."

"*Grandpa*," Sarah complained.

Solomon winked and placed Betty in her case before leaving the room. I heard his footsteps echo down the hallway as the smell of aftershave faded from the room, overpowered by Sarah's orange scent.

"I worry about him," Sarah said as she sprayed my hair with a water bottle. The water droplets on my neck itched, but I couldn't do anything to scratch them or wipe them off.

"The way he's been talking lately," she continued, "his dementia seems to be getting worse. It's like he thinks he can talk to you or something, not that you're not awake in there. If you are, I'm sorry you're trapped. That would be awful."

It is. Trust me. But it's not so bad right now.

"Listening to him talk to you like he just did…I worry Grandpa Solomon is going crazy."

Oh, he's crazy alright, but not for talking to me.

Sarah ran a comb through my wet hair, pulled out her scissors and tipped my head forward. I felt the cold metal of the scissors against the back of my neck.

"I say he sounds crazy," Sarah continued, "but here I am talking to you exactly the same way. Maybe I'm the one who's crazy."

Snip. The first pieces of red hair began to fall onto the barber's bib.

You're not crazy, I said in my mind. *You're kind, pretty, and very nice to come cut my hair. But you're definitely not crazy and you have no idea how glad I am that you're talking to me.*

Sarah continued cutting my hair, and it looked like a red forest was being chopped down as the red clumps gathered on the bib. Thankfully Sarah kept talking, telling me all about her first week of school in the 9th grade—what her teachers were like, which classes she was taking, and songs she was learning on flute for the band, etc…The whole conversation made me miss school more than ever. The only part I wished she had skipped was all the gossip about the 'cute boys' and who liked who. Nothing hurts a man's ego like hearing a pretty girl talk about all the cute guys she likes. Guys who are not him, that is.

Sarah finished trimming around my ears, careful not to snip them by accident like Solomon had joked about, and took out a small brush to sweep the loose hair off my face, ears and neck.

"I really wish I could lay you over a sink and wash your hair," Sarah said. "In fact, how do they wash your hair—and your body for that matter?"

Now this is an awkward conversation. Good thing you can't hear me, I said in my mind. *The nurses give me a sponge bath or use medical wipes to wash me. They close the curtains on this side of the room, undress me, and check for bed sores while they wash. You know how people have those bad dreams about being naked in front of a crowd, well that dream is my reality two to three times a week. Luckily it's not in front of a crowd, usually it's just in front of Nurse Penny who's old enough to be my mom, and luckily you can't hear a word I'm saying.*

"Oy vey! She may not be able to hear you, but I can," Solomon called from the hallway before shuffling into our room. As he entered, so did the scent of aftershave which collided with the fragrance of oranges.

"Grandpa. Who are you talking to?" Sarah asked, her forehead filled with creases of concern. She had a glop of green hair gel in her hands as she started rubbing my head, working the gel into every inch of my hair.

"I was talking to the kid. He was telling us about how he gets a sponge bath from—"

SOLOMON DON'T YOU DARE! I shouted with all of the mental force I could muster.

Solomon reeled back a step, putting his hands to his temples. "Oy, kid! That hurts. Never shout like that again. Your voice is still ringing in my head."

"*Grandpa!* Are you okay?" Sarah asked, rushing to Solomon's side, her hands still coated with a thin layer of residual hair gel.

"I'm fine child. Aaron just needs to learn to control his voice. He can be quite loud and obnoxious when he puts his mind to it…get it…put your mind to it."

Solomon let out a small chuckle, followed by a hacking cough. I was not amused.

"But Grandpa, what are you talking about? Aaron hasn't said a word. He can't talk, remember?" Sarah's face was so full of concern that I thought she might cry.

You'd better stop talking out loud to me, I said in my mind. *You're scaring Sarah and I think she might cry. She's really worried about you.*

Solomon rubbed his temples one last time and nodded at my comment.

"Sarah, my dear, I'm not going crazy. For some reason, I can hear Aaron speak when no one else can. We have a special connection, he and I, and I can talk to him through his mind palace."

Sarah narrowed her eyes and her face relaxed into a look of pity. "Oh, Grandpa. I'm so sorry you have dementia and have to go through this. I know Aaron's here all the time and I'm glad you have someone to talk to, but you're not alone. I'll come visit you. You don't have to pretend to talk with Aaron."

She doesn't believe you, I said. *No one will believe you and if you start telling people you can read my mind they're going to worry you're dangerous and move you out of this room. You've gotta stop talking like this in front of other people. I don't want them to take you away, Solomon. You're the only friend I've got, and I can't go back to being alone.*

I realized a tear was trickling down my cheek. I'd never been able to cry since contracting Cryptococcal Meningitis. Though I had cried in my mind dozens of times, I could never release any actual tears. *Had I just made that tear come?* I thought.

"Aaron, if there's anyone who will believe me, it's my little Sarah," Solomon said. He shuffled out of my view and over toward his bed. He reappeared with a piece of paper and a pen.

"Sarah, I want you to write down a sentence. Anything you want, and show it to Aaron and only Aaron. I'll go to the corner of the room and close my eyes and tell you what you wrote."

"Grandpa, please. You're not a magician and I think you need some rest."

"Oy, Sarah! I know I'm not a magician!" Solomon barked, causing Sarah to flinch. Solomon took a deep breath and sighed. "I'm sorry I yelled, sweetie. Just, please, humor this old crazy man."

Sarah reluctantly nodded, a look of pity crossing her face as Solomon shuffled to the corner of the room and out of my sight.

Sarah scribbled something on the paper and held it up to my face, making sure to use her body to block any view her grandfather might have of the paper.

I read the paper to Solomon in my mind. *This is a dumb game and I'm worried about you, Grandpa.*

"This is a dumb game and I'm worried about you, Grandpa," Solomon repeated out loud.

Sarah's jaw dropped. She looked at the paper and then back to her grandfather in disbelief, who was still turned around facing the corner. "How did you do that?" she asked.

She looked around the room and all around my head as if searching for a clue. "Is there a mirror hidden somewhere? Do have a camera hiding? Are we on that *Candid Camera* TV show?"

Solomon chuckled. "No mirrors and no cameras. Go ahead and write down another sentence."

Sarah wrote on the paper again, taking much longer to write this time. When she held up the paper, the text was tiny, making it hard to read, and the sentence was now a short paragraph.

Silly Sally sells shimmering sea shells by the shiny sandy sea shore. Sometimes Silly Sally sings silly sea songs as she sells shimmering sea shells by the shiny sandy sea shore.

You've got to be kidding me, I thought as I slowly read the paper to Solomon. Even my mind was getting tongue tied as I read it, that's if minds were capable of being tongue tied.

Solomon read the tongue twister back to Sarah, verbatim.

"No way," Sarah exclaimed. "How many fingers am I holding up?" she said, holding up three fingers in front of my face.

"Three," Solomon called out.

Sarah shook her head in amazement, dumbfounded by what was happening. "Okay. If this is for real, I'm going to ask you a question that only Aaron would know. What is the name of my third period teacher and who is the boy that I like who sits across from me in that class?"

I groaned in my mind. *Yeah, more talking about boys she likes— my favorite topic in the world,* I thought before telling Solomon the answers.

"Your teacher's name is Miss Horsehind—interesting name—and the boy's name is Donald, kind of like Donald the Duck. Although, I should let you know, sweetie, it's not polite to talk about the boys you like with another boy. I think you made Aaron uncomfortable."

Sarah turned and stared at me, her hand went up to her open mouth and she gasped. Her blue eyes seemed to take me in for the first time as she looked at my face through her pink glasses. After another moment, she dropped her hand from her mouth and a smile beamed across her face, dimples forming on her freckled cheeks.

Sarah grabbed my floppy hand and shook it. "Hi, Aaron. Let me reintroduce myself. My name is Sarah Clements. It is a pleasure to meet you and I really hope we can be friends—oh, and I really hope you like your new haircut," she said, holding up a mirror.

CHAPTER 10
LET'S SWING THIS JOINT

Fall swept into the Bay Area of California like a fast moving wave. It was October, and I could smell the faint hint of leaves on the nurses and on Sarah whenever they entered our room. The mixture of oranges and fallen leaves made for an interesting scent on Sarah. It wasn't a bad smell, just interesting, which fit her perfectly. For the last two months, since Sarah learned I was still awake in my head and could communicate with Solomon, she had come to visit every day after school.

She made it her mission to try and help me catch up in my studies after my two-year hiatus from formal education, other than *Sesame Street* that is. This proved difficult since Solomon quickly became bored whenever he played the conversational middleman between Sarah and myself. Often, Solomon would leave the room to take a break as spokesman from my mental chatter and Sarah would continue teaching while he was gone. Often, she would do her homework at my side, explaining math problems, reading her textbooks out loud, telling me about her history lesson on World War II, and so on. I loved every minute of it.

I came to find out a lot about Sarah during those first few months. Not only was she a science fiction and comic book geek, like me, but her dad raised her to love the 49ers and the Giants, which she did wholeheartedly, keeping me up to date on all of the latest team news.

She told me about the bakery her mom worked at and how Jesse had named their new black lab puppy, Bandit.

"Jesse's really been having a hard time with dad gone," she told me while Solomon was out of the room. "But I think having Bandit around is helping him out a lot."

With Solomon gone, I couldn't ask any more questions about her dad, but luckily she kept talking to me.

"He's in the NAVY, you know. Dad was stationed at a local training base here in California, but then he received orders to go to a port in South Carolina this past summer. He and mom are having marriage problems. They don't think I know about it, but I do."

I know the feeling, I said in my mind.

"Dad wanted us to move out to South Carolina, but he knew he was going to eventually ship out, and my Mom didn't want to move with the school year about to start. But then I heard her arguing with my dad late one night and she said, 'Maybe it's best if we separate for a while. Maybe we need time apart.'"

I'm sorry Sarah. That's hard. I know. But on the bright side, at least you know where your parents are.

"So we stayed here, and Dad went to South Carolina. I'm glad we stayed, though. He's stationed on the U.S.S. Carr awaiting orders for a one-year tour. If we had moved out there, he would still be gone, but we would be stuck in a new place. Plus, if we had moved, you never would have met Grandpa Solomon, and I would have never met you."

This thought hit me harder than a line drive by Mark McGwire. Over the past two months, my life had drastically changed for the better, all because of Solomon and Sarah. The thought of losing them, let alone never having them in my life, filled me with dread.

"So what about your parents?" Sarah asked. "Oh right. You can't tell me. When Grandpa gets back, you can answer. Plus, I'm still trying to get him to answer questions about World War II for my history report. We are supposed to interview a veteran, but every time I ask him, Grandpa just nods and says, 'Oy, the war is over, thank God, and that's all you need to know about it.'"

Maybe refusing to answer was something Solomon and I have in common. It'd been three months since my parents left for Hawaii, and they hadn't been back to visit since they left. I didn't want to talk about my parents. I had no real answers to tell Sarah if she asked about them. Talking about them only made me angry and depressed. Maybe war is the same way.

***

"Have you heard from the boy's parents?" I heard Solomon whisper to Nurse Penny in the hallway. My eyes had closed for the night and my mind teetered on sleep, but Solomon's question woke me and I struggled to keep my thoughts fluid so he would not notice.

"Oh, no, we have not heard a peep from his parents," Nurse Penny answered. "But their payment is still on time each month, and there's no change in address or phone number. Dear me, I tried leaving a message on their phone, but there was no answer, and their answering machine was full. I do hope they are okay. Imagine that poor boy all alone. It's a crying shame, dontcha know."

Solomon released a gruff sigh. "I just worry about the kid. It's not right that his parents haven't visited him. Do you think you could get me his home address or phone number? I'd like to call his folks myself, or have my granddaughter go visit them and make sure they are okay."

I heard Nurse Penny sigh this time. "Oh, Solomon. I'm sorry. But I can't do that. You know I can't share the personal information of a patient's family."

I couldn't even share *that* information with Solomon. He had asked me before to give him my parents' phone number and address, but I had no idea. I explained to him how I got sick the day we were moving here, and by nightfall I was completely paralyzed. I never learned my parents' new address or phone number.

"Oy, there's gotta be something we can do to find his parents," Solomon pleaded. "If they don't want to visit their son, that's fine," he added—a tone of bitterness in his voice. "That's their choice, albeit it's a horrible and despicable choice. But the kid has a right to know what's going on, and they should at least let the staff at Restwood Suites know, in case you need to get a hold of them."

Nurse Penny had come to see Solomon's attachment to me as endearing, but she still did not believe Solomon could hear my thoughts. He had tried to get her to do the same test as Sarah, but Penny would not play along, simply using her calm voice to tell Solomon he needed to rest.

Penny sighed again. "Oh, boy. I tell you what. I have the afternoon shift off tomorrow and I will try and go visit their home before I come in. I'll admit, it's strange they haven't visited or answered our calls, but are still paying the bill for him to stay. It's a real mystery, dontcha know."

"Thank you, Penny," Solomon replied. "You truly are a beautiful ray of hope in this world."

I heard Solomon's shuffling steps as he entered the room again. His heavy scent of aftershave grew stronger as he neared my bedside. If I could have opened my eyes, I would have, but instead I laid there, pretending to sleep and keeping my thoughts fluid.

Solomon rested his hands on the metal bar along the side of my bed. I felt the slight vibrations of the bar as his grip tightened.

"Aaron," he whispered. "I'll find your folks for you."

There was a long pause and Solomon's breathing grew heavier. I worried he might fall asleep and collapse by accident, but then he spoke again.

"A father should never stop talking to his son. No matter what..." he said calmly, but then his voice suddenly rose a notch in volume and pitch. "The show's got to go on no matter what, I tell you. I don't care if Oswald and Stew are both puking their guts out in the bathrooms. This is our first big gig in Chicago, and we either find another trombone player or we play without them."

Solomon, I'm awake. What are you talking abo—but before I could finish my thought, I felt my mind pulling backwards as I fell into swirling darkness. The darkness spun me around and around, building a queasiness in my stomach. As suddenly as the spinning started, it stopped.

I was in another room of my mind palace, but it was more of an auditorium than a room. I stood by myself in the center of a circular stage surrounded by rows of plush red chairs spanning out in every direction.

The stone palace walls had spotlights bolted into them, shining bright white, cool blue, and deep red lights directly onto me from all sides. The loud sounds of clapping and cheering echoed in the auditorium, which kind of freaked me out, since there was no one else in there but me. At my side, my hand brushed against something cold and metal. Looking down I saw a trombone, but not just any trombone, it was *my* trombone from school.

As soon as I picked up the instrument, the clapping ceased and the room went silent. In the silence of the room, I lifted the trombone to my lips, closed my eyes, and played a B-flat, holding the sweet sounding note for as long as possible. The sound reverberated throughout the circular auditorium, its echo playing into itself. When my lungs finally gave out, I ended the note and took a deep breath, my eyes still closed shut.

But as I inhaled, expecting a breath of fresh air, my nose was assaulted by the smell of cigarette smoke and my ears were treated to the soft sounds of a bass, piano and trumpet playing a jazz ballad.

I opened my eyes, surprised to find the room had changed. Instead of standing in the middle of the circular stage, I found myself off to the side of a different stage, just behind the open curtains. Further backstage, about fifteen feet away, stood a short, black man, dressed in a fancy tuxedo. He had a thin, tight-lined mustache and his head was cocked back, looking upward into the red face of an angry, twenty-something, Solomon Felsher.

"Sol, little brother, we can't go out there and swing this joint without any trombones. They're half the brass section for Pete's sake!"

"JJ, *little brother*, we're not cancelling this gig. I didn't just quit my job at the railroad, pay to get us here to Chicago, only to turn tail and run because Oswald and Stew drank themselves sick our first night here," Solomon scoffed. His face was still beet red, which was a sharp contrast against his white tuxedo and curly, jet black hair.

"It looks like Oz and Stew aren't the only ones drinking themselves silly tonight. Your face is flusher than a good poker hand," JJ retorted. "Be reasonable, Sol. If we go out there and try to swing it like Benny Goodman, without our trombone section, it's going to sound weak and they will laugh us off the stage. We'll never get another gig in this town again."

"Well, if we cancel now, we'll never get another gig in this town either," Solomon argued, shaking his head in disgust.

JJ rested his hand on Solomon's shoulder. "Listen, Sol. You're my best friend. You really are like a brother to me. You're the reason most of these clubs even let a black man musician like me inside. I know you quit your job and paid for us to get here, and I know your pop's not talking to you because of it. You've sacrificed everything to get us to this point, but, Sol, unless you can get another trombonist to fill out the brass, I'm not going out there and playing drums. I'd rather drop this gig and try again later than be laughed at on our first night in Chicago."

Sensing someone was watching him, Solomon turned his gaze toward me and stared in disbelief. This caused the other man, JJ, to turn my direction as well. Soon, both were staring at me with dropped jaws.

Worried there was something gnarly on my face, or drool running down my chin, I rubbed my face with my right hand and felt the thin wisps of a mustache along my upper lip.

"What in the world?" I said out loud, still rubbing the stache with my right hand. "Since when can I grow a mustache?"

I turned my head to avoid their gaze and saw a calendar hanging on the wall to my side. It looked like an old pinup calendar with a girl in a long red dress. The calendar read *Dazzling Dolls* across the top in fancy lettering, and the month was set to October 1940.

"What in the world?" I said again. Then I realized my left hand was holding something heavy at my side. Looking down, I saw a long, skinny, black case. Without opening it, I knew what was inside—a trombone.

"Seriously. What in the world?" I whispered a third time.

"Say, kid. Come over here a minute," Solomon called, his red face beaming with a full smile.

I looked down at myself and I was wearing a white shirt and I felt a hat on my head, but my right hand instinctively went back to rubbing the mustache on my upper lip. I walked slowly toward Solomon and JJ, worried about where this dementia dream was heading. "Listen, Solomon. I know what you're thinking and it's not going to happen. You're dreaming and you need to wake up."

"Oy, listen to this kid," Solomon said with a chuckle, slapping JJ across the back. "I was just dreaming that we had an extra trombone player and out of the blue, bam, you pop up right in front of us holding a trombone. I assume you can play?"

"Well…" I hesitated, not sure how to answer. "It's been a while since I performed."

"Perfect. You're hired. I'll pay you $1 for the night and an extra $0.50 if you don't embarrass us."

"A buck fifty? That's it?" I said out loud, not that I knew what the exchange rate was for 1940, but c'mon, only $1.50?

JJ laughed at this. "Solomon the Cheap. The kid's not dumb, Sol. You better pay him straight."

Solomon smiled. "I like you, kid. What's your name?"

"My name is Aaron."

"Well, Aaron. My name is Solomon Felsher, but you can call me Solomon the Great or Solomon the Amazing. All my friends do. I tell you what. I'll pay you $2, the same as those drunk-as-a-skunk putzes, Oswald and Stew. Plus, I'll throw in an extra $1 if you don't embarrass us. Three bucks ain't bad for a night's work in Chicago. What do you say?"

Solomon held out his hand to shake on the deal.

I tallied my options. It didn't look like I was going to wake Solomon from his dementia dream. The thought of playing trombone in front of a live audience terrified me, but at the same time, the thought of playing the trombone again was too good to pass up.

I grabbed Solomon's hand and shook. "Deal."

"Attaboy," Solomon said with a wink. "Say JJ, go get Stew's jacket and tie for the kid. It might be a little big on him, but it'll do. C'mon kid, let me run through the music with you quick. We go on in twenty."

JJ left to track down a matching tux and bowtie while Solomon pulled out a stack of swing tunes and jazz ballads.

"So how old are you, Aaron, sixteen? Seventeen? I remember being like you, sneaking into New York clubs looking for a chance to sit in and play with a band. It takes moxie to do what you're doing. I like that in a fella."

"Umm…I'm only fourteen."

Solomon's head reeled back and his eyes went wide. "Oy, vey! You're only fourteen! I say, nice job with that mustache, kid. You sure fooled me. I can't believe I'm paying a fourteen-year-old three bucks. Do me a favor and don't tell the other fellas. They'll think I'm losing my negotiating touch. If anyone asks, you're seventeen, got it?" Solomon gave me a wink and a nod of his head.

"Okay," I answered timidly.

"Now for the music. What's your range?"

"I can play a high B-flat and a low F."

Solomon furrowed his brow and nodded. "Good enough. How's your sight reading?"

My shoulders slumped. I was a horrible sight reader.

"Not so good," I said honestly, "but I'm decent at improv."

Solomon ran his hand through his curly black hair, his mind thinking through possibilities.

"Okay. I probably won't need any improv tonight, but I will need sound—lots of bright, full, swinging sound. I'm missing two trombonists, so you've gotta play for two tonight. I've already written the chord progressions above the staff on all the music. Just play the chord notes the whole time and do your best to follow the rhythms—and give me lots of *full sound*. I'll try to pick songs that will be easier for you to follow."

JJ returned holding a tux jacket and a bow tie.

"Perfect. You've got ten minutes to get dressed and warmed up, but conserve those chops. We're playing a three-hour set tonight. Let's swing this joint!"

CHAPTER 11
MACK THE KNIFE

I never got a chance to warm up since I spent the whole ten minutes fumbling with my bow tie. Luckily, JJ came back to get me and fixed my tie in a matter of seconds.

"Alright, kid," JJ said with a grin. "It's show time."

I followed JJ out onto the stage and he pointed to a seat next to three trumpet players sitting on a row behind the saxophones. In front of the band stood Solomon in his gleaming white tuxedo, with his saxophone, Betty, strapped around his neck.

In front of our stage was a wide dance floor with round tables covered in deep maroon table cloths surrounding the dance floor. Waitresses in short black dresses walked around the candlelit tables bringing food, drinks and selling cigars and cigarettes. The place looked classy, like out of an old-time movie.

I felt the first trickles of sweat roll down my neck as the nearly blinding stage lights broiled us alive. Between the smoky haze and the bright lights, my already troubled nerves were on the brink, causing my stomach to churn. But then a man walked onto the stage, standing off to the side, and spoke into a big, round microphone.

"Ladies and gents, guys and dolls, The 226 Club presents to you for your live entertainment, *King Solomon & His Swinging Fellas.*"

"Well that's not a very subtle name," I said under my breath.

The trumpet players next to me must have heard what I said, since they all struggled to keep a straight face as they stifled laughs.

But the crowded club paid no attention to us in the background. All eyes were on King Solomon as the crowd cheered and clapped.

Solomon gave a long bow to the audience and then turned around to the band.

"Alright you bunch of ninnies. Let's show Chicago how it's done and get this place hopping with a little *Sing, Sing, Sing.*"

I followed suit as everyone quickly raised their instruments. Thanks to Solomon's Jazz Appreciation lessons, I actually knew the tune to this song.

My hands trembled as I placed the trombone mouthpiece to my lips. Besides the single note played in my mind palace auditorium, it had been two years since I really played the trombone. Solomon gave me a knowing smile and winked.

"1, a 2, a 1, 2, 3, 4," Solomon counted off energetically, and JJ laid out a steady beat on the tom-toms before the band exploded into a sweet cacophony of brilliant, swinging sound.

Song after song we played into the night. I had no idea how late it was, but it didn't matter, we were feeling the groove and the people in the club were dancing the night away. Three of the songs we played were tunes I had actually learned in Jazz band, at least a variation of the same song, which made it easier to play along. At first I was timid, scared to make a misstep and play during a rest, but quickly the timidity left, replaced by the swaying of the music. I did like Solomon asked and I played full of sound.

It didn't take long for my face and jaw muscles, otherwise known as chops, to feel the burn. I was exercising muscles long forgotten. It was also strange to play with the mustache, but luckily it was a tight and thin one and it didn't get in the way too much.

We were playing the last song of the night and everyone in the band, except me, had played multiple solos on songs. But King

Solomon had played solos on every song, which wasn't a bad thing since the man could play. Every time he soloed, the crowd ate it up.

Solomon was playing an improv solo at the front of the band and he turned and gave me a head nod, which I had come to learn was his signal that it was time for a certain band member to solo next.

My face went pale and my heart, which had been beating in sync with JJ's drums, fell out of rhythm, skipping multiple beats.

Solomon nodded again for me to stand up and I froze—my rear stuck to the chair. With an arched eyebrow, while still playing his fluid improv, Solomon gave me a final head nod and winked.

Fine. This is only a dream. You can do this, I thought to myself.

My body stiffly rose from my chair, and my emotions screamed at me to sit back down. Solomon wrapped up his solo and the crowd cheered. Then he waved a hand toward me, putting me on display for the audience and I started to solo. My cheek muscles were on fire as I flexed them and blew into the trombone. My arm felt like Jell-O as I slid the trombone's slide up and down, pulling the slide to the notes in my head. I played a horrible sounding note and nearly collapsed with fear, but luckily with the trombone, if a note is off, all you have to do is move the slide a little further in a long glissando until it fits.

Soon the notes were pouring from my mind, to my lips, through my arm, and out the beautiful brass instrument resting on my shoulder. I started swaying back and forth to the music, feeling the intense high of the solo as I grooved with the music. I sensed the time for my solo coming to a close, and I knew how I wanted to wrap it up. I could hear the high-pitched C note I wanted to end on, but I had never played a clear High C in my life, let alone after a three-hour marathon of playing that had left my chops dead.

But the crowd cheered louder as I played and a bolt of renewed energy flew through my body. I started my build up for the finish, getting higher with each note—a D, then an F, an A, B-Flat and then finally the C. I thought my lips would fall off and my cheeks would explode, but I played that High C note clear as a crystal, holding it true for eight solid beats.

Releasing the note, the crowd went wild and I couldn't help but grin ear-to-ear as I bowed my head and sat back down in my chair. I lifted my trombone back up to my lips, but my chops were completely toast and no more notes would come out, so I faked playing the last few measures before the song ended.

"Oy! Not bad, kid. Not bad at all. I'll admit, when I heard you climbing up for that High-C note, I was a bit worried you wouldn't pull it off, but then *BHAM*, you nailed it like the Israelites taking down the walls of Jericho! Here's your take for the night," Solomon said, handing me a $10 bill backstage. "We're playing another show tomorrow night if you're interested. What do you say, kid? Are you in?"

"Sure," I answered reluctantly, not knowing how long I would be stuck in Solomon's mind. Solomon's last dream had only lasted one night, and time seemed to work differently in his dementia dreams than it did in reality. Who knew how long I might be stuck in 1938 Chicago?

"Swell, kid. How about I buy you a soda? My treat. Our adoring fans await."

Solomon led me out a stage door and into the club, where a thick haze of cigarette smoke filled the air. The same small jazz trio that played before us was back on stage. I found out from Solomon they were the club band and played as fillers each night.

We walked amongst the candlelit tables of the crowded club, various people stopping Solomon, and myself by association, to shake our hands and tell us how much they loved our music. Most of the men in the club were dressed in slick suits, and the women wore dazzling evening gowns of varying colors. No one wore the flapper hats anymore, like Zelda Fitzgerald had worn at the Dempsey fight, but besides that, the styles had not changed too much from thirteen years earlier.

We made our way to the bar, and Solomon ordered a scotch on the rocks for himself and a Coca Cola for me. We took our drinks to a nearby table as Solomon continued to shake hands with passing fans. The rest of the band was out and about the club, mingling at tables and dancing with various ladies on the dance floor.

A pretty young waitress came to our table. She wore a simple black dress with a ruffled skirt that ended just above her knee. Her hair was blonde, and she wore a black hat in the shape of an army cadet hat, with a tall red feather sticking out the side.

"You boys sounded great up there," she said in a cheerful voice, flashing a confident smile. "What can I get you to eat? Donny, the owner, says it's on the house."

"I'll take a burger and fries. Do you have those?" I asked, unsure if burgers and fries had been invented yet.

The waitress gave me a wink. "Of course, kid. And how about you Mr. King Solomon. What can I get for you?"

For the first time in my life, Solomon was silent. He stared at the waitress with his eyebrows slightly arched and his mouth partially open. He looked like he was about to speak, but no words came out.

"Are you doing okay, sweetie?" the waitress asked, a look of concern crossing her face. "Anything I can get you? You need some ice water? Fresh air?"

Solomon's mouth was agape a few seconds longer before he closed it and seemed to come to his senses. "Uh, yeah, uh…sorry about that miss…?"

Solomon held out the word and flashed his most charming smile, waiting for her to give him her name. The waitress rolled her eyes, a slight grin tugging at her lips.

"Miss Winter, but you can call me Dolores, Mr. King."

"Oy, please call me Solomon. All that Mr. King business is unnecessary."

"Okay, Solomon. So now that the cat's no longer got your tongue, is there anything I can get you?"

"To be truthfully honest, my dear Dolores, there's only one thing in the world I would love to have right now and I'm not sure it's on your menu at this fine establishment."

Dolores smiled, showing a row of pearly white teeth, and playfully raised an eyebrow. "I don't know about that," she said. "Our chefs are pretty amazing. I'm sure they can whip up something special just for you. Tell me what you want and I'll see what I can do."

"Wonderful!" Solomon proclaimed. "If anyone can help me out tonight, it's you Dolores. The only thing I'm hoping for tonight is a single dance with the most beautiful woman in the room. The only problem is she's working as a waitress here tonight, but I'm hoping she can sneak away for a single dance before taking our orders. What do you say, dearie? Give me one quick dance, and you will truly make me feel like a king for the night."

Dolores blushed, tilting her head slightly to look off to the left toward the bar before rolling her eyes back to Solomon. Solomon stood up from his chair, his white tuxedo gleaming brightly against the sea of men wearing dark suits. He held out his hand, offering a forlorn smile with puppy dog eyes.

"Just one dance?" he asked in a silky voice.

Dolores shook her head slightly, holding back a smile. "Okay. Just one dance, and then I got to get back to work. But answer me this. How is me dancing with you going to make you feel like a king?"

Solomon took Dolores by the hand and grinned. "Simple, my dear. I'll be dancing with a beautiful queen."

Dolores stifled a giggle and rolled her eyes. "You're something else, Solomon."

"As are you," he replied, placing his hand on Dolores' back as he led her to the dance floor. He turned his head around and gave me a wink, flashing a big grin.

Their single dance turned into two, then three, then four dances. Not only was Solomon a talented musician, but both he and Dolores were like professionals out on the floor. Light on their feet, they moved in perfect harmony with one another, gliding around the dance floor. Other dancers began to form a circle around them, clapping and cheering for Solomon and Dolores as they moved to a quick, swinging tune from the club band. As the song ended, the crowd cheered and applauded the duo. Solomon took a bow, pointed to Dolores and clapped enthusiastically. Dolores gave a slight curtsy to the crowd, her face flush with embarrassment, and she grabbed Solomon's hand, dragging him back toward our table. The couple was full of smiles and laughter as they walked back toward me, hand-in-hand.

"Oy, Dolores my dear. You can dance! Wouldn't you say so, Aaron? She was the dancing queen tonight. You know what? That's a great title for a song. Dancing Queen. I gotta remember that one."

I clapped my hands together and gave a slight bow to the couple. "You two were amazing together out there. I've never seen dancing like that in person before."

"Yeah, you were an original Fred Astaire out there," Dolores said, her dimples forming like Sarah's when she smiled.

"And you were Ginger Rogers," Solomon replied, taking Dolores by the hand, bowing, and kissing the top of her hand, all in one smooth motion.

Dolores blushed and rolled her eyes again, her smile widening. But something caught her attention from behind Solomon. Like night and day, she pulled her hand away from Solomon and her smile withdrew to a scowl.

"Let go of my hand," she hissed. But the hiss was not out of anger. It seemed more of a warning or out of fear.

Solomon's red face, which I attributed to the mixture of his scotch and the exertion of the dancing, reared back in surprise. "Why, what's wrong?" he said, reluctantly pulling his hand away. "I hope I didn't offend you. I, I…"

But Solomon was cut off by the bellow of a giant man coming up behind him.

"Dolores, who is this putz you're dancing with?

The intruder had slick black hair, a scar down his left cheek, and a tuxedo that appeared to be two sizes too small as it squeezed around his bulging neck and arms. He also stood a few inches taller than Solomon, which was impressive, since the young Solomon was at least six-foot two-inches tall himself.

The man pushed his way past Solomon and grabbed Dolores roughly by the arm.

"Mack," she said nervously. "We were only dancing. Plus, you and I only had the one date. We are not an item. We are not a pair, and you need to let go of my arm or I'll get Donny."

Mack snorted cockily. "Donny? Really? You think that fat, penny-pinching, greedy old Jew is going to do something? Donny ain't nothin'. He answers to me and my bosses. I used to enforce this club for Al Capone himself, back in the day before he got pinched," Mack hissed. "Donny doesn't own this nightclub—we do. Don't you forget it, sweetheart."

Mack yanked on Dolores' arm, pulling her toward him. She winced in pain, but held her head up pridefully, shooting a contemptuous glare at Mack.

"Hey!" I yelled, standing up to protest, knowing I would get creamed if I tried anything. But Solomon gently put his hand in front of me and motioned for me to sit.

"Let go of the lady," Solomon commanded Mack through gritted teeth. His red face turned five shades darker as he stared at Mack, full of loathing.

"Excuse me," Mack said with a laugh. "What was your name again? Solomon, right? You're the one with the colored, pet monkey who plays the drums."

Mack lifted his thick hands up to his armpits, and said, "ooh-ooh-ooh-eee-eee," pretending to be a monkey.

"Don't you ever talk about my friend like that again!" Solomon growled.

Mack snorted. "Relax, pal. I think you've had a bit too much to drink. Why don't you sit down and have another drink on me while I take Dolores, here, away for the evening to remind her who owns what."

Solomon did not sit down and I saw two more, equally menacing men, make their way to Mack's side.

Solomon raised his finger and pointed it directly at Mack. "I'll only give you one more chance. Let Dolores go or I'll make you let her go."

Dolores' eyes went wide and she shook her head, trying to dissuade Solomon. The section of the club where we stood began to grow silent as onlookers realized what was happening.

Mack nodded to his companions at his side. "It seems our friend, Solomon, has forgotten how to sit and be quiet. Why don't you two take him out back and give him a lesson."

The two thugs grinned and took a step toward Solomon, but before they reached him he hit both men with a one-two punch to the noses, quicker than lightning. Blood poured down their faces as both men stumbled backwards and fell to the ground. The two goons lay on the floor, dazed and confused.

Mack released Dolores and pushed her away. He tilted his thick neck side-to-side, cracking it, and lifted his fists up to fight.

"Okay, wise guy. You have no idea what you've just brought down on yourself."

Mack threw two powerful jabs, but Solomon put up his hands to block the blows before returning two quick jabs of his own. He hit Mack in the face with both punches, but they only seemed to make the monster-of-a-man angrier.

Mack retaliated with a left jab and then a right cross. Solomon avoided the jab, but the right cross caught him square in the jaw, sending him reeling backward onto our table. Solomon blinked his eyes and opened them wide as his face lay on the table looking at me.

"Fella has got some power to those punches," he mumbled to me, opening his mouth and rubbing his jaw.

Solomon shook his head, gave me a wink, and popped back up to face Mack, who was pointing and laughing at him. I noticed a few more of Mack's gang had shown up, pushing people back to give Mack space. From the corner of my eye, I saw JJ shaking his head furiously before ducking out of view.

Mack threw another cross and then a wide hook, but this time Solomon deftly moved out of the way, landing succinct blows to Mack's side and kidney. Mack winced in pain this time, which Solomon took note of as he pounded Mack's kidney with three more sharp blows.

This caused Mack to hunch over, his hands resting on his knees. A handful of men closed in on Solomon to intervene, including the first two goons Solomon had knocked down. With blood on their faces they rushed Solomon, who punched them both in the noses a second time, sending new streams of blood running down their faces like a faucet. Three more men grabbed Solomon and pinned his arms behind his back while Mack straightened himself up, wiping blood from his lip.

Mack stared at Solomon with a look of murderous rage. Reaching into his jacket he pulled out a switchblade.

"I've had quite enough of you, *King* Solomon," he said mockingly while shaking the knife in Solomon's direction.

"Mack, stop!" Dolores pleaded.

Mack turned toward Dolores and sneered. "Don't you worry, babe. When I'm done with this putz, you and I are going to have a long talk back at my place."

Dolores' face went livid. "I don't think so," she said. "I'm never going back to your place with you!"

Like a professional NFL punter, Dolores kicked Mack straight in the groin with her black, pointed shoe.

Mack doubled over in pain and dropped the knife. But this didn't stop Dolores. Before Mack could cover himself with his hands, she unleashed another kick, with the power of a trained dancer, into Mack's groin a second time. And while the brute gasped for air, Dolores grabbed a nearby wine bottle from a table and brought it down with such force across the back of Mack's skull that I thought she had killed the man when he collapsed to the floor.

Mack's goons turned to her in shock. But before they could do anything about it, JJ and the rest of Solomon's band, pushed through the growing crowd and collided with Mack's men in a fist full of fury.

Taking a cue from Dolores, I grabbed my Coke bottle and smashed it across the back of the head of one of the goons still holding Solomon. The man went down just enough to release his grip, which freed one of Solomon's arms. Solomon swung a heavy hook into the other man holding him and finished the man off with a few more punches. He turned toward a man trying to grab Dolores and Solomon's face looked angrier than a wolverine, not that I've ever seen a real wolverine, but I've read the X-Men comics and that's who he reminded me of.

Within a few minutes, Solomon and his band mates mopped the floor with rest of Mack's men. A short, fat man with balding hair pushed his way into the circle, his shoulders slumping as he took in the scene.

"Donny," Dolores said, tears forming in her eyes for the first time. "I'm sorry Donny. He was going to kill Solomon and then take me back to his place. I couldn't let him, I just couldn't..."

Donny looked at her, shook his head appraisingly, and gave a tight-lipped grin. "You kids need to get out of here right now! Come with me."

I was last in line as Donny led us back behind the stage and rushed us down the hallway, past our dressing room, toward a back exit. Everyone kept going, but I stopped at the dressing room, realizing Solomon had forgotten Betty, and darted inside.

"Kid, hurry up!" Donny called as I came out of the room and sped down the hallway toward the exit door he held open.

The sticky summer air hit me as I ran outside into the dark night of a deserted alley.

"When that giant fool wakes up there's going to be hell to pay. Here, take this," Donny said, pulling out a sizeable stack of money from his wallet and a pair of keys. "You kids get to the train station and get on the next train out of town. Dolores, use my Plymouth parked around the corner. You kids can probably squeeze in there. Leave my car at the station, and I'll have someone pick it up later."

"But what about my drums and all our instruments," JJ protested.

"Kid," Donny said with a smirk. "I just gave you one thousand dollars. I think you can buy yourself new instruments."

JJ's jaw, along with the rest of the band mates, dropped.

"Betty," Solomon whispered, with a look of panic. "I've got to go back and get Betty!"

Dolores tipped back her head and arched an eyebrow. "Who's Betty?"

"It's his saxophone," I replied, holding up the case with the gold inscription on the side. "And don't worry, Sol. I grabbed it for you on the way out. You left it in the dressing room next to a bowl of fruit."

Solomon let out a gasp and wrapped me up in a bear hug. "Kid, you just saved the day!"

Donny rolled his eyes. "Wonderful. You've got your instrument back. Now you all need to move it."

"Sir, thank you," Solomon said, hurriedly offering his hand to Donny. "I apologize for the trouble this caused you."

Donny shook Solomon's hand firmly. "No apology necessary. Thanks for protecting my best waitress and my only niece. But now the lot of you need to get out of town. And Dolores, don't try to come back until I say it's okay. Call me when you get out of town and let me know where you are. I'll keep in touch and let you know when it's safe to come back to Chicago. Mack the Knife may not be the brightest bulb in the lamp, but he has a long memory."

Tears streamed down Dolores's face as she wrapped her uncle in hug. "Thanks, Uncle Donny."

Donny wiped the tears away from her cheek and smiled. "Take care sweetheart. B'ezrat HaShem. I'll see you again. Now, go. Get out of here before they wake up. If there's a round two with Mack and his crew, they won't be using fists this time. Shalom aleichem."

"Shalom aleichem," Solomon and Dolores replied back in unison.

We all gave our final thanks to Donny and followed Dolores around the corner to a big, black boat of a car. But before we got in, Donny pulled Solomon back with a firm grip and whispered in his ear. Thanks to my super-hearing, which apparently still worked in dementia dreams, I caught every word.

"Listen to me, kid. I may have just wished peace upon you, and I am thankful to you for protecting my niece, but if anything happens to my little Dolores, or you so much as defile her sacred womanhood before getting married, which you will need *my* blessing to do, Mack and his goons will be the least of your worries. *Capisce?*"

Solomon bobbed his head up and down emphatically.

"Good, now get," Donny said with a pat across Solomon's cheek.

Solomon scooted in next to Dolores, who was at the wheel of the big black Plymouth, and wrapped his arm around her tight. After the rest of the band stuffed themselves into the car like a bunch of clowns at a circus, I put my foot on the running board to get in, but my foot slipped, and I fell backward, unable to regain control. My head hit the cement with a thud, and all went black.

CHAPTER 12
HAPPY HANUKKAH

Solomon full-out belly laughed as he sat in the recliner across from my bed, while I recounted the story of the Chicago 226 Club to him. "Oy, I'd forgotten half that story, except for meeting Dolores and my fight with Mack the Knife."

Wait, that was Mack the Knife?' I asked with my mind. *As in "The" Mack the Knife from the song?*

Solomon huffed. "Yes and no. The original *Mack the Knife* song came from a German opera, if you can imagine that. Rumor is, one night at the opera the organ stopped working. So the pit, which was a jazz band, had to improvise an accompaniment to a song about a killer named Macheath, who was known as Mack the Knife, and the first version of the song, as you know it, was born."

But I thought you said he was the real Mack the Knife, I asked.

"Oy, he is. His name was Mack and he killed people with a knife. People called him Mack the Knife. One night I told Louis Armstrong and Bobby Darin all about my run-in with ol' Macky and they loved the story. Louis had his fair share of run-ins with the rival Chicago and New York mobs in his day. He was such a money-maker when he played at the clubs that the mobs fought over him, even threatening Louis at gun point, trying to force him to play in their clubs exclusively so they could manage his career. I was never popular enough to have that problem. But luckily for Louis, he always slipped away unscathed."

So Louis Armstrong sang the song about you?

"Kind of. When he heard my story about actually going to fisticuffs with Mack the Knife, he felt inspired to sing his own version of the opera. It did okay on the charts, but when Bobby Darin made his version a few years later, back in '59 I think it was, the song hit number one and that lucky crooner got himself a Grammy for it."

Solomon shook his head and sighed. "Oy, maybe if I was a better singer I could have made it big like those two. Even Ella Fitzgerald got a Grammy off the song when she improvised it at a live recording. The only thing I got from it was this scar," Solomon said bitterly, pointing to a thin, white, nearly invisible scar, running along the top of his bushy eyebrow.

Well, you did get Dolores, I offered, trying to cheer him up. It seemed the more he talked about his famous friends, the more his attitude turned bitter.

Solomon's frown upturned into a smile. "You're right. I did find my sweet Dolores. I would trade all the music and all the fame and riches in the world for her."

She was very pretty, and the way you two moved on the dance floor together was amazing.

"She was more than pretty, Aaron my boy. Not only was she the most beautiful woman in any room, but she was the kindest, smartest, most talented, and toughest person I ever knew. And I'm a better man for it."

Solomon's mood seemed to completely change as he talked about Dolores.

So what happened to you guys after you left Chicago? Where did you go? Did you go back to New York?

Solomon shook his head. "Me, Dolores, JJ and the boys headed south to Dallas, Texas. We had already hit all the nightclubs we could in New York before we came to Chicago and we were going nowhere. So we tried to make it in the south. We went from Dallas to Houston, to New Orleans, Mobile, Nashville, Atlanta and then back to New Orleans. Those were the days—my favorite year of touring I ever had, probably because Dolores was with me.

"But it was tough at first. Only a few of the white dance halls and clubs would let us play, since JJ's black and I'm a Jew. So we started hitting all the colored clubs and picked up a bit of a following, making new friends along the way. But when we went back to New Orleans, JJ met a sweet girl named Violet. He and Vi fell in love and got married. Then a few of the boys decided to go back to New York, and one-by-one, King Solomon's band evaporated. I subbed in little clubs, playing sax to make some extra cash, until one day we got word from Donny that Mack the Knife had been killed in a gang shootout. The next day, Dolores and I hopped on a train to Chicago, and a week later, with Uncle Donny's blessing, we were married on December 7, 1941, a day that would go down in infamy—the day Pearl Harbor was bombed."

Really? I asked. *You were married on the same day as the Pearl Harbor bombing?*

Solomon just nodded, his eyes looking far off as he stared to the side. I had not yet studied World War II, but I knew about Pearl Harbor. Everyone knew about Pearl Harbor.

"Such a happy and a sad day," Solomon continued. "Made it kind of hard to ever forget your anniversary. It was a day of pure joy for Dolores and me, but a day of sorrow and anger for all of America. It was the day the U.S. officially entered the war, and millions of lives would be changed because of it."

***

"Chag Sameach, Aaron my boy," Solomon proclaimed.

"That means Happy Hanukkah," Sarah said matter-of-factly. She smiled brightly, revealing a row of her hot pink braces.

Well, Chag Sameach back to you guys, I replied in my mind.

It didn't matter that I was not Jewish, at least not full Jewish. My grandparents on my mom's side had been relatively faithful Jews, but my Mom never talked about it, and my grandparents died before I was born. I knew almost nothing about Hanukkah, so Solomon and Sarah took it upon themselves to tutor and include me in the festivities.

Solomon placed his yarmulke, or kippa as he called it, on his head, and Sarah wrapped her head in a beautiful purple scarf. Solomon explained they wore these during the lighting of the menorah and during special ceremonies and prayers. He turned off the lights in the room, allowing the golden sunset to slowly give way to nightfall. The corner streetlamp outside our window flicked on, casting a dim, yellowish hue in the darkened room.

The menorah Sarah brought for us sat on small table placed in my line of sight next to the TV. It was gold colored and had nine candleholders—four on each side with one large holder in the middle. Solomon held a larger candle in his left hand and spoke reverently.

"This larger candle is called the shamash. It is lit first to give us light and to light the others. We celebrate Hanukkah in remembrance of the miracle of oil, when only one-day's worth of oil burned for eight days after a small group of Jews revolted and reclaimed the Holy Temple."

All was quiet in the room, including my own thoughts, as Solomon continued.

"I will now recite the Hanukkah blessings—

"Baruch Atah Adonai Eloheinu Melech HaOlam…" Solomon spoke the blessing in Hebrew and then translated it into English.

Blessed are You, O Lord Our God, Ruler of the Universe, Who has sanctified us with Your

*commandments and commanded us to kindle the
lights of Hanukkah.*

*Blessed are You, O Lord our God, Ruler of the
Universe, Who made miracles for our forefathers in
those days at this time.*

*Blessed are You, O Lord Our God, Ruler of the
Universe, Who has kept us alive, sustained us and
brought us to this season.*

Using a match, Solomon lit the large shamash candle, and
then used the flame of the shamash to light the smaller candle Sarah
had placed on the far-right of the menorah. The flames flickered and
danced in the darkened room and we watched them with a quiet
reverence.

Then Solomon clapped his hands, not just once, not just
twice, but repeatedly, producing a steady beat. His shoulders began to
sway as he started humming a tune. Carefully he shuffled in a dance
around the room as he clapped. I remembered how graceful he had
been on the dance floor in the Chicago Club, and felt a bit of sadness
as I watched him gingerly shuffle his feet to the beat.

But Solomon showed no signs of sadness. His eyes were
closed and a wide smile spread across his face as the candlelight
illuminated his bouncing, gray curly hair. He continued to hum the
unknown tune and sway to his slow, steady beat of claps. The tempo
of his clapping began to creep up faster, and faster, and as his tempo
increased, so did the volume of his humming. His humming was loud
now, reaching a pinnacle with the speed of his clapping, and then
Solomon broke into lyrical song.

*Hanukkah, oh Hanukkah, come light the menorah
Let's have a party, we'll all dance the horah
Gather 'round the table, we'll give you a treat
Dreydels to play with and latkes to eat.*

Sarah giggled at her grandfather as he beckoned with his hands for her to sing and dance with him. She began clapping and dancing at his side, the edges of her purple scarf fluttering in the air as she twirled. When the second verse began, Sarah added her voice to Solomon's and I felt a chill down my spine. Sarah had an amazing voice.

And while we are playing the candles are burning low
One for each night they shed a sweet
Light to remind us of days long ago
One for each night they shed a sweet
Light to remind us of days long ago.

The song ended and Solomon wrapped Sarah in a big bear hug. "Oy vey, you have a *beautiful* voice, my little Sarah. It reminds me of your grandmother."

Sarah sounded like an angel, I said in my mind, still amazed such a powerful voice came out of a fourteen-year-old girl.

"Even Aaron liked it. He said you sounded like an angel."

If I could blush, I would have, but even in the dim glow of the candles I could see Sarah was doing enough blushing for both of us.

"Thanks, Aaron," she said sweetly.

I didn't know you could sing, I said. *You never mentioned going to choir at school.*

Solomon relayed my message to Sarah with a bemused smile on his face.

"That's because I don't sing in the choir. I don't like to sing in public. Consider yourself lucky you heard me at all, and I'm not that good."

Are you kidding me? With a voice like that you should try out for Star Search. There's no reason you shouldn't be in the choir singing solos. You've got to let that light shine and share your talent.

96

Solomon shared my message and Sarah eyed him incredulously. "Is that really Aaron talking because it sounds a lot like you, Grandpa?"

"Oy, I'm hurt," Solomon said, feigning protest. "Those were all Aaron's words, truly. He recognizes what your mother and I have known for years. You have a gift, and you should share it. Your grandmother Dolores had an amazing voice as well, but she refused to sing in public. No matter how much I coaxed her or how much everyone told her she sounded like Billie Holiday, she wouldn't sing in public."

Sarah rolled her eyes at Solomon and then looked at me. "I'll make you a deal, Aaron. If you can tell me to join the choir with your own lips, I'll do it."

Solomon harrumphed. "Sarah. That's ridiculous. The boy may never speak out loud again. You can't do—"

Deal, I said in my mind, interrupting Solomon.

Solomon turned toward me and arched an eyebrow. He let out a low chuckle and gave me a slight nod of approval, followed by a wink.

"Aaron agrees to your terms. But you'd better watch out, Sarah. When Aaron sets his mind on something, he can accomplish anything. The boy has a beautiful mind, like a palace. Just you wait and see."

Sarah stepped closer to me, bringing her face in front of mine. She squinted her eyes slightly and pulled her lips into a tight smile, causing the freckles on her cheeks to move upwards. "Fine. It's a deal."

"Wonderful. Now that we have that settled, who's ready to lose money spinning the dreydel?"

Under the lights of the menorah, we played the dreydel game for another hour or so. Sarah spun for me on my turns, and true to Solomon's word, he took all of the pennies we started with and won the game.

As we played, Solomon explained the history of the dreydel. The more time I spent with Solomon, the more I felt like he was my personal history tutor who would not only tell me about history, but take me on special fieldtrips into his mind to see the past.

"Dreydel became a tradition when the ruling Seleucid Empire outlawed the Jews from study and worship. So the Jews would often meet secretly to study the Torah together. If a patrol came near they would pull out the dreydel and begin playing to hide what they were really doing. The Seleucid's just thought they were gambling and left them alone. Then after the Maccabee rebellion, the tradition carried on as part of the Hanukkah. So," Solomon said as he gathered the last of our coins, "Hanukkah reminds us that God still performs miracles, and he has not left us, and the dreydel teaches us to remember the sacrifices of those who came before."

And, I interjected, *to never play against you with more than pennies.*

Solomon chuckled and gave me a wink. "You learn quick, kid."

A soft knock tapped on our door, interrupting Solomon's win. A second later the door slowly swung open, allowing the bright lights of the hallway to enter our candlelit room. I could not see who entered, and no one spoke, but I smelled a familiar scent I had not smelled in months. Chlorine.

CHAPTER 13
MISSING PARENTS

DAD? I shouted in my mind.

Solomon arched an eyebrow and harrumphed. "So. Are you Aaron's long-lost father?" he asked. His words had a sharpness to them that no one in the room could miss. Solomon stood from his chair and extended a hand to the stranger.

"Uh, yes. Yes, I am Aaron's father, Robert Greenburg. And who are you?" he asked with a confused voice.

This made sense since my dad had never met Solomon and I could see how finding an old guy with a New York accent, and a pretty teenage girl, hanging out in your paralyzed son's room, with candles lit in the darkness, might be confusing.

Solomon introduced himself with his usual bravado while Sarah turned on the lights. I saw my dad's tanned hand come into view as it shook Solomon's hand.

"I wasn't aware Aaron had a roommate. That's…that's good," my dad said as he stepped into my view. He turned to look at me, his face frozen in sadness.

"Well, if you ever bothered to visit your son you might know a lot of things," Solomon spoke, sounding like a teacher disciplining a student.

My dad's face visibly flinched at the dig, but he said nothing, his eyes still locked on my face.

Solomon continued his interrogation. "Where have you been? I know that the management has been trying to reach Aaron's parents for a few months. Aaron, I mean management, was worried something had happened to you."

My dad said nothing, bowed his head and turned to walk out of the room, leaving my view.

"Oy vey! You've got to be kidding me. You're leaving. Just like that. Oh, no you don't. Not like that. This boy needs his father, and he needs some answers."

"Listen," my dad finally spoke. I could hear the rising agitation in his voice. "I'm glad Aaron has a roommate, but I'm his father. I'm sixty-one years-old, and I don't need advice from a stranger telling me what to do. You don't know me and you have no idea what it's like to lose a son and...to lose a wife."

MOM! What happened to mom? I screamed in my head.

My screaming caused Solomon to flinch and he pressed a hand to his forehead. He gave me a look to calm down and patted my foot softly from where he stood at the end of my bed.

"Robert. May I call you Robert? I know exactly what it's like to lose my wife and to lose my son. But you have not lost your son. He is here. He's not gone. Now tell me what happened to your wife?"

My dad didn't say anything for a minute. He took a few steps back into the room and I could barely see him in my peripheral vision.

"Say," my dad asked in a surprisingly calm voice. In fact, he sounded almost happy, or curious. "Is that a saxophone laying on the couch? What did you say your name is again?" he asked Solomon.

"My name is Solomon Felsher, and yes that is my saxophone. I am a jazz musician and recorded quite a few songs in my day."

My dad took another step closer and into my view. He drew a sharp intake of breath and wrung his hands together near his chest. "Did you happen to record the song *No Life Without You*?

Solomon nodded. "Yeah, back in '52. It was one of my biggest hits...to be honest, it was my only hit. We broke the top 100 charts for a single week."

My dad's shoulders fell forward and he broke into a mixture of laughter and crying.

Dad? What's wrong? What happened to Mom? What's going on? I pleaded in my mind.

"Robert? What's wrong?" Solomon said with an air of authority. He placed a hand on my dad's shoulder and gave it a comforting squeeze.

"I...it..." he said between sobs. "oh, that...that was our song...*No Life Without You* was our song...we played it at our wedding...and now...I have no life without her...she left me."

What? I cried in my mind as I watched my dad fight to hold back his tears. *What do you mean she left? She's not dead, is she? Solomon, you've got to ask him for me. I need to know what happened.*

"Robert," Solomon said with a voice full of compassion. "I'm going to leave you and your boy alone. Tell him what has happened. I know he can't answer you, but he's there. I promise you your son can hear you and *he* needs you to talk to him as much as *you* need to tell him what's happening."

Solomon turned and gave a nod to Sarah. "Come on sweetheart. Let's give them some privacy and go get some Jell-O."

If I could have cried, I would have. If I could have gulped to pull back the lump in my throat, I would have. If it had been possible for me to scream at the top of my lungs, I would have. But all I could do was watch—watch as my Dad pulled up a chair in front of me and stared with wet, swollen, red eyes.

He simply stared at my face, saying nothing, and I said nothing in return.

He wiped away his tears, sniffed, and after a few more minutes his eyes began to soften as he continued looking over my face. His lips twitched upward and he let out a soft chuckle.

"You have your mother's eyes, and I can't believe how grown up you look. It seems like yesterday you were just a babe in your mother's arms. Now, in a few weeks, it will be a new year—1988. You'll be turning fifteen. So much has changed. So much."

My dad paused for a minute, looking into my eyes. "Aaron," he continued. "I don't know if you can hear me. But if you can, I'm...I'm so sorry..."

He exhaled and took a deep breath. "I'm not very good at this, am I? I'm not very good at anything I suppose, especially being a father or a husband. We went to Hawaii, and your mother and I fought the whole trip. It was my fault. I don't know why, but I kept pushing her away. She left Hawaii three days early. She packed her bags while I was in the shower and left. There was a note on the bed that said she couldn't take it anymore, and we needed some space. She flew to her Aunt Sheila's home in Denver and has been living there ever since."

My dad inhaled, taking another long, deep, breath. The redness in his eyes began to clear and the shakiness of his voice disappeared, replaced by a calm sadness.

"At first I convinced myself I didn't care. *Good riddance*, I thought. But I was lying to myself. When I returned home, she kept calling, trying to talk with me and telling me to go check on you, but I was too prideful. I refused to answer the phone, and I couldn't bring myself to come see you. That is, until tonight."

What happened Dad? Is Mom coming back? I asked.

"It's been four months since we separated. Tonight she left a new message. She said that it was clear I wanted nothing to do with her and that she had hired an attorney and wants a divorce. She wants full custody of you, Aaron, and wants to relocate you to Denver."

Divorce? I thought. I hyperventilated in my mind. *Denver? I can't go to Denver. I can't leave Solomon and Sarah. I can't be alone again. Solomon? Come back in here. I know you're just outside the door and you heard everything my dad said. You've got to stop this. You've got to help me.*

I heard Solomon's shuffling feet as he entered the room, accompanied by the smell of aftershave and Sarah's sweet orange scent.

My dad looked up toward Solomon and was about to speak, but Solomon waved his hand dismissively.

"I heard. Sorry for eavesdropping. I may be old, but my ears keep growing bigger like a satellite dish and my hearing is better than ever."

My dad let out a brief chuckle. "I really am the worst father and husband, aren't I?"

Solomon shook his head. "Oy, you really screwed this one up, but you know exactly what you need to do. You love your wife, and you love your son. You haven't lost them yet. Take it from someone who has. Go to Denver and get your wife back. Quit being a putz, and go back on bended knee, begging for forgiveness, and do whatever it takes to save your marriage. And then come back, with your wife, and see your son. Because, Robert," Solomon said pointing his finger toward me. "Your son can hear you. And no child deserves to be ignored by their parents."

My dad turned his attention back toward me and I felt the cold, wet tingle of a single tear roll down my face. *Oh my gosh*, I thought with an air of excitement. *I'm actually crying.*

But my dad didn't seem to notice.

CHAPTER 14
LIGHTSABERS & LETTERS

Did you hear from my dad? I asked Solomon as he entered our room.

Solomon ignored me as he carefully placed Betty back in her case. He had been out in the rec hall playing saxophone for the other residents of Restwood Suites. After a few weeks of careful coercion, he had convinced the manager, Mr. Wilson, that the residents needed a Valentine's Dance and that he would provide live music entertainment at no cost.

Apparently, the idea of a *free* band appealed to Mr. Wilson's cheapskate personality, and he agreed to allow a dance. Now Solomon was practicing on Betty every day in preparation for the first annual Restwood Suites Valentine's Dance. Solomon was bringing in a couple of his old buddies, one of them being JJ, to help him put together a small band for the event. Even Barry, the janitor, was in on it. When Barry found out about the dance, he offered his assistance on electric bass guitar. Since Solomon was missing a bass player, he readily accepted.

Solomon? I asked again. *Did you hear from my dad? Did he call the front desk, or did I get a letter in the mail today?*

Solomon locked the case on Betty, turned toward me, and sadly shook his head. "No, I haven't heard from your dad since last week. I tried calling him from the front desk, but there was no answer at his new number in Denver. But don't you worry, Aaron, my boy. Your dad is a good man, and he loves your mom. He will win her back."

I sighed in my mind. As much as I hoped he would, I wasn't so sure. My mind played back all of the arguments they'd had since I became sick. Mom had tried to be patient while Dad distanced himself, but she couldn't be patient forever.

Only two more weeks until the Valentine's dance, I thought, trying to change the subject. *Are you and your new band going to be ready?*

Solomon snorted. "Oy, Barry needs a bit of work, but he's doing fine. But don't you fret. We will sound great. Just wait until my buddies JJ and Tom get here next week. With some good percussion from JJ, laying down a solid beat, and Big Tom's trumpet, our little quartet will swing this joint, at least as much as old fogies like us can swing."

JJ seems like a nice guy, and he had your back in that fight with Mack the Knife.

"Good ol' JJ. He's been my best friend since we were pups in the Bronx. We got separated during the war. I went to the front lines in France, and he was a fighter pilot with the Tuskegee Airmen. But a few years after we both got back, he started playing gigs in Southern California, and we connected again, playing off-and-on together ever since. We even took a trip with our wives, back in '72, to go visit the Holy Land."

Wait, is JJ Jewish? I asked.

Solomon shook his head. "No, he's Muslim. I know what you're thinking—a Muslim and a Jew as best friends, but it's true. We both call each other 'little brother.' He says it to me because he's two months older than I am. I say it to him because I'm a foot taller than he is."

And where did you meet Tom? I don't think you've ever told me about him before.

106

Solomon smiled and let out a chuckle, his eyes wandering off as if remembering a funny story. "I met Big Tom in the Army band. Great trumpet player and an even better friend. He's a Mormon, you know, from Utah. Big as a tree, but smart as a whip and clean as a whistle."

So a Jew, a Muslim and a Mormon get together at a rest home to play in a jazz band...sounds like the beginnings of a bad joke.

"And don't forget Barry. He's a Baptist," Solomon added with a chuckle. "We're a regular mixed-up group. But I tell you what, Aaron. It's good to have a melting pot of friends. You need a little variety in your life. It's like music. We're all different and play our own instruments, but to make music, real, beautiful music, you gotta blend together."

Solomon gave me a wink. "It's all about playing in harmony."

I thought about that for a moment—blending and harmony. The idea was so simple and it made sense, but still, the world fought, people fought, parents fought.

So what was World War II like? I asked. *How did you blend and find harmony when you had to fight—when you had to kill?*

Solomon frowned and chewed the corner of his bottom lip.

"Listen, Aaron, I'll tell you the same thing I told Sarah," he said softly. "The only thing you need to know about the war is that it's over and we won. Let's just say there was very little beautiful music during the war, and we had to fight to get it back. But some things are worth fighting for."

Before I could respond, Solomon retreated to the bathroom and out of my sight. I had the feeling he wanted to be alone and that I had struck a nerve asking about the war. But while he was in the restroom, Barry came down the hall, whistling a tune as he entered our room. With a slosh of his mop in the bucket, the scent of pine cleaner filled the air.

"Hey there, Aaron. What's shakin' my friend?" Barry called. "Where's that crazy cat roomie of yours?"

In the bathroom, I answered.

Barry shot a glance at the bathroom door as he continued mopping. "I tell you what, I've been practicing with Solomon at night—you know getting ready for this dance—and man almighty that old cat can play."

No kidding. You should have seen him in the 40's.

"When I told the missus I was dusting off my bass guitar to play with Solomon and his band, she freaked out with excitement. She can't hardly wait to come to the dance and hear us play. Told me the first time she saw me playing my bass guitar with my garage band back in high school was the day she fell in love with me."

Barry finished up one half of the room and moved in and out of my view as he rolled the bucket along and mopped the floor.

"Too bad we can't get you out of this room to go to the dance," Barry continued. "Maybe I'll bring the missus by to meet you, if you don't mind visitors. I've told her all about you."

I don't mind at all. That'd be cool.

"Well, tell your friend Solomon hello for me and that I will be back tonight to practice after work. Check you later, Aaron."

See you Barry.

After Barry left, I started to worry about Solomon. He had been in the bathroom a long time, at least twenty minutes, and I couldn't hear any sounds coming from the bathroom. There was no flushing, no running water.

Solomon? Are you okay? I called in my mind.

No answer.

I couldn't tell if he was giving me the silent treatment for asking about World War II or if something was wrong.

Solomon! I mentally yelled. *I'm sorry about asking about the war. I just want to know if you're okay. Can you answer me?*

My super hearing picked up faint moaning from behind the bathroom door, but I couldn't understand what he was saying.

Solomon? What is it? What did you say?

Solomon's moan turned into a chuckle and he spoke raggedly. "Tom, can you believe it? We just played for Roosevelt, Churchill and Stalin. No one's going to believe us back at home."

Before I could call back to Solomon, familiar black swirls filled my mind and I felt myself falling backward.

Not again, I thought, trying to keep myself from getting sick as my mind spun faster and faster.

But even as I complained, deep down I felt a twinge of excitement. Since Solomon's arrival, I had not been able to pull myself into my mind palace anymore. At least not at will. The only time I went there was right before Solomon pulled me into one of his dementia dreams. It was like a waiting area before I could enter Solomon's dreams. But even my mind palace wasn't what it used to be for me. There, I was usually all by my lonesome in the castle, but in Solomon's dementia dreams I could move and talk to other people. In his dreams, I could relive history. In his dreams, I felt alive.

The spinning stopped, and I opened my eyes, surprised to find myself outside. I stood on the weapons training area on the palace grounds, with the castle a few hundred feet off in the distance. The training ground was basically a giant dirt patch stuck between the castle and a thick forest of trees. There were large circle targets for archery on one side of the dirt field, wooden practice dummies on the other, and rows of weapons in the middle. My eyes lit up as I looked over the traditional weapons like swords, spears, rifles and pistols, all lined neatly on wooden racks.

But further down the racks, I came across the not-so-traditional weapons, such as baseball bats, crowbars, potato guns, ninja stars, whips, and my personal favorite, lightsabers. Of course, I was immediately drawn to the lightsabers. I picked one up and flipped the switch on the black, cylinder handle.

PSSSSSZEWW the lightsaber hissed, shooting out a greenish-brown beam of laser light.

"That's weird," I said, scrunching my eyes to get a better look at the laser sword. The color was puke green with brownish swirls in it. "You know what it looks like," I continued out loud. "It looks like camouflage. Never seen a camo lightsaber before."

Not that I had seen any lightsabers up close like this before. But the camo color didn't deter me from swinging the lightsaber around like a space ninja. I attacked a few wooden practice dummies anchored in the ground next to the weapons.

ZWOOOOOM FVISH...ZWOOOOM ZWOOM FVISH

The camo lightsaber cut clean through two of the wooden dummies, leaving them both headless.

"Way cool!" I exclaimed.

I prepared to destroy another wooden dummy when something hissed by my ear and landed in the middle of the dummy's forehead with a loud *THUNK*!

Lodged a few inches into the dummy's head was a thick, black arrow with black feathers on the end.

I turned to where the arrow had come from, only to see two more arrows flying speedily in my direction. I jumped to the side, wildly swinging my lightsaber, hoping to cut down the arrows before they hit me. But apparently having a lightsaber doesn't make one a Jedi. I missed both arrows, with one whizzing by my face and the other tearing through my T-shirt just under my armpit.

"Youch!" I screamed, touching my side where the arrow had grazed my skin along my rib cage. A line of blood began to drip from the razor thin cut.

Since when does my mind palace attack me? I thought. But before I could ponder the question further, a set of four arrows came flying at me from the same direction. Luckily, I noticed them early enough and dashed to the side, out of the way as the arrows impaled the wooden dummies where I'd been standing.

I searched the thick forest, looking for the archers, but saw no one. The arrows just appeared out of nowhere, flying from the tree line.

Maybe they are just targeting the wooden dummies and I was in their path, I thought. But then eight more arrows came flying through the air directly toward me where I stood, a good ten feet off to the side of the dummies.

"Guess I am the target," I said, running out of the direction of the growing onslaught of arrows.

As soon as the arrows hit the ground where I had been standing, another volley, with more arrows than I could count, launched into the air in my direction. The swath of arrows was so large, there was no way I could move out of their path fast enough. But still, I turned and ran as fast as my legs could move.

Out of the corner of my eye I saw the cloud of arrows zooming closer and closer.

I'm not going to make it, I thought with desperation.

But then, just a few feet ahead, I saw a deep hole in the ground, maybe six feet wide. I pushed myself harder, dropping the lightsaber as I pumped my arms—willing myself to get to the hole in time. I dove in headfirst, just as the arrows sailed over me. But instead of hitting solid ground, I kept falling, and falling, and falling. I closed my eyes and screamed as I fell, until the world suddenly turned upside down, and I was standing, feet-first, on solid ground.

I felt myself take control of my body, and I blinked my eyes. The bright sunlight blinded me, and I raised my arm to block the sun, but the air was filled with the cold chill of winter.

I was wearing a thick green jacket, boots, and I felt a hard helmet on my head. Instinctively I reached up to my face, seeing if my mustache was back, but was surprised to find it was replaced with the sharp scruff of whiskers that extended along my chin, jaw and neck.

"This is weird," I whispered.

I heard the loud hum of airplanes, watching them land and take off a few miles in the distance. And my super sniffer smelled the gagging scent of diesel fuel exhaust floating in the air.

"No way," a voice yelled from the other side of a dirt road. "The captain flew you two bums all the way to Iran and then back to France, just to play for Roosevelt, Churchill and Stalin? I don't buy it."

I looked across the muddy dirt road and saw Solomon, dressed in an army uniform, standing by a fire with a handful of other soldiers. There were rows of brown tents in the background along with a few cinderblock buildings and dozens of military jeeps and trucks parked nearby.

"Oy, you don't know bupkis, Cantrel. I'm telling the honest truth," Solomon replied to the crowd of men, placing his hand over his heart. "Just ask Big Tom. Tom's a Mormon and he never lies. Ain't that right, Tom?"

Solomon nodded toward a tall, well-built man with blonde hair who was sitting off to the side. "It's true," said another soldier. "Big Tom's a straight shooter. Never heard him tell a lie in my life." This caused a collective nod amongst the other soldiers.

Tom smiled at the compliment and gave a single, slow nod. "We played for them in Tehran at a dinner party. We were with some other British and Russian soldiers in a mixed orchestra. Played some Bach, Beethoven, Tchaikovsky. It was a nice night."

Tom was a slow talker with a deep voice, and the more he spoke, the more I realized that he sounded like John Wayne.

"So there was no swinging with the Ruskies?" one of the other soldiers joked.

Solomon laughed. "I'm not sure old Stalin could swing if he were a monkey. I tell you what, though. That guy scared me. You should have heard him. He said he wanted to execute 50,000 German soldiers to stop them from building up another army. Not just war criminals, but regular Joe Schmo soldiers like you and me."

"What did Roosevelt have to say about that?" one of the soldiers asked.

Solomon shook his head. "I think President Roosevelt thought Stalin was joking. He said maybe 49,000 would do the trick.

But you should have seen Churchill. He went off the handle and stormed out of the room. That Stalin scares me. I'm not so sure he was joking. I think he was just testing the waters to see if he could really get away with it."

"Hey, isn't that the mail carrier?" Big Tom asked slowly, pointing directly at me.

The soldiers turned toward me and whooped with excitement, jumping up from their makeshift log chairs. For the first time, I realized I had a large satchel around my neck and a handful of letters in my hand.

"Hey kid. Come on over here, next to the warm fire," Solomon called, beckoning me with a wave of his gloved hand. "No use freezing while we read the mail."

I walked across the muddy road, my boots sloshing in the puddles from rutted tracks in the dirt, and the group of soldiers attacked me like moths to a porch light. They grabbed the letters from my hand and began sorting them, calling out names as they handed out the mail.

"Wizowsky. Smith. Topham. Cantrel. Felsher."

Solomon took a single letter addressed to him and a smile tugged at the corners of his lips. I moved closer and watched as he carefully opened the sealed envelope with his pocket knife. Standing just to the side, I read the letter as Solomon mumbled the words out loud.

> *Mazel Tov, my dearest Sol,*
>
> *I have the best news to share with you. Your son, Michael Joshua Felsher, was born on November 15, 1943. Oh Sol, he's amazing. God has blessed us with the most beautiful baby boy. He has your eyes and a full head of curly, black hair. I only wish you were here with us. I'm doing fine, and I am back home with little Michael. He's sleeping well at night and your mom's been over to visit and help around the house.*

Donny sent us some money for the baby, and we have plenty of food and everything, even with the rationing.

Solomon, I know I already said it, but we have the most beautiful baby boy, and I know he's going to love you just as much as I do. I can't wait until this blasted war is over and you can come home to be with us again. I miss you more every day. Stay safe, and don't try to be a hero and get yourself killed. But I know you better than that. So, God willing, if you're going to be a hero, be a smart one and stay alive. Not only do you have me, but now you have a darling baby boy waiting for you at home. Be safe. Please.

I don't know when you will get this letter or how long it will take to get a letter back from you, but until then, know my heart is yours and that I love you deeply.

Your loving, beautiful, gorgeous, amazing wife,
Dolores

Solomon raised his head to the air and cheered. "I'm a dad! Can you believe it fellas? My wife just had a baby boy—Michael Joshua Felsher. I'm a father!"

The group of soldiers clapped and cheered along with Solomon. In turn, they grasped his hand in congratulatory handshakes. Solomon turned toward me and I extended my hand.

"Mazel Tov," I said, gripping his hand. I couldn't help but smile as Solomon beamed with more excitement than I had ever seen on his face.

"Yes! Mazel Tov! You must be Jewish," Solomon asked.

"Not really," I responded, "but I have a good friend who is."

"Well thank you, my friend. It is a good day, indeed, and God has poured out his blessing upon me."

A soldier pulled out a flask and held it up to Solomon. "To the happy new father. Here, Solomon, take a swig. It's the best whiskey in the camp."

Solomon smiled and shook his head dismissively. "Thanks, Cantrel, but I don't drink."

"What? Did you convert to Mormonism?" one of the other soldiers joked.

"Hey. I resemble that remark," Big Tom joked back.

"No, I'm still a Jew, but I've learned that alcohol tends to get me into more trouble than it's worth."

"Ah, alcohol. The cause and solution to all of life's problems," the soldier named Cantrel joked, before taking a swig of whiskey and passing it around.

"Congratulations. You will make a fine father," Tom said, clapping Solomon on the shoulder. "I've got three little rascals at home, and they will change your life forever and make you a better man than you can ever be on your own."

The whiskey bottle made its way to me and I stared at it, holding it gingerly in my fingertips, remembering I was only fourteen.

Solomon took the whiskey from my hands and passed it along.

"Don't worry kid," he said with a wink. "I've got some hot water boiling and a little cocoa mix I've been saving. You can have a drink with Tom and me."

I sat down next to Solomon and Tom by the fire. The tea kettle hung over the flames and steam exited the kettle until it started to whistle. Solomon passed me a tin cup and used his gloved hand to grab the kettle, causing the whistling to stop. He poured the boiling water into each of our cups and Tom dumped a single scoop of dark brown cocoa mix into our cups.

"L'Chayim. Cheers," Solomon said, raising his tin cup into the air.

"Cheers," Tom and I called back, tapping our cups to Solomon's.

I took a sip of the hot cocoa and felt the sweet taste envelope my tongue as warmth rushed down my throat and into my belly.

"Oh, this is good. I miss eating and drinking," I said out loud.

Solomon arched his eyebrow and Tom gave me a strange look. I hurriedly put the cup back up to my mouth and took another sip. But as I did, I heard the high-pitched whistle of the tea kettle sound through the air. I looked at the kettle, which was on the ground in front of us and no longer in the fire, but the whistle continued, growing deeper.

Fearful recognition fell on both Solomon and Tom's faces.

"INCOMING!" Solomon yelled, diving toward me and tackling me to the ground.

CHAPTER 15
FOXHOLES IN FRANCE

The first explosion landed a hundred feet away, hitting a parked jeep. I felt a wave of heat wash over my face, and my ears popped. Solomon rolled off me and grabbed me by the coat collar, pulling me up.

"Get to your foxholes," he screamed to the surrounding men. My ears rang like church bells, and his voice sounded muffled as he screamed. The men appeared to know the drill. Grabbing their rifles, they dashed down the muddy road and into a field, disappearing from view.

"C'mon kid. Stick with Big Tom and me."

Solomon and Tom grabbed their weapons and Solomon passed me a rifle. New whistles filled the air, followed by explosions. It seemed the whole world was blowing up. As we reached the field, I heard the rattle of machine guns and sparks of light flew through the air from a line of trees up ahead.

Bullets whizzed everywhere, spraying the dirt only a few feet in front of me. I froze in place until two strong hands grabbed me from below and dragged me down. At first I didn't realize what was happening as my body sank into the ground. I thought I was being buried alive. But as my eyes adjusted to the dark, I realized I was in a large hole, at least seven feet deep and six feet wide. Solomon and

Tom stood at my side, their faces grim. There was a small ledge of dirt built into the wall facing the enemy and I saw rounds of stored ammunition stacked on the ledge.

"Are you okay, kid? Were you hit?" Solomon asked.

I shook my head, unable to answer.

More explosions hit the ground around us, shaking the earth.

"They're getting closer," Tom yelled over the ripping sounds of machine gun fire and explosions. "Their mortar shells are zeroing in."

Solomon nodded. "We can't let their line advance on us. How did they get so close? Command gave us no warning they were coming!"

Solomon mumbled some words in Yiddish, which I assumed were swear words, grabbed his rifle, and stood on the ledge so he could peer over the side. There was a break in the enemy machine gun fire, and Solomon popped his head up and fired a half dozen rounds into the woods.

"Did you see any of them?" Tom asked.

Solomon shook his head. "They're staying hidden behind the tree line, but I don't think they could see me. The grass was just tall enough to hide my head."

"My guess is they wait until nightfall to advance. Keep pounding us with mortars to try and wear us down," Tom spoke.

Solomon nodded in agreement.

"What about the planes?" I asked. "Can't they just fly over and bomb them?"

"Good idea kid," Solomon replied. "Only one problem. The Nazi's are too close and there's a good chance those bombs would hit us as well as the Krauts."

Solomon rubbed the scruff on his chin as the mortar shells continued to whistle and explode above ground.

"What are you thinking?" Tom asked.

"Oy vey, I was thinking we should have stayed in Tehran," Solomon joked. "But since we're here, we can't let them take the airstrip. Our planes will be taking off as we speak, trying to get away in case the airstrip is compromised. We've got to hold off the Krauts until nightfall and try to move our guys into position along edge of the tree line and flank them. I'm going to crawl over to Wizowsky and Topham's hole and see if their radio is working and try to contact the Cap. Then we will decide what to do."

Big Tom shook his head. "No you're not. You just became a father. I'll go."

"No way," Solomon argued back. "You've got a wife and three kids back home yourself. I'll go."

The two continued arguing back and forth until I held up my hand.

"I'll go," I said, the words choking in my throat as I spoke them. The two men stared at me. I gathered my courage and spoke more confidently. "I'll go. I don't have a wife or kids. Let me go."

Solomon shook his head and smiled. "You got courage kid, I'll give you that. But you don't know where all the foxholes are and you could get lost crawling around out there. Thanks for the offer, but I'll—"

But before he could finish, Tom was crawling out of the hole like a big cat. Once on the surface, he turned his head back over the edge and winked at Solomon. "You're a better shot than me, Sol. Give me some cover, and I'll be back in a few."

Tom disappeared from view as he stealthily crawled through the tall grass.

"Why that stubborn, no good, crazy Mormon. When he gets back I'm gonna—" but Solomon couldn't finish. He just sighed and nodded toward me. "Kid, come help me lay cover fire for Tom."

I followed Solomon up onto the two-foot high dirt step, fumbling with my rifle as we crouched below the edge of the foxhole. I tried to figure out how to load the rifle, dropping both the weapon and the ammunition at the same time. Solomon wrinkled his brow and shook his head.

"On second thought, put that rifle down, take my binoculars and be my spotter. 10 o'clock, 11 o'clock, 12 o'clock, 1 o'clock, 2 o'clock," Solomon said, waving his hand in each direction as we stayed crouched below the surface. "We will start at 10 and work our way back and forth across the tree line. You see an enemy, tell me where and try to guide me into the target. Got it?"

I nodded, taking the binoculars from Solomon.

"Okay, here we go," Solomon said. The mortar shells continued to drop around us and it took me a second to realize Solomon had already popped his head up and was firing at the trees.

Carefully, I put my head just above the edge of the foxhole and peered into the binoculars. I could barely see above the grass in front of me and tentatively poked my head up a little higher until the trees came into view.

"10 o'clock," Solomon called.

I turned my head towards 10 o'clock and searched for the enemy. Solomon let off slow, methodical rounds, taking his time as he moved across the tree line.

"I'm aiming for the trees," Solomon called. "You see that big one with the black hole half-way up the trunk?"

"Yes," I called back.

"Tell me if you see any movement when I hit it."

Solomon pulled the trigger and I watched as the tree sprayed splinters of bark on the right side.

"Wait. I saw something move a few feet to the right and behind the tree. There's a lot of shadow under the trees, but I think someone is back there."

Solomon kept his eye glued over his iron sights and fired again. This time the dark spot moved closer to the edge of the tree line and I saw the clear face of a man in a gray uniform. He was holding his shoulder, red blood seeping through his knuckles.

"You got him," I mumbled, but my words came out forced. The enemy soldier looked like a teenager with blonde hair under his helmet. He was only a few years older than me, his face contorted in pain and blood pouring through his fingertips.

Solomon kept his rifle raised, but turned his head toward me. "Kid, I need you to focus. This is war. It's hard, it's sad, and it's deadly. You won't make it out without scars, but right now we have to focus if we want to protect Tom and the other guys. We have to fight, because if we don't, who will?"

I nodded slowly and gulped. "Okay. I'm ready. Let's keep going."

We moved back and forth across the tree line for hours, spotting six more Nazi soldiers and six more hits for Solomon. But with every shot, I couldn't shake the image of the blonde-haired teenager, his face wrenched with pain, and red blood seeping through his fingers.

The sun began to drop below the horizon and nightfall approached. The darkness made gunfire easier to spot and locate enemy positions, causing the Nazi mortar shells and gunfire to nearly slow to a stop. Silence filled the air, with the occasional mortar shell and machine gun fire blasting through the night sky to keep us at bay.

"You fellas mind giving me a hand," Tom called from above the hole, causing me to jump.

"You made it!" I shouted with excitement as we helped Tom back into the foxhole.

"That I did, but not without a scratch," Tom replied, pointing to his right pant leg which was tied with a blood-soaked cloth. "One of them got me with a lucky shot. Hit my calf as I was crawling. Hurts like the dickens, but I'll be fine."

"Oy, you lucky dog. You had me worried. What took so long?"

Tom shrugged. "You try crawling like a snake for four hours. It's slow moving. But I got a hold of the Captain and all of our men in the foxholes. He said we are to hold this position and keep the Krauts from advancing. Apparently, the kid wasn't far off with the plane idea. We've been bombing the Krauts to Timbuktu behind their lines where we were safe from friendly fire. The remaining Krauts in front of us are cut-off from behind and the Captain says troops are moving in to encircle them. We just need to wait out the night, let them run down on ammo a bit, and by morning they'll be trapped."

Solomon shook his head incredulously. "I hope it's that easy. But right now I'm worried about you. We need to get you to a medic. Your leg doesn't look so good."

Tom waved him off. "The closest medic is up the road a few miles. It's too dangerous. I'll be fine, though. Cantrel used a bit of his fire whiskey to clean out the wound before we tied it off."

Solomon sighed and pulled up the collar of his jacket. "Good thing it's not freezing outside or anything. I assume Cap gave the command for no fires tonight?"

Tom nodded the affirmative.

"Oy, it's going to be a cold, long night."

We huddled close together in our foxhole as the temperature plummeted. The Nazis continued to fire mortar shells randomly through the night and shot the occasional flare into the sky to shed light on the grass field between us.

Solomon and I took turns on watch, peeking above ground, while the other one huddled close to Tom to try and keep each other warm. All three of us began to shake as the night wore on, and I felt my teeth chattering in my skull.

"If daylight doesn't come soon, we are going to freeze to death," I stuttered through my shaking lips. I had never been so tired or so cold in my life. Part of me wished the enemy would come so we could die fighting instead of freezing.

"Only another ten minutes or so until sunrise," Solomon said, struggling to control his own shaking body. "You think you can make it that long, Tom?"

Tom did not answer. His eyes were closed and I realized he had stopped shivering.

"Big Tom?" Solomon called shakily. "Oy! Wake up! No sleeping, soldier."

But Tom didn't move. His body went limp as he laid between Solomon and me.

I pulled off my glove and reached my frozen fingers to his equally frozen neck. There was no pulse.

"We've got to do CPR," I said, remembering my CPR lessons as a Boy Scout.

"CPR," Solomon called anxiously. "What are you talking about?"

Ignoring Solomon, I laid Tom on his back and began doing the chest compressions with my gloved fists. I pushed as hard as I could, putting my full body into it, and felt his ribs crack under my weight.

"What are you doing? You're not a medic!" Solomon exclaimed as he knelt down at Tom's side.

"No. But a paramedic taught me this when I was a kid. We've got to get his heart beating and get him breathing again. Here, you keep pushing down on his chest, like this, right in the center. Push hard and push down at least two inches at a quick tempo. It's okay if his ribs crack or break. Those can heal, but we have to get his heart going."

Solomon obeyed and continued performing chest compressions as I kneeled over Tom's head, put my lips to his, and blew. The initial thought of *gross, I'm kissing a man*, flickered into my mind, but then it quickly disappeared as I focused on saving Big Tom's life.

"C'mon!" I yelled before continuing mouth-to-mouth.

Solomon kept beating on Tom's chest.

THUMP-THUMP-THUMP-THUMP

Tom's face was turning purple. He still wasn't breathing and I couldn't feel a pulse.

A crack sounded through the foxhole as one of Tom's ribs broke. Solomon pulled away in shock, stopping the chest compressions.

"Don't stop!" I yelled. "Keep pushing hard. Don't stop for anything!"

Like a good soldier, Solomon went back to work pushing into Tom's chest. Another rib cracked but Solomon didn't stop this time.

As he pushed, I bent over to give Tom another round of mouth-to-mouth. After five breaths I stopped. Still no pulse. Still no breathing.

How long has it been? I thought with dread. Tom's face was a full shade of blue and it felt like minutes had passed—too many minutes.

Forgetting this was only a dream, I said a silent prayer, hoping someone heard my pleas. I didn't know what else to do. Suddenly, Tom opened his eyes and sucked in a gulp of air.

"Tom, you're alive!" Solomon shouted with excitement. "You big dumb lumberjack. You had me scared to death."

Tom groaned, wincing in pain as his chest heaved up and down for air. "What...happened?" he mumbled between gasps. "I...I feel like a tractor...landed on my chest."

Solomon and I laughed, letting our tension ease.

"The kid saved you," Solomon said. "You were dead as a doornail. No heartbeat and you weren't breathing. But the kid saved you. Some crazy thing called CPR."

Tom took deep, steady breaths, clearly still in pain, and gave me a slight head nod.

"Thanks kid," Tom spoke in a weak voice, "I owe you one."

Solomon shot me smile and winked. "You did good, kid. Real good."

I smiled back. I noticed that the gunfire outside had ceased and I heard men shouting in English that it was all clear. Like a light switch, the wave of euphoria I felt from saving Tom washed away and I fell back against the dirt wall of the foxhole, shaking with exhaustion. I looked up at the opening of the foxhole toward the sky. The darkness of the night gave way to the soft glow of sunlight on the horizon. I smiled at the welcoming light of a new day, closed my eyes, and drifted off to sleep.

CHAPTER 16
MY FIRST DATE

Solomon, quit ignoring me and answer the question! What really happened that night Big Tom got shot? Or what about at the Chicago club? I was only there in your dream, so if I wasn't there, who really played the trombone at the club and who really saved Tom's life?

Solomon continued to ignore me as he played Betty. He gave the appearance that he was absorbed in his music, but I could tell he was listening to me and my questions. He just chose to ignore them. It was strange—well, strange for Solomon. Sometimes he would tell me stories on end from his past and share details from the dementia dreams with a crystal clear memory. But whenever I asked him why this was happening or who was really there in my place from the moments I lived in his dementia dream—he avoided the questions and either changed the subject or said his memory was fuzzy.

It made no sense, and Solomon was not helping. I waited until he finished the last crescendo to a song called *April in Paris*. His friends, JJ and Big Tom, were arriving today in preparation for the Valentine's Dance taking place the following night. Solomon was making sure he had every song down perfectly before they arrived.

Solomon, I said, once he put Betty back in her case. *You've got to answer me. Since those were dementia dreams and I wasn't really there, someone had to do those things I did, right? Someone saved you from falling off the ledge of your building on the way to the Dempsey fight. Someone played trombone at the club, or you would have never gone on with the show. Someone had to have helped save Tom, since I know he's alive and will be here any minute. Why won't you tell me?*

"Oy, kid, always full of questions. I don't know what to tell you. I'm old, and my memory is fuzzy in places. I think it's this dementia. Maybe you can ask JJ and Tom when they get here. They were there too you know."

Fine. Maybe I will.

"Good, now stop bothering me. I need a nap before they arrive. All that standing is killing my back."

Solomon shuffled out of my view and within minutes I heard him gently snoring in his bed. His ability to fall asleep in an instant made me jealous. And his inability to remember who was really with him from those dreams made me crazy.

Those were pinnacle times in his life, I thought. *How could he not remember?*

Annoyed with Solomon, I lay there in bed, since that's all I ever do, and silently watched the clock spin round and round. I tried to pull the clock into my mind palace to play Clock Watch, but it wouldn't work.

That was another thing that had changed since Solomon arrived. Somehow our mental connection changed my ability to enter my mind palace at will. None of it made sense, and I wasn't sure if it ever would make sense.

With nothing else to do, I stared at the wall, officially bored. Luckily, my boredom did not last long, as I heard someone open the door and the sweet scent of oranges entered the room.

Sarah, I whispered in my mind, careful not to wake Solomon.

Sarah tiptoed into our room and over to the foot of my bed. "Hey Aaron. How's it going?" She whispered.

I'm okay, I guess. Your grandfather is driving me nuts, but what else is new.

"I see Grandpa is asleep. Too bad you can't talk to me. I really wish you didn't have this sickness and that we could totally talk like normal people without a translator."

You and me both. But someday I'll talk again. I keep practicing, trying to make my mouth move or make a sound on purpose. Nothing yet, but someday.

"I guess if you did learn to talk again, I would have to sing in the choir. So maybe I take it all back," Sarah teased. She flashed her pretty smile, pink braces and all, and patted my leg.

Solomon stirred in his bed and snorted, but continued sleeping.

"Anyways," Sarah whispered a little softer. "Grandpa keeps talking about the Valentine's Dance tomorrow and I think maybe I'll come."

My heart sank a few inches. Now Sarah would be at the dance as well, while I stayed in my prison of a room.

"I was wondering, well, I wanted to ask, will you go to the dance with me? I mean, that's if you're not going with anyone else."

Whaaa? What did you just ask me? I mean, yes! Of course I would love to go with you, but I don't see how that's possible. I'm stuck here, in case you forgot. Plus, I can't actually answer you while your Grandpa is asleep. But seriously, you want to go to the dance with me?

My heart started beating faster and a flash of heat rose in my cheeks. *Am I doing that?* I asked myself as my cheeks grew warmer and warmer.

"Aaron, you're blushing," Sarah whispered excitedly. She came to my bedside, close to my face and grabbed my hand. This only made me blush more.

"I take it that's a yes? You'll go with me to the dance?"

"It's a yes," Solomon grumbled, with his back still turned to us as he lay in bed. "The kid's more excited than a five-year-old at Disneyland."

Hey, you were awake? I asked.

Solomon rolled over to face us and let out a long yawn.

129

"With all the racket your mind was causing, of course I was awake. And don't you worry kid, I'll make sure you get all spiffy'd up for the dance. If you're going to take my granddaughter out on a date, you better look and act the part of a gentleman. Understand?"

A date? I asked, fear gripping me. *Is this really a date? My first date? And with Sarah? Solomon, is this really happening? Am I dreaming now, because this is crazy! How am I going to take Sarah to a dance? Plus, she's way too pretty to go out with me.*

"He's blushing again," Sarah teased. "What's he saying?"

Solomon chuckled, sitting up in bed. "He says he's delighted to take out the most beautiful girl in the world. And he hopes he doesn't step on your toes when you dance together."

I did not say that! Wait, I'm supposed to dance? How in the world am I supposed to dance?

Sarah tried to stifle a giggle, but failed. "Wow, he's really blushing now. I didn't think a person could turn so red." She giggled again. "Don't worry Aaron. We are going to have a great time and I already have a plan to help you dance. It's going to be totally awesome!"

Oh boy. On second thought, maybe I shouldn't go. Maybe this is a bad idea.

Solomon patted me on the shoulder. "Don't worry kid. We will take care of everything. You just bring that charming personality of yours and I'll make sure you get polished up spic and span."

Sarah hung around for another hour, telling us all about the dress she was going to wear for the dance. It was a pink gown with big puffy sleeves and tons of shimmering sequins. The more she talked about it, the more I had the sneaking suspicion she had been planning this for more than one day before the dance. And the more she talked about her dress, the pink rose corsages she made and how Solomon was going to dress me up all fancy, the more I felt my nervousness building up like a giant pit in my stomach.

Sensing my uneasiness, Solomon thankfully changed the subject.

"How's your mom and little brother?" he asked Sarah. "I haven't seen them in a while. Is your mother too good to come see her old man?"

Sarah rolled her eyes. "You just saw them last week, Grandpa. And they're doing...okay. Mom's been having a bit of a hard time with Jesse since Dad left for South Carolina. But other than that, we're doing fine. Oh, and I think Mom and Jesse are going to come to the dance as well. Jesse really wants to hear you play with the band.

Solomon grunted his approval at this idea. "And what about your dad? How's Chief Warrant Officer Richard Clements?"

Sarah shrugged and let out a quick sigh. "We got a letter from Dad the other day. It said they were headed to the Middle East on his ship, the U.S.S. Carr. Jesse thinks Dad is going to war and that he's going to die. He's mad at Mom for not moving to South Carolina so we could have stayed with him before he shipped out."

And how do you feel? I asked in unison with Solomon. I wanted to say *Jinx,* but figured now was not an appropriate time.

Sarah looked up at Solomon and frowned.

"I'm okay, I guess. I'm worried about Jesse and Mom. Mom tries to hide it, but I saw her crying in her room the other day. She's struggling. I think she really misses Dad, but now he's gone for who knows how long, and maybe...he really could die in a war."

"Don't you talk like that," Solomon scolded. "Your father is going to be just fine. We're not at war out there. He's just on tour and will come back to you safe and sound."

Sarah frowned. "We may not be at war now, but we might be soon. I read in the paper that the war between Iran and Iraq is getting worse, and that's why we are sending extra Navy ships out there. We're supposed to protect the oil tankers from both sides to keep the oil flowing. But just last week one of our ships was hit by an Iranian missile, and 37 U.S. sailors died. Then we attacked some Iranian oil platforms in retaliation. It all scares me, Grandpa. What if a real war breaks out? What if Dad gets caught in it and he gets killed like those other sailors?"

Sarah began to cry and Solomon stepped in front of my bed to hold her tightly. The thought of war brought back the memories of the last dementia dream and I felt a familiar sadness swell over me. An image of the blonde-haired Nazi teenager popped into my head and a tear trickled down my cheek.

"My dearest little Sarah," Solomon spoke gently, "I hope your father does not have to fight. War is hard, it's sad, and it's deadly. But sometimes we have to fight to protect our freedoms and way of life, because if we don't, who will? Your father is a very brave man, and he loves you, your brother, and your mother very much. You always remember that, understand?"

Solomon wiped away her tears as Sarah nodded. Then he turned to me with a serious face. "And you, Aaron. You've got to get those thoughts under control. It took me years to come to peace with those memories you're replaying in that head of yours, and I really don't want to see them in your mind anymore. Your mind palace is a clean and peaceful palace. Why fill it with such sadness?"

"What are you talking about Grandpa?" Sarah asked. "Did you and Aaron share another dream?"

Solomon nodded to Sarah. "Yes, but not one that I want to share with you, my child."

But Solomon, it's not like I can just forget what I saw! I helped you kill a bunch of—

"No one is saying you have to forget it," Solomon said firmly, cutting me off. "Accept it and learn from it, but don't dwell on it. Dwelling on it will do you no good. Remember what else happened that night. We helped save the base, the other soldiers, and Big Tom. Remember the good."

"Did I hear someone calling me good?" a deep voice drawled from the doorway. I smelled the faint aroma of garlic enter the room.

"No, no, no. He's not the good one. I'm the good one," called a second, high-pitched voice, accompanied by the smell of cinnamon.

Solomon turned to face the door and gave a toothy grin. "JJ, Tom, you old dogs finally made it. I thought maybe you had gotten lost again, like that time in Tijuana when the police chased us out of the concert venue and clear across the border."

"You should be so lucky," Tom's deep voice answered. "And they were chasing you, not us, remember."

'Yeah, yeah," Solomon said with a wave of his hand.

"Solomon, you rascal," joked the high-pitched voice of JJ. "Little brother, what in the devil are you doing to this poor child? You always had a knack for making the girls cry, but this?"

Solomon harrumphed. "First, if there's anyone *little* here, it's you, short-round. You seem to be shrinking in your old age, my little brother. Second, this is my granddaughter, Sarah. Her father just shipped off to the Middle East with the Navy. She's worried about him. Oy, I'm sure you two louts can empathize with her situation."

Tom and JJ came into my view as they offered their apologies and encouragement to Sarah. It was amazing to see them in their old age. Besides the wrinkled face and bald head, Big Tom still looked strong with his broad shoulders and thin midsection, accentuated by the dark brown leather jacket he wore over a blue polo shirt.

JJ on the other hand, looked completely different. He was still a head shorter than Solomon, but weighed at least a hundred pounds more than his younger self, with a full head of gray hair. He wore a gray suit coat with big gold cufflinks and a giant gold watch.

They each gave Solomon a friendly hug and extended their hands to Sarah.

"Pleasure to meet you," Sarah said, color coming back to her face as she gave them a smile and shook their hands. "Grandpa has told me so much about you two. Playing with you again is all he's talked about for the last month."

"No I have not. I couldn't care less about you two bums. My granddaughter exaggerates. It's a condition she has. She does it all the time. The doctors can't figure out a cure."

"Whatever, Grandpa," Sarah replied, giving Solomon a quick elbow to the ribs, much to the amusement of JJ and Big Tom.

Finally, taking notice of me, Tom looked down and squinted, causing deep creases to fan out around his eyes. "Well, I'll be. Say, Solomon, doesn't this kid look like the spitting image of that young fella who saved my life back in the war? I can't remember that kid's name for the life of me, but I'll never forget his face, and this kid looks just like him. Kid was my guardian angel."

JJ pushed his glasses up the bridge of his nose and gave me a once over. "You know who he reminds me of, that trombone player back in Chicago. You know, Sol, the club where you met Dolores. Just give him a little mustache and bingo, it's like I'm back in 1940 again."

Wait. They remember me? But how can that be? I wasn't there? It was just a dream, right? I asked Solomon.

Solomon looked at me and shook his head. "Fellas, that was a long, long time ago. My memory is not what it used to be. Let me introduce you to Aaron Greenburg, my paralyzed roommate."

But Solomon, they said I look just like the kid in the war and at the club. How is that possible? What's going on?

Solomon continued to ignore me. "Say, why don't we go run through the charts a few times? I'll go find Barry, the resident bass player who will be joining us."

"Sounds good to me," Tom added in his deep voice, still staring at my face. "I still can't believe how much Aaron looks like the same kid. This world sure is a funny place."

JJ nodded in agreement. "Say, Sarah, since your grandpa is a feeble old man, maybe you can come help Tom and me unload the drum set."

"Sure," Sarah said excitedly. "Is that okay with you Grandpa?"

Solomon nodded. "Go on child. I'll be along in a minute."

Sarah gave me an excited smile as she waved goodbye. "See you tomorrow, Aaron. I can't wait for you to see my dress and to take you to the dance!"

Right. The dance, I thought, causing my stomach to squirm. I had completely forgotten about the dance since Tom and JJ arrived, making comments about remembering me, or at least remembering a boy like me.

So are you going to talk to me or keep ignoring me? I asked Solomon after the others left the room.

"Oy, I haven't decided yet. I don't know what you want me to say!"

Why do they remember me? Do I really look like the same kid?

Solomon shook his head. "To be honest, I have no idea what those kids looked like. I just know they were there. When I try to picture their faces, I see nothing."

Really? You can't see the face of the kid, or kids, from any of those moments?

"Oy, that's what I just told you. I thought you were paralyzed, not deaf?" Solomon practically growled.

Hey, don't get smart with me, old man. At least I'm trying to understand what's going on. All you do is ignore it. This thing between us, with the whole mind reading and shared dreams, it's weird—like Twilight Zone weird.

Why can't you remember who was there in real life, and why do they think I look like the same person from the dreams we shared?

This isn't normal. None of it is. This isn't something you just ignore.

"I'm not ignoring it!" Solomon shouted. He pounded his fist against the little table in our room. "I...it...when I try...I think and it's gone. It's just gone."

Solomon's anger turned to tears. "Things are gone. I feel them slipping, and then they're gone. Blank. Missing."

I sat in stunned silence, watching the tears flow down Solomon's face.

After a minute, Solomon sighed, a long, pitiful sigh, and wiped his eyes with the cuff of his shirt sleeve. His bushy eyebrows seemed to droop as he looked back up at me.

"I'm sorry I yelled at you," he spoke softly.

It's okay, I thought back to him. *I didn't realize—*"

Solomon put up a hand to stop me. "No. It's not okay. I'm sorry. It's just, my mind keeps getting jumbled up inside and I can feel it slipping—like an old transmission going out. It's happening more often and it…it scares me."

Solomon paused for a moment before continuing. "I don't know why we can communicate like we do, but we can. I don't know why JJ and Tom say you look like the kids from those times in my life. I can't remember who was really there. I try to remember, but it's like a blank spot in my mind, and I give up trying to understand it."

But you can't give up. Don't you want to know why it's happening? I asked.

Solomon grabbed his saxophone case and turned back to me. "Kid, some things in life just are what they are because God allows it to be so. Maybe we're not meant to know *all* the answers. Maybe we're not ready for them yet. Knowing them now won't change a thing, and trying to figure it out will just take up our time and leave us with more questions. I'm old, and I don't have much time to waste. I prefer to live life as it comes, and maybe, just maybe, I'll get the answers to my questions after I die."

CHAPTER 17
RED BANDANA

You've got to be kidding me! I thought to Solomon as he held a mirror up in front of me. *Where did you get this suit? It's way too big, looks like it's from the 50's and it smells like mothballs and Old Spice—hey wait a minute, this is your suit, isn't it?*

Solomon chuckled. "Oy, kid, quit your complaining. You've never looked better. I bought that suit for $200 back in 1959 for a concert in Miami where we opened for Bobby Darin. That was a lot of money back then. It was custom tailored and it was Dolores' favorite suit."

Other than being a little too big, Solomon's dark pin-stripe suit actually looked pretty good on me, especially with the bright red tie and silver cufflinks he added. But the way my super sniffer picked up the musty-dusty smell of the old suit made me want to cough and sneeze. That's if I could control myself to do either of those things.

When was the last time you had this thing dry-cleaned? I asked.

Solomon furrowed his brow and tapped his chin. "Oh, at least twenty years ago. I haven't been able to fit in this suit since the 60's. But don't worry, I shook it out and hung it by the shower to steam out the wrinkles before getting you dressed."

I looked at myself in the mirror. Even though I was skinny as a rail and did nothing but lie in bed all day, I could see the changes in my face. I looked older, more mature. Or maybe that was just my neatly combed red hair, which was slicked over and stiff as a rock from all the hair gel Solomon used on it to get me ready. Or maybe it was the suit and tie that made me look older. Either way, Solomon was right. I did look pretty good, and I hoped Sarah would notice.

I caught the scent of peppermint entering our room, and Nurse Penny greeted us with her cheery voice. "My, oh my, dontcha look handsome, Aaron. And Mr. Felsher, you're looking mighty spiffy yourself."

"Why thank you, Penny. I had to squeeze a bit to fit into this old penguin suit," Solomon said, adjusting the bow tie of his black tux. "Hopefully, I can still play with my waist being squeezed like a boa constrictor in these pants."

Nurse Penny laughed.

"And how does Aaron like his suit?" she asked.

After the first month of Solomon talking out loud to me, Nurse Penny decided to just go along with it. Solomon had never tried to hurt me, and she didn't see the harm in a crazy old man talking to a supposedly brain-dead boy. Granted, I don't think she believed we could really communicate with each other, but she seemed content to play along.

"Oy, the kid is beaming inside and out. He feels like a million bucks and is ready for his first date with my granddaughter."

This caused me to blush and I felt the heat rising to my cheeks again.

"See, look at that. He's even blushing," Solomon chuckled and patted me on the shin.

Nurse Penny raised her eyebrows and pulled her head back in surprise. "I think you're right. He is blushing. Oh my goodness! Aaron, do you understand what we are saying? Are you blushing on purpose?"

"Of course he understands what we're saying," Solomon replied. "But you're asking the wrong questions. If you want to see him really blush, why don't you ask him if he thinks my granddaughter is pretty? The kid lights up like a menorah every time she walks into the room."

Solomon, quit it! I yelled in my mind. But it was too late. Solomon was still holding up the mirror in front of me and I watched as my cheeks burned redder than a Valentine heart.

Nurse Penny's surprised face turned into the widest smile I had ever seen and she put her hand over her mouth. "Oh my, oh my!" Nurse Penny said, hyperventilating. "I knew he was awake in there! Dontcha know I just knew it! I've got to tell Mr. Wilson and your parents, Aaron. They've got to get your doctor back in here to check you out immediately!"

Solomon shook his head. "My dear Penny, why don't you wait until after tonight's festivities before telling everyone," Solomon suggested.

Nurse Penny shook her head with excitement. "Oh, no, no, no. We have to tell them right away. This can't wait. This is big news!"

Solomon rested a hand on Penny's shoulder. "Penny, please. Let the boy enjoy his first date and dance. If you tell the doctor now, he may not get to go. His parents are still in Denver and calling them tonight won't change anything. Just let him enjoy the evening before calling in the cavalry."

Nurse Penny looked a little deflated as she mulled over Solomon's plea. "Oh, fine. I guess it won't hurt to wait until tomorrow. This is a night to celebrate, but first thing in the morning I'm calling everyone and we are getting that doctor back in here to see Aaron."

"Wonderful," Solomon replied with a wink. "Did you bring his special transporter? It's time to get him strapped in and head to the dance."

Nurse Penny left my view and I heard the soft squeak of rolling wheels as she pulled something into the room.

"Here's his contraption/dolly/thingy," Nurse Penny said with a hint of worry. "Oh, I hope it works okay."

Solomon, I'm not so sure about this, I thought nervously. *Are you sure we can't just use a normal wheelchair?*

"Nonsense. This is going to work," Solomon replied. "Have a little faith in Solomon the Great. I taught MacGyver everything he knows."

The month prior, Solomon had demanded that Mr. Wilson upgrade our room with a color TV. Reluctantly, Mr. Wilson gave in. But ever since, Solomon had been on a *MacGyver* kick, watching all the reruns that came on TV.

But MacGyver's not real, I responded. *Plus, he uses duct tape and a Swiss Army knife to make stuff.*

"Exactly!" Solomon exclaimed, causing Nurse Penny to jump. "My ingenuity is unreal. But don't worry. I used more than duct tape and a knife to make this beauty. I also added some belts, pieces of 2x4, a foam mattress pad, a piano dolly, a red bandana, and a comfy green cushion from a stool in the cafeteria. It will work great, won't it, Penny?"

Nurse Penny looked less convinced as she squinted her eyes and shrugged her shoulders. "It's not exactly what I would call a pretty design, but we tested it on Solomon and it should function just fine."

Great. That's reassuring, I thought as Solomon and Nurse Penny helped me out of bed and into Solomon's custom contraption.

***

I look ridiculous, I moaned in my head as Solomon pushed me down the hallway.

"Oy, are you kidding me? You look fantastic," Solomon replied. "When was the last time you stood up like a normal human being, besides the dreams, which don't count. Plus, the wheels make you two inches taller."

Solomon rounded a corner in the hallway and pushed me into the rec room, which was decorated with hanging Christmas lights and dozens of red and pink balloons.

I look like Frankenstein in the movie when they wheel him up on a dolly to strap him to the electric bed, I complained to Solomon. *Whatever you do, DO NOT let Nurse Penny take a picture of me like this.*

Nurse Penny had forgotten her camera at her desk and left us in the hallway to go grab it. She had just bought a brand new Canon SLR and was planning to take pictures of the dance, promising to get a good picture of Sarah and me together.

Solomon ignored my complaints as he wheeled me through the rec room. A handful of other residents had started to gather for the dance, some of them giving me strange looks as I passed. Although I had been at Restwood Suites for over two years, none of the other residents knew me since I never left my room.

As we approached the makeshift stage where JJ, Tom and Barry were testing mics, JJ lifted his head and stared at me, his mouth agape. "What have you done to that poor boy? He looks like Frankenstein in that movie."

See, told you!

"Oh, you hush," Solomon chastised JJ. "You look like Igor from the movie. Aaron looks great! Even better than his looks, he's standing up for the first time in nearly three years, thanks to me."

"It's true," Barry offered. "I've never seen Aaron out of his room the whole time I've worked here. It's good to see you up and about, Aaron, my man."

It had been a long time since I'd left my room, and I had to admit that I *was* standing up, but not by my own power. Solomon had rigged a wide piano dolly with a 4x4 beam bolted to the center that ran straight up in the air like a mast on a ship. But instead of sails being attached to the mast, I was the attachment.

Solomon had run a thick leather belt through my pant loops on the side of my waist, then around a u-bolt anchored into the 4x4 posts, and back through the belt loops on the other side of my waist. He also ran two other belts under my legs, which reminded me of a rock climbing harness I had once used in Boy Scouts, and wrapped those belts around the post as well. Another belt went around my chest and under my armpits to attach me to the post. And to finish it off, Solomon used a long red bandana to secure my head to the post so it didn't flop around.

I groaned in my mind as I thought about the bandana.

"I like the red bandana," Solomon told me as he wheeled me to a stop. "It matches your tie. Plus, it makes you look like that cool kid, what's his name again...Johnny Depp, that's it. You look just like Johnny Depp in that new show *21 Jump Street*."

I was pretty sure no amount of bandanas were going to make me look cool while strapped to this contraption.

Luckily, there was a foam pad attached to the post that cushioned my backside, and the green stool cushion Solomon snagged from the cafeteria made a nice pillow behind my head. Still, I looked ridiculous and I wished I could go back to my room so Sarah would never see me like this.

"*AARON!*" Sarah screamed from across the darkened rec room.

Too late, I thought. *Solomon, I hate you so much right now!*

Solomon chuckled and went back to helping the rest of the band finish the audio checks.

"Aaron, I can't believe it!" Sarah exclaimed. As she rushed toward me, her pink dress with the flowers and puffy sleeves, came into view. A giant pink hair bow, with a rose in the center of it, was nestled in her frizzy light-brown hair, which bobbed as she ran to my side. It was exactly as she had described

You look amazing, I mumbled in my mind.

"He says you look beautiful, sweetie," Solomon called from the stage. "And I couldn't agree with him more."

Sarah's cheeks turned pink, like the rest of her outfit. "Ahh, thanks Grandpa, and thanks Aaron. But I can't believe you, Aaron. You're standing up! Grandpa got it to work. And you look so handsome in your suit and tie. I kind of dig the red bandana too."

Now it was my turn to blush.

From the stage, Solomon snorted into the mic. "Oy, see, I told you the bandana was cool."

I'm pretending to roll my eyes at you, I said to Solomon.

"This is perfect," Sarah squealed. "Now we can dance together!"

Sarah grabbed my hands, sending tingles up my arms, and she slowly pulled me back and forth, causing the dolly to roll and sway with her motion.

"Look at you move," she squealed. "And I almost forgot, I have something for you."

There was a gleam in her eyes as she dropped my hands, which flopped back to my side, and pulled out a little pink rosebud and metal pin from the tiny pink purse strapped around her shoulder. Reaching out, she pinned the rose to the lapel of my suit.

But I didn't get you anything, I thought.

"But don't worry," Sarah continued, as if reading my mind. "I made a matching corsage for myself."

From her purse, she pulled out a small wristband covered in pink roses and fluffy white plant stem thingies. She slid the corsage onto her wrist, held it up, and winked at me.

"There. It's official. We are now at our first dance!" Sarah grinned at me from ear-to-ear and wrapped me up in a hug. Her orange scent enveloped me and I wished I could return her smile and hug her back, but instead I just hung there, strapped to the post like a wet noodle.

Much to my disappointment, Sarah released me from her hug and I heard a few more footsteps enter the rec room, bringing with them the scents of grass and baked bread.

"Testing, Testing. Say, Talia and Jesse, can you hear me in the back of the room?" Solomon called into the mic.

Though they were out of my line of sight, I heard Jesse shout back excitedly, "I hear you, Grandpa. Can I try? I wanna try. Oh, and can I play on the drums? I wanna play on the drums!"

Sarah grabbed my hand and turned the dolly so her mom and brother came into view.

"Mom, Jesse, check out what Grandpa made for Aaron. Isn't it totally awesome?"

Jesse wrinkled his nose and tilted his head to the side as he looked at me. Talia just raised her eyebrows, trying to hide her surprise.

"Well, that's new," Talia replied. "I bet it feels good for him to stand up and get out of that room. A change of scenery is always nice. I think it's great you're doing all of this for him, sweetie."

She's talking about me as if I'm not here, I sighed inside my head. I was used to people doing this, but something about Sarah's mom doing it, as I stood next to Sarah, made me sad.

"It's like he's on a giant skateboard," Jesse commented, reaching out to touch the 4x4 mast. "Can I ride around it with him?" Jesse asked. But before his mom could respond, he jumped on the back of the dolly behind me, grabbed the mast, and used one leg to push off like a scooter. We went flying forward and the dolly began to spin in a circle.

"Weee!" Jesse called as he continued to push us forward in long spinning circles.

Although Jesse took me by surprise, I found myself enjoying the ride. It had been a long time since I had ridden a bike or a skateboard, and the sensation of rolling along, even spinning, brought back memories.

Jesse pushed us in a tighter circle and soon we were spinning faster than a carnival ride.

"JESSE!" Sarah and her mom yelled in unison. Their yelling must have caught Solomon's attention as his voice boomed through the microphone.

"Jesse Solomon Clements!" Solomon barked. "Oy vey! Kid, get off of there this instant!"

The loud rebuke caused Jesse to stop pushing immediately and the dolly slowly came to a halt.

It's okay, I called to Solomon. *It was actually kind of fun.*

"Jesse! I can't believe you did that!" Talia scolded. "This is why I didn't want to bring you tonight. You can't just grab anything around you and play with it. What if you had tipped the boy over? You could have seriously hurt him, or yourself!"

It's okay, really. We are fine, and like I said, it was kind of fun.

But my response fell on deaf minds until Solomon reached us.

"Talia, it's okay. No harm was done. In fact, I think Aaron even enjoyed it."

Talia grabbed Jesse by the arm and the boy dipped his head down toward the ground.

"Don't try to excuse Jesse's behavior. He's been acting up like this all the time since Richard left and I've had just about enough it. Do you understand me, young man?" she said, her finger wagging and her eyes narrowing like laser beams into Jesse.

Solomon sighed. "Sarah, why don't you take Jesse and Aaron over to the punch bowl to get a drink while I talk with your mother for a bit."

Hey, don't let her try to give me a drink," I rapidly called to Solomon. *I can't swallow, remember. If Sarah tries to give me a drink I could drown.*

"Oy, I almost forgot. Sarah, sweetie, don't actually try to give Aaron a drink. You could accidentally drown him."

Sarah's face paled at the thought and she nodded. "Right. No punch for Aaron. Come on Jesse, let's go, and try not to break anything."

I felt the warmth of Sarah and Jesse's hands as they each grabbed one of my hands and pulled me toward the punch bowl, which had little bits of raspberries floating in it. As we wheeled away from Solomon and Talia, JJ, Big Tom and Barry began warming up on the drums, trumpet and bass. Even with the added noise of their warm-ups, my super hearing still picked up bits and pieces of Solomon and Talia's back and forth conversation.

145

"I don't know what to do…I keep trying…"

"Write Richard. Tell him how…"

"…fights at school."

"Is he winning?

"Dad. He needs…"

"Sarah tells me…"

"…and Sarah is hurting too."

"It will be okay, Talia. Just love them…be patient…will be okay."

I felt for Jesse and Sarah as I listened to Talia and Solomon talk about them. I knew what it was like to have a missing parent. I had two of them. The last letter I received from my dad was over three weeks ago. He was still in Denver and said he and my mom were trying to start over. Mom was still staying at my aunt's house, but they were starting from scratch by going on a few dates a week.

"It's like we're finding each other all over again," Dad had written. "It's a funny thing. A couple of sixty-year-olds dating like we are in our twenties. It's been really nice. We are actually talking, too. Not just regular everyday conversation, but talking, like we used to."

When Solomon read me the letter, I was excited and happy for my parents, I really was, but deep down I wished they would find me all over again. Sometimes I felt more like an orphan than a child with living parents. But I couldn't blame them. I knew why things were the way they were. Sometimes I just wished life could be different.

CHAPTER 18
KING & QUEEN

"Welcome everyone to the Restwood Suites Valentine's Dance," echoed the nasally voice of Mr. Wilson through the speakers. "We want to give a special thanks to Solomon Felsher for assembling our live entertainment tonight."

The small crowd of fifty or so residents clapped and cheered.

"It's now 6pm, and we will end the dance promptly at 8 pm," Mr. Wilson continued. The crowd of aging residents booed in response.

"Now, now. We don't want to keep you up too late. And remember to use caution. You're not spring chickens. We don't need any falls and broken hips or broken necks tonight."

The residents booed louder, and Mr. Wilson frowned.

But before the annoying manager could respond, Solomon took the microphone from Mr. Wilson and shooed him off the stage. "Thank you Mr. Wilson. Remind me to call you if I ever want to anger a large number of senior citizens. You have a real knack for it."

This caused Mr. Wilson to harrumph and storm out of the room.

"What a lovely man. Now that the prison warden has left, let's get this party started with a song that's fitting for tonight and one of my personal favorites. *My Funny Valentine.*"

The crowd cheered and residents partnered up all along the open floor of the rec room. The band began to play the slow love song and they sounded surprisingly good together. But just like that night in the Chicago 226 Club, it was Solomon's mesmerizing saxophone sound that stood out, carrying the melody.

Sarah took my right hand in her left hand and placed her right hand on my left shoulder.

"I guess I'll lead," she playfully joked, and began gently pulling me in a slow circle as she swayed back and forth.

She deftly avoided the other Restwood residents shuffling around the dance floor as she pulled me and the dolly around the center of the room.

"I'm glad you agreed to come tonight," she said, taking a step closer. "I know you were nervous about it and I'm sure this dolly thing isn't that comfortable."

It's actually not too bad, I responded in my mind. *Except for the belts harnessed around my legs and groin. Those are starting to give me a serious wedgie, and they could use a little more padding. But it's a good thing you can't hear a word I'm thinking or this conversation would be really awkward.*

"I know I've said it before," Sarah continued, unaware of my internal monologue, "but I really wish we could talk to each other normally. But even so, it doesn't really matter that you can't talk to me like normal or move like normal. When I talk with you, even when my grandpa's not there to play the middleman, I can tell you're listening and that you care. I feel like I can tell you anything."

Sarah spun me around another couple and squeezed my hand. "Thanks for being such a great friend."

Normally when a girl you like calls you a friend, a guy might feel a little let down. But the way Sarah said it and the sincerity in her voice, I couldn't think of a better compliment than to be her friend.

Thank you, I answered, *for being my friend, too.*

Sarah and I danced off and on for another hour as Solomon and his crew played song after song. I recognized a lot of the tunes as ones I had played with Solomon back in Chicago, but there were still a few new songs I had never heard before, like *Zorba the Greek*. The way Big Tom played the insanely fast trumpet part was amazing. And then when Solomon joined in, he and Tom playing in unison and then harmony—I was blown away.

I smiled inside as I watched my fellow residents dancing and enjoying the party as if they were in their twenties again. I easily imagined them as their younger selves doing the foxtrot and swing dancing around the dance floor.

The thought made me happy, but sad at the same time.

Sarah squeezed my hand and nodded her head to the side. "Check out Jesse," she said, spinning me so I could see him.

Jesse was dancing with his mom and the two were giggling as Jesse twirled her out with one hand, like Solomon had shown him earlier. Then Jesse spun under his mom's arm and the two laughed, their faces full of smiles.

I'm not sure what Solomon had said to the kid after he talked with Talia, but Jesse had been a model of behavior the whole night, except for when he snuck onto the stage while the band took a break and started banging on the drums. Needless to say, JJ was none too thrilled with Jesse's uninvited solo.

I watched as Sarah's face brightened at the sight of her mom and brother smiling and laughing as they danced.

"It's good to see them so happy. They deserve it," Sarah said. "And I think it's your turn to take the lead and give me a twirl."

Sarah gave me a mischievous grin as she jumped on the dolly, wrapped her arms around me in a hug, and with a single push, sent us into a dizzying spin.

My heart beat like a jackhammer as Sarah's frizzy hair reached just below my chin and she burrowed her face into my chest.

"Today has been a good day," she said.

Yes, it has, I answered. *I'm not sure how it can get any better.*

The song ended and Sarah hopped off the dolly and the crowd clapped for the band.

149

"Thank you, thank you," Solomon's voice boomed over the speakers. "You have been a wonderful audience tonight. It's almost 9pm now and I've been repeatedly warned by our prison warden, Mr. Wilson, that we are one hour past our curfew, and we need to end this show immediately."

The crowd booed. I couldn't see Mr. Wilson in my line of vision, but my super hearing picked up his nasally voice mumbling something about ungrateful old fogies.

"But before Warden Wilson locks us back up in our cells, I want to dedicate the final song to two of my favorite young people. Seeing them on the dance floor brings back memories of from my youth. To my dearest granddaughter, Sarah, and to my roommate, Aaron, will you please come up to the front of the stage to be crowned the Valentine Dance King and Queen."

Solomon, what are you doing? Since when is there a Valentine Dance King and Queen? I asked.

"Since I decided tonight," Solomon answered into the mic, much to the confusion of the audience who could not hear me.

Sarah pushed me closer to the stage and I saw the dark circles of fatigue settled around Solomon's face. Up close, he looked so tired and worn out from the night's event, but under the dimness of the rec room, no one else could tell.

Are you okay? I asked Solomon. *You look a little beat.*

"Oy, I'm fine, but we better hurry," Solomon said as Tom and Barry each handed him a golden paper crown from Burger King. His eyes seemed to flicker for a moment as he placed the crowns on top of our heads.

"Here are your crowns your majesties. And now, for one last song," he continued. His eyes blinked a few times and he squinted. "I need to hurry and wrap this up so I can get back to Dolores. I have a recording gig at Verve Studios tomorrow and she's going to flay me alive for coming home late again."

Solomon, what are you talking about? Are you okay? Can you hear me? I asked.

"Oy vey, of course I can hear you! Stop shouting. My head hurts and baby Talia has a bad fever and David just got the chicken pox. He's playing baseball on the All-Star team. Getting so big and strong, like Jack Dempsey. If I get this recording contract, we'll be set, Dolores and I. Set I tell you!"

Solomon. Not now. Not another dream. Pull yourself together.

I saw JJ, Tom and Barry come to Solomon's side. They put their arms around him, holding him steady as he swayed on his feet. Solomon dipped his head, his gray curly hair bobbing like springs as his chin touched his chest.

Talia ran into up to the stage, as did Nurse Penny.

"It's okay, Sol. We're here. It's okay," I heard Tom whisper in his low, deep voice.

"Did I get the contract at Verve?" Solomon mumbled, his head still bowed down.

JJ looked up at Big Tom with a pained expression in his eyes.

"Yeah, you did, little brother," JJ answered, but his body language implied it was a lie. "We got the contract."

Solomon lifted his head, a smile twitching at the corner of his lips. "Good, good. Dolores will be so happy. We can get out of that hole of an apartment and—wait...what..."

Solomon's eyes seemed to flicker as he blinked rapidly and shook his head side-to-side.

"What was I saying? I seem to have lost my train of thought," Solomon continued, raising his head back up and rounding his shoulders to stand up straight.

He looked down at Sarah and me as we watched him from the foot of the stage. We were still wearing our Burger King crowns, though mine felt crooked on my head, and he clapped his hands together.

"Oh, right. Congratulations to the King and Queen, Aaron and Sarah. This final dance is dedicated to you. May we always cherish the memories of youth."

The room was silent. Sarah squeezed my hand hard as Talia and Nurse Penny reached Solomon on the stage.

"Dad, I don't think that's such a good idea," Talia spoke softly. "I think it's time to call it night. Let's go get you ready for bed, okay?"

Deep creases appeared along Solomon's forehead as he arched an eyebrow.

"Talia, what on earth are you talking about? Why would we stop now with one song to go? And JJ, Tom, Barry, why are you hanging on my arm like I'm a supermodel?" Solomon said, pushing their supporting hands away.

"Dad, it's time to call it a night," Talia said more forcefully.

The room remained silent, as everyone watched the scene play out on the stage.

Before Solomon could speak, JJ waved a hand toward Talia. "It's okay, Talia. Just one more song. That's all. It will be good for him," JJ spoke softly.

Talia looked to Tom for support, but he only offered a nod in agreement. "One more song," Tom's deep voice spoke.

Talia turned to Nurse Penny, pleading for backup. But she also nodded her consent and my super hearing listened in as she whispered into Talia's ear.

"Thank goodness. I think he's come out of the episode. He should be okay for one more song. Dontcha worry. We'll get him back to his room and settled for the night as soon as he's done. Trying to stop him now will only get him riled up and might send him into another episode or make things worse."

Talia frowned and gave her dad a concerned look. "Fine. One last song."

"Wonderful. Now that I have your approval, which I didn't need," Solomon muttered under his breath, "we will play the final song of the night, *No Life Without You.*

Reluctantly, Sarah wheeled me a few feet away from the stage, her face full of concern for her grandfather.

"Is he okay?" she whispered to me.

I didn't have an answer for her, not that she could hear me if I did.

Solomon looked straight at me and gave me a wink as he put his lips to his saxophone. He seemed to be back to himself again, but he had never lost it like that before, at least not in public. Though I hated to admit it, Solomon was getting worse.

The sweet sound of Solomon's saxophone echoed through the room as he began playing the song, *No Life Without You*. It was a slow ballad with deep harmonies and chords between the trumpet and sax. The chords resonated through my body as Barry plucked a slow, deep bass line and JJ played soft brushes on the snare drum and cymbals.

Holding my hands, Sarah slowly pulled me back and forth and we swayed to the song.

This was my parents' song, I said to Sarah. *My dad said this was the song they played at their wedding.*

But Sarah did not answer. She just stood there, in her beautiful pink dress, wearing her Burger King crown, holding my hands and pulling me back and forth. Even though she was right here in front of me. Even though I knew she was my friend and cared about me, at that moment, I felt like she might as well have been on a different planet. Everything around me felt distant, just like my parents—there, but not really there. I felt alone.

The song continued, reaching the bridge from the chorus line, but I couldn't enjoy it. All I wanted to do was leave, get put back in my bed, and wait for my eyes to close so I could escape into my sleep.

As the song crescendoed back to the melody, I caught the faint, familiar scent, of lavender from somewhere to my side.

Someone smells like the lavender detergent my mom always used to do our laundry, I thought to myself, wondering how I had missed that all night. The smell sent my emotions downward, adding to my loneliness.

But as Sarah continued to pull me around in a slow circle, the smell grew stronger until it seemed to be right on top of me. I felt a hand touch my shoulder

"Pardon me, but may I cut-in?" a sweet, familiar voice spoke. "It's been a long time since I danced with my son."

Sarah's eyes grew with acknowledgement, and the hand on my shoulder turned me around toward them. There stood my mom, wearing a bright yellow dress with her gray hair pulled up in her normal bun. She smiled at me, her lip quivering as tears rolled down her cheek.

"Aaron," she wept. "I'm so sorry I left you."

I wanted to cry. I wanted to shout for joy. I wanted to reach out to hug her.

But I couldn't. Focusing all of my newfound energy and excitement, I pushed my thoughts as hard as possible against the walls of my mind and made the first audible sound to pass through my lips in nearly three years.

"aaaahhhh," I groaned.

Great, I thought. *Not only do I look like Frankenstein, but now I sound like him.*

CHAPTER 19
DR. IDIOT DOES MATH

"Okay, Aaron. I want you to focus on me and try to make a sound whenever I hold up the correct answer," Dr. Idiot explained as he leaned over my bed, less than a foot away from my face.

How can I not focus on you? I said in my mind. *I can't tell where your nose hairs end and that mustache begins. And your breath smells like tuna. For the love of Pete. Hasn't he ever heard of personal space...or breath mints?*

Solomon chuckled off to the side where he relaxed on his own bed. The room was crowded as my parents, Sarah and Nurse Penny all stood behind Dr. Idiot against the back wall by the TV. But this didn't deter Dr. Idiot. He seemed to like the attention.

"What's so funny?" Dr. Idiot asked Solomon.

"Oh nothing, Doc. You didn't happen to have tuna for lunch, did you?" Solomon asked.

Dr. Idiot nodded and then furrowed his brow in confusion— which was the normal look most people gave Solomon.

"Here. Catch," Solomon said, tossing a small plastic case of Tic Tacs toward the good doctor.

Surprised, Dr. Idiot fumbled the catch in the air and the bottle of Tic Tacs landed on my stomach.

Solomon chuckled. "Nice catch. I thought doctors were supposed to have good hands."

Dr. Idiot looked flustered. "Why on earth are you throwing Tic Tacs at me?" he asked.

"I was giving you a subtle hint. Aaron's right. You are an idiot," Solomon snorted. This caused Sarah to giggle from the back wall by the TV. "Aaron says your breath smells like tuna. Oh, and you may want to invest in a nose and beard trimmer."

"Why, I've never—Nurse!" Dr. Idiot exclaimed. "Would it be possible to have Aaron's roommate removed while I perform my tests? He is quite rude and distracting."

Nurse Penny stepped into view, giving an apologetic smile to Dr. Idiot. "Oh, Solomon is harmless, Dr. McPhearson. But if he acts up again," she said, giving Solomon the evil eye, "I will boot him out in a heartbeat, dontcha know."

Dr. Idiot harrumphed. "Fine. But, I need absolute silence as I run these tests. I'm not sure what brain capacity Aaron has regained so we need a quiet environment for him to concentrate. Now for the first question. Aaron, I want you to groan when I hold up the correct answer to this math problem."

Dr. Idiot held up a flash card with the equation $1 + 1 = ?$

Are you kidding me, I groaned in my mind, making sure not to groan out loud yet. Thanks to Sarah's help, I'd actually kept up fairly well with math as she did her algebra homework with me at my bedside.

Dr. Idiot held up a flashcard with the number 4 on it. He held it for a minute in front of my face as I remained silent. Finally, he held up another flashcard. This time it had the number 1 on it. I remained silent as Dr. Idiot held the new card in front of my face for at least two minutes.

"I want to be sure to give him time to work through the calculation," Dr. Idiot explained to everyone in the room.

Solomon, this is going to drive me crazy! I said in my mind. *We need to move this along or I'm going to have to start calling him Dr. Snail.*

"Or Idiot Snail," Solomon said out loud, causing everyone to turn toward him.

"Sorry," Solomon said. "Pardon the interruption. Continue Doc, though you may want to pick some harder problems for Aaron. He's a smart boy."

Dr. Idiot shook his head dismissively and rolled his eyes at Solomon. Then he held up the next flash card with the number 2 written on it.

"AAAAAAHHHHHHH," I groaned with all the sound I could muster, hoping he would speed things along.

Dr. Idiot's jaw dropped, nurse Penny clapped, and my mom cried with excitement while my dad gave her a hug.

"Amazing! This is fantastic. Let's try another one!" Dr. Idiot exclaimed.

After easily solving the problems $2 + 3 = 5$, $10 - 1 = 9$ and a handful of other addition and subtraction flash cards, Solomon rose from his bed and shuffled over next to the Dr. Idiot.

"What do you think you're doing?" Dr. Idiot insisted as Solomon held up a piece of paper with an algebra equation.

$$8x - 3 = 3x + 17$$

Nice. Now here's an actual mental math challenge, I said to Solomon.

"Nurse Penny, please remove this man from the room. I cannot have him interrupting my testing. There is no way Aaron can solve this problem."

Nurse Penny took a step toward Solomon and rested her hand on his forearm. "Come on Sol, let's let Dr. McPhearson run his tests, okay."

"Penny, just give him a second to figure it out. I promise you the kid can solve this problem. Dr. Idiot on the other hand, I'm not so sure about him."

"You know," piped in my dad from the back wall. "I would like to see if he can answer it as well. I don't see what it hurts to try."

"Same," said my mom. "Let's try it. Maybe he can do it."

"Oh, he can solve that one," Sarah said. "It's an easy one."

Thanks Mom, Dad, Sarah, I replied in my mind.

Dr. Idiot huffed. "I *highly* doubt he can solve it, but to appease everyone in the room, we will test him. And, for the record Mr. Felsher, I already solved the problem and I will write down the answer myself to make sure there is no cheating."

"Be my guest," Solomon replied nonchalantly, stepping away from the foot of my bed.

While Dr. Idiot scribbled a bunch of numbers on flash cards, I worked through the algebra problem in my mind.

$$8x - 3 = 3x + 17$$

subtract 3x from both sides

$$8x - 3x - 3 = 3x - 3x + 17$$

that equals

$$5x - 3 = 17$$

add 3 to both sides

$$5x - 3 + 3 = 17 + 3$$

that equals

$$5x = 20$$

20 divided by 5 = 4

$$x = 4$$

"Okay Aaron. I know you can't answer this equation yet, but don't get upset or down about it. Eventually, after years of therapy, we may someday get you back to this level. But to settle the issue so we can continue our planned testing, we will try anyway."

"Hey, Doc. Since you're so sure of yourself, how about we place a friendly wager on whether Aaron can answer the equation or not? Say $100 bucks?"

Dr. Idiot snorted. "I don't bet on my patients. That's highly unethical. Now let's get this over with."

Dr. Idiot held up a card with the number 6, but instead of leaving it up for two minutes to "let me process the answer," he only left it up for five seconds before holding up a new card with the number 12. Then 2, 15, 5, and finally 4.

"AAAAAHHHHH," I groaned.

"Attaboy, Aaron!" Solomon called as everyone in the room cheered—well, everyone except Dr. Idiot, who stood dumbfounded with his mouth agape and his eyes bulging.

"You're lucky you didn't place that bet," Solomon said with a wink to Dr. Idiot. "I would have gladly taken your money."

"This is beyond amazing," Dr. Idiot whispered, ignoring Solomon's jab.

My mom rushed to my bedside and gave me a hug. "Oh, Aaron. My sweet boy Aaron. You're back!" my Mom said excitedly, still hugging me.

Mom, I replied quietly in my mind. *I never left.*

But my words fell on deaf minds, except for Solomon, whose smile turned downward at hearing my thoughts.

"So what's the next step, doctor?" My dad asked enthusiastically, stepping next to my mom. "How do we get our boy back?"

"Uhm, well, uh…" Dr. Idiot babbled for a few seconds. "Uh, the first thing we need to do is get Aaron out of this rest home and moved back to the hospital for full-time care and treatment. We will run a series of tests, including PET scans, CAT scans, MRI and MEG. I will also schedule physical and speech therapy sessions to see what results therapy can produce. I must be honest. I don't know what the final outcome will be with Aaron. We are in unchartered waters here. We need to run further cognitive tests, but it appears Aaron may be fully awake and aware inside his mind. The next step is building back those connections between his brain and his body."

While my mom, dad and Nurse Penny bustled with excitement, my mind went numb with one thought. I saw Solomon and Sarah, standing side-by-side behind my parents and Dr. Idiot. Their faces showed they were thinking the same thing I was.

I was leaving Restwood Suites. I was leaving them.

CHAPTER 20
SOLOMON TAKES A TRIP

"We're going to run another MEG," Dr. Idiot said. "Now that we have the imaging from your MRI, we want to layer that image with the readings we get from this MEG machine and compare those to your previous tests."

Yippee, I said in my mind. *More tests.*

"Now I want you to try and make a noise again and respond to my flash cards. It's been three weeks since you last made a noise and we need to see what's happening inside that brain of yours. Or we could cut you open and take a look, but the Magnetoencephalography is a much safer approach," Dr. Idiot said with a chuckle.

Ha. Funny. Thanks for not cutting me open, Dr. Idiot. And you still need a breath mint, I spoke to his deaf mind.

Dr. Idiot closed the heavy metal door of the shielded room. As I learned from my first experience with the MEG, the machine had sensors, called S.Q.U.I.D.S. hooked up in a dome around my head. The S.Q.U.I.D.S. read the magnetic impulses my brain gave off as neurons fired, to see what was working in my head and where.

But the MEG was so sensitive that the scan had to take place in a room shielded from other magnetic signals and electrical equipment. A television and even the magnetic waves from the earth itself could throw off the readings without the shield.

"Okay, Aaron, let's start out slow. Which flashcard spells *cat?*" Dr Idiot asked.

He held up a card that read dog, then cow, and finally cat. I tried to groan, just to end the stupid test, but nothing would come out. I pushed against my mind, trying to focus on making the sound.

Nothing.

I screamed in my mind.

I HATE THIS!
WHY CAN'T I MAKE NOISES ANYMORE?
NO ONE CAN HEAR ME!
I'M ALONE AGAIN.
TRAPPED IN THIS HOSPITAL.
RUNNING THESE STUPID TESTS WITH DR. IDIOT
ALL DAY.
I'M ALONE.
I'M GOING CRAZY.
I CAN'T GO BACK TO THIS.
I CAN'T.

"We are getting a fair amount of brain activity this time, but still no vocal response," Dr. Idiot spoke with disappointment. "I just don't get it. You've been here five months and we were making such progress at first, but it's like you're reverting—going backwards. I see the brain activity, but without your abilities to answer, I'm not sure how we can communicate with you to help you improve."

Just send me back, I pleaded. *Let me go back to Solomon and Sarah.*

I wept in my mind as a new bout of depression hit me like a punch from Mike Tyson. I'd been gone from Restwood Suites for five months, and I felt more stir crazy and confined than ever before. My mind went through constant waves of imprisonment, claustrophobia, depression, anger, fear. Even during the first two years of being trapped in my mind, I had never felt this bad.

It was like being put in prison, locked away in solitary confinement, and then being released, only to be thrown back into solitary. Not that I actually knew what being behind bars in solitary felt like, but I imagined this had to be similar.

Dr. Idiot gave me a dozen more tests with flashcards and then poked and prodded various limbs to see what reading came up. Finally, after an hour of testing, he called it quits.

"That's enough for today, but we will keep trying," he said. "Your mind is firing neurons all over the place, unlike when you were first diagnosed. But this is a new frontier of discovery. Your meningitis is very rare, and the road to recovery is unchartered."

Dr. Idiot sighed and looked at his watch. "Shoot. I'm late," he said, exiting the shield room without so much as a goodbye or a hand wave.

I sat there strapped in the MEG seat, looking straight ahead at the blank white walls of the shield room. Everything in the hospital was white. From the walls to the curtains and from the lights to the linoleum floor—all white.

I guess that was supposed to give it a clean feeling, which makes sense since it's a hospital, but what it really gave me was a blank feeling of emptiness. I wished I could close my eyes and go to sleep. Sleep was the only escape I had now, with no one to talk to. But sleep wouldn't come. I sat there for what seemed like hours, waiting. I thought they had forgotten me in the room until finally, two orderlies opened the shield door and lifted me into a gurney to take me back to my room.

They laid me in bed and I stared at the white wall in front of me. I found myself missing my old room in Restwood Suites, with the dumb painting of a bowl of fruit, watching TV, and most importantly, talking with Solomon. Gradually the sun set on the Pacific Ocean, shining through the window in my room, and painted the wall with orange and reddish hues.

Finally, some color, I said to myself and sighed in my mind. *That means night is coming and I can forget my worthless life and fall asleep.*

There was a soft tap on my door and I heard it swing open and then close again. Someone was breathing heavily and a familiar scent of aftershave filled the room.

"Oy, pull yourself out of it kid," Solomon spoke, wheezing between breaths. "You've got the blues worse than Billie Holiday and B.B. King put together."

SOLOMON! I shouted in my head. *Is that really you? I'm not going crazy am I? I mean, maybe I am. Where are you? I can't see you!*

"Shhh, slow down kid. It's me," Solomon said, breathing heavily as he shuffled into my line of sight.

The light from the sunset began to fade, darkening the room, and I was surprised to see Solomon wearing a trench coat, sunglasses, and a San Francisco Giants ball cap pulled on tight, forcing his gray curly hair to explode out the sides.

Solomon? Why are you dressed like that? You look like you're about to open your trench coat and try to sell me a fake Rolex.

Solomon harrumphed. "I break out of my prison, to come see you in your prison, and then you insult my attire? It's not like the white curtain they have you wearing is exactly high fashion."

Whatever, I said. *I'm just surprised and happy to see you. You have no idea how boring the last few months have been. I'm starting to go crazy.*

Solomon's breathing was haggard as he spoke, pausing to catch his breath. "Tell me about it, kid…I'm the one with dementia…remember…I know all about…crazy."

Solomon removed his sunglasses and pulled up a chair. He winced and let out a long exhale as he slowly eased himself into the seat.

Are you okay? I asked, eyeing Solomon closely. The old man tried to hide his discomfort, but he looked more ragged and weak than I had ever seen him before.

Wait a minute. I continued. *How did you get here? Did Talia bring you?*

Solomon furrowed his brow and smirked.

No way! I exclaimed. *You didn't, did you? You came all the way here, across the bay, by yourself?*

"Oy, Aaron," Solomon said, taking deep breaths between phrases. "I've only been here two minutes...already you're burying me...with your questions. No...Talia did not bring me...I'm a seventy-three year-old man...I'm perfectly capable...of riding the BART train...into the City...on my own."

Before I could respond, Solomon held up a finger, pausing our conversation.

"I just need a moment...the stairs up to the 9th floor...were harder than...expected."

You walked up eight flights of stairs to my room? What? Are you crazy?

Solomon wagged his finger again and ignored my questions. Annoyed Solomon would try something so dangerous, I sat in silence, watching as the man closed his eyes and continued taking long, deep breaths. After a few more minutes, his breathing began to steady and he opened his eyes and gave me a wink.

"Ah, that's better. Those stairs must have been the stairway to heaven, because they almost killed me," Solomon said, chuckling at his own joke.

You are ridiculous, Solomon. Why didn't you just take the elevator? I asked.

Solomon removed his sunglasses and waved them in the air. "Can't you see? I'm in disguise! Those new elevators all have fancy cameras in them now. I can't let the Russians and the Nazis see me in their zones. I've got to stay disguised, like they trained me."

Solomon. What are you talking about? There are no Russians or Nazis here. This is a hospital.

"The hospitals are their favorite place to send their spies. They can see how many are injured, steal supplies, get information from unknowing patients. You've got to be careful in hospitals."

I sighed in my mind. *Man, it's good to see you, but this was a bad idea for you to come all the way here, by yourself. You don't sound well and how are you supposed to get home? You don't look too good either.*

Solomon shrugged. "Restwood isn't my home. I haven't had a home since Dolores died. But enough about me. How are you doing, Aaron. Does that klotz, Dr. Idiot, have you fixed up yet? We gotta get you healed and on the first ship back to the states. No more fighting for you. The war is over and with that shoulder of yours, they won't assign you to the spy game, you lucky dog."

This was not good. Solomon wasn't making any sense. It sounded like he was going into a dementia dream, but instead, he was seamlessly going back and forth between living in the past and the present. Had his dementia really gotten this bad in only a few months?

Sounds like a plan, I said, playing along. *No, Dr. Idiot doesn't have me fixed yet. In fact I seem to be getting worse.*

"That's no good," Solomon answered dramatically, waving his hands in the air and standing up from his chair. He paced the room as he continued to talk. "But you're a fighter, kid. You'll pull through it. We gotta get you fixed up for your parents and the ladies that will be swooning over you like that new actor, Carey Grant. Did you know he was a Brit, and his real name is Archibald Leach? I met him a few times, you know. In New York and Hollywood. Nice guy. Tough childhood. But boy I tell you what, that man goes through more wives than I do pairs of socks. Glad I got Dolores to keep me on the straight and narrow. She's the only woman for me. I wonder..."

But Solomon never finished the thought. He just paused and then started pacing back and forth again.

Solomon, why don't you relax and take a seat, I said, trying to calm him down. *That's it. Just take a seat and relax.*

Solomon nodded his head slightly and rubbed his eyes. He followed my invitations and took a seat back in the chair at the foot of my bed.

"Oy vey, my legs are so sore and stiffer than a board," he said, rubbing them as he sat back down. Solomon stared at me for a few minutes and smiled, flashing his toothy grin. "It's good to see you, Aaron. How's Dr. Idiot treating you? Are you getting any better?"

And just like that, Solomon was back, clear-eyed and in the present. But, I wasn't sure how to respond. Should I tell him he'd just been out of it, or continue the conversation as normal? I struggled to keep my thoughts fluid and conversational so Solomon wouldn't know what I was thinking. His mind seemed jumbled enough without my non-conversational thoughts clouding his.

"Earth to Aaron. Is everything okay?" Solomon asked, snapping his fingers. "I asked you a question. In polite conversation, especially with an old roommate who just traversed half of the Bay Area to see you, that's when you respond."

Yeah, sorry about that, I said, deciding it was best to just ignore the dementia moment and enjoy talking like normal while Solomon remained coherent. *Yeah, I'm doing okay. The therapy and tests are long and boring, and I don't seem to be getting any better. In fact, I seem to be getting worse.*

Solomon shook his head dismissively. "Don't worry, kid," he said with a wink. "You're a fighter, just like good ol' Jacky Dempsey. You'll pull through."

Thanks, I responded, remembering Solomon had just told me the same thing a minute ago. I hoped it was true—that I would get better. But for the first time in my life, I wanted something more than to get better myself—I wanted Solomon to get better. Watching him like this was like watching a flower in full bloom start to wither away and shrivel as winter came.

We sat in the dark room, talking for hours and catching up on our time apart. Solomon seemed like his normal self, telling me all about how Sarah had signed up for space camp and was spending the summer at NASA in Houston, Texas. Jesse had made the baseball All-Star team, and Talia was taking him to a tournament in

Sacramento this weekend. I found out Sarah's dad was okay and, so far, they had stayed out of any serious confrontations.

I told Solomon all about my treatments and tests and how my parents came to visit me every afternoon. They had moved back in together, got their old jobs back, and things were looking up for my folks.

As the night drew on, my internal clock told me it was almost time for the nurses to come for my nightly checkup.

The nurses will be coming soon, I told Solomon. *You better go hide in the bathroom for a few minutes until the coast was clear. You can stay tonight if you don't mind sleeping in the reclining chair, but you've got to call Talia first thing in the morning and get a ride back to Restwood. I bet she and Nurse Penny are worried sick about you.*

"Yeah, yeah. I'll call them tomorrow. But I need at least one night out of that prison," he said, shuffling into the bathroom.

Truth be told, I probably should have forced him to call Talia right away or let the hospital nurse find him sitting in my room so she could sort it out. But, I didn't want him to leave yet. I needed a vacation from my prison as much as he did from his.

As Solomon closed the bathroom door, I heard footsteps just outside the main door to my room. Light crept out from under the bathroom door and I heard the nurse enter my room from the hallway.

SOLOMON! I shouted. What are you doing? *Turn off the light! The nurse is coming in the room right now!*

I heard a grumble from the bathroom and the glow from the light flicked off.

Luckily, the nurse, who I called Nurse French Fry, since she smelled like French fries, did not seem to notice the light turning off in the bathroom. I had never seen the face of Nurse French Fry. She was the night nurse and never came into my line of sight when she visited, preferring to stay to my left side, checking my vitals and fluids. She didn't roll me over, change me, or check for bed sores like the day nurses. All I knew was that she smelled like French fries, which made me hungry every night.

The nurse mechanically completed her duties, without saying a word, and exited my room.

You can come out now, I called to Solomon. *The coast is clear.*

"Not sure now is the best time," Solomon called back. "I just realized it's been a while since I last used the facilities. I might be a minute...or two."

CHAPTER 21
DRIVING LESSONS

Solomon peacefully snored in the reclining chair in the corner of my room. My eyes had not yet closed on their own, and I stared at the dark wall ahead of me, waiting to fall asleep.

I listened to Solomon and felt a pang of guilt for letting him stay overnight. This was mixed with the sadness of knowing I would probably never see him again. After the stunt he pulled, escaping Restwood Suites to visit me, I doubted he would ever be able to leave on his own again under Mr. Wilson's watch. And who knew what was going to happen to me. I wasn't improving, but according to Dr. Idiot, it sounded like I would never leave the hospital.

"Your rehabilitation and progress may take years," Dr. Idiot had told me. "I want to keep you close by where I can monitor and evaluate you daily. What's happening in your mind is remarkable and new territory for the medical field. You may be the key to unlocking new mysteries, and I will be the one to document and publish the findings."

To Dr. Idiot, it seemed like I was a pet science project to help him win the science fair. Basically, I was never going to leave, and after tonight, I would probably never communicate with another living soul again.

Solomon groaned, interrupting his steady beat of snoring and then began to mumble. "You'll get home...soon, Aaron. No more war...death...you'll get home."

Solomon, I whispered in my mind. *It's okay.*

His mumbling ceased and he went on sleeping peacefully. Finally, my own eyelids began to close, covering my sight with darkness, and I slowly drifted to sleep.

My eyes were still closed when my mind woke up and I felt like I had only slept for a few minutes. *Is it morning already?* I groaned in my mind to Solomon. But no one answered.

Sol? I asked. *You there?*

I tried to open my eyes and was surprised that my eyes obeyed me. But instead of lying in a hospital bed with a white hospital gown, I found myself sitting in a dank, dark dungeon cell, wearing a pinstriped black and white prison suit. The suit was more like a pair of itchy burlap pajamas that scratched at my skin as I stood up and looked around the tiny cell.

There were no beds or any furniture and the walls were made of thick stone, except for the black metal bars lining the front. A mouse skittered in front of me along the dirt floor and disappeared into a small hole at the base of the rock wall.

Standing up, I rushed to the iron bars and tried to look for a way out. The bars wouldn't budge, and I realized there was no doorway or gate in the iron bars. Somehow, I'd been trapped inside the cell with no way in or out.

A small torchlight from the hallway outside my cell provided the only light as I paced back and forth. "Why would my mind palace trap me here like this?" I thought out loud. "I didn't even know there was a dungeon in the castle. How am I supposed to get out of this nightmare?"

I paced until my stomach started to growl and my mouth began to dry. I smacked my lips together, wishing I had something to drink. I noticed a moss-covered section of stone along the wall where water trickled down into a crack and disappeared.

I'm not drinking from that, I thought, hoping my mind palace would soon let me out. I figured eventually I would be freed and pulled into one of Solomon's dreams. That seemed to be the pattern.

Time passed—for how long I didn't know—but I found myself dozing on and off. I hoped I would wake up in Solomon's dream or back in my bed in the hospital. But when I awoke, I was still there in the cell, trapped. By this time my mouth and throat were completely dry, and my body ached with fatigue. I tried to stand and nearly fell over from exhaustion.

Why are you doing this? I thought to my mind palace. *Let me out of here. Or at least give me some food and water.*

I heard the faint trickle of water from the wall as it rolled down into the crack.

I stood, trying to reach it and fell to my knees. Reluctantly, I crawled through the dusty floor, dragging myself to the mossy rock

I stuck out my tongue and let it touch the moss, feeling the cold trickle of water hit it and enter my mouth and throat. Immediately, I spat it out, gagging and retching onto the floor. The water tasted like sewage strained through a dumpster and served out of an old sneaker.

I threw up and felt what little strength I had leave my body with the contents of my stomach. I laid on the ground, going in and out of consciousness.

What happens to me if I die in my own mind? I thought, wondering if maybe it was the only way to free myself from this pain. I felt like I had been stuck in the cell for days, months, years—it all blurred together.

"Hello?" I whimpered as I lay on the dirt floor. "Someone? Can anyone hear me? Please, help." A salty tear fell down my face and landed in the dust beneath my head.

"Anyone?" I continued in a whisper, my strength nearly gone. "Why did you trap me here? I didn't do anything. Why am I here? Please, let me go. Help me."

The loneliness, the hunger pains, the weakness, were all worse than anything I had ever felt. It was worse than the first two years of being trapped in my mind alone, before Solomon arrived.

"This isn't fair," I whispered, my strength nearly gone. "I'm going to die in my own mind palace. Someone...help...me."

I struggled for breath and felt dust enter my nostrils and throat as my head slumped into the dirt. As my eyes began to close, for what I was sure would be the last time, the tiny gray mouse scurried in front of my face, holding a thimble full of water. He pressed the water to my lips and I felt the cool liquid touch my tongue and trickle down my throat. The drops of water sent tingles throughout my body, and I felt a small wave of renewed energy.

"Help is coming," squeaked the little mouse, before disappearing back into his hole.

Shakily, I pushed myself back up to sit against the wall. Even with the drops of water, I was still weak. From down the corridor outside my cell, a rumbling sound stirred far off. At first it sounded like distant thunder, deafening as it echoed down the hallway. I put my hands over my ears and closed my eyes as the thunder grew louder and louder, shaking every bone in my body.

Just as suddenly as the thunder began, it stopped. I opened my eyes and coughed as swirls of thick dust hung in the air around me. As the dust settled, caking onto my skin and clothing, I stared in awe at the most beautiful white stallion I had ever seen, standing on the other side of my prison bars. Granted, I had never seen a white stallion before, but this animal was nothing short of majestic.

It turned its rear toward me and, without warning, kicked the iron bars with its powerful hind legs. The cell rang with the clash of the metal from the horse's hooves and the prison bars. I scooted to the corner of the cell as the horse reared up its legs and released a second powerful kick.

CLANG!

The echo rang in my ears, but when I looked at the bars, nothing had budged. The horse neighed with frustration and raised its legs a third time, sending one more powerful kick sailing into the iron bars.

This time the bars exploded with a *BOOM!* Looking up, I saw a thin opening where two of the bars had disintegrated. The horse turned its head toward me, looking straight at me with one of its large brown eyes. It neighed softly and bowed its head. Without a second thought, I scrambled out of my prison, and the horse knelt down so I could climb on its back.

The horse had no saddle, and I gripped its thick white mane as it stood and galloped down the dark corridor. Wind whipped past my face as the horse sprinted faster and faster. The darkness seemed to go on forever until I saw a small light at the end of the underground tunnel. The light grew larger as we sped toward it, and I shielded my eyes from its blinding rays.

The heat of the light warmed my skin, and I felt the thick mane of the horse dissolve into a steering wheel in my hands.

"Oy, watch the road, private!" a voice barked in my ear. My eyes popped open, rapidly squinting at the blinding light.

"Who taught you how to drive?" Solomon's familiar voice asked.

Ignoring Solomon, I continued to blink my eyes to get accustomed to the brightness of the noonday sun shining high in the sky.

My hands gripped the steering wheel of an army jeep as we plowed along a lumpy, dirt road, jostling us side to side. A forest of various trees lined both sides of the road and the air smelled like fresh pine, mixed with the burnt scent of fire.

"WATCH OUT FOR THAT HOLE!" Solomon yelled, pointing to a small crater in the road right in front of us.

I swerved hard to the left, causing a young looking Solomon, dressed in army gear, to lean into me as we careened off the road toward a large tree. Reflexes kicked in and I swerved hard right this time, whipping us back across the road toward the trees lining the other side.

Taking my foot off the accelerator, I slammed onto the brakes, but nothing happened. Spinning the wheel left again, but not nearly as hard as the previous two turns, the jeep pulled back onto the road. I furiously pumped the brake pedal to stop the jeep, but it continued to coast along the road, only gradually slowing down.

"Kid! You trying to kill us? The war is *practically over* and I don't intend to die now."

"Sorry," I sputtered, my mind still wrapping itself around being freed from the prison cell. My body felt strong again and the memory of the cell felt like a distant nightmare.

"Hit the brakes already, kid," Solomon called.

"I'm trying to," I shouted back. "But the brakes won't work. Plus, I've never driven a car before!"

I pointed to my feet where I continued to slam the brake pedal over and over again with no apparent effect as we continued to coast down the dirt road.

Solomon bent his head down to look at the pedal and broke into a boisterous laugh.

"Ho ho ha ha haa," he carried on. "Private, the brakes are not working because your klutz of a foot is pressing the clutch, not the brake."

Using my feet, I awkwardly searched for another pedal to push, accidentally jerking us forward as I slammed on the gas again, until I finally found the brake pedal and slammed us to a stop.

Luckily, we were both wearing army helmets as our heads whiplashed forward, tapping the glass in front of us but not breaking it.

"Oy, you weren't kidding, were you?" Solomon asked, giving his head a slight shake. "You really don't know how to drive properly. I'm amazed we made it this far without dying."

"Sorry, sir," I said sheepishly, blood rushing back to my white knuckles as I released the steering wheel from my kung fu grip.

"*That's Lieutenant Felsher, sir,* to you, private. In a couple of months, when we're back home in the states, you can call me Solomon. Got it?"

"Uhm, yes sir, Lieutenant Felsher."

"Good. Now we've got another five miles or so to reach the coordinates the Colonel radioed for us to meet him at. How about I give you a driving lesson on the way. It would be a shame for a good looking kid like yourself to go home and not be able to drive the ladies out on dates. Sound good to you?"

"Really?" I asked a little too excitedly.

Solomon nodded and flashed a toothy grin. "Seriously, kid. What are they teaching you guys in basic? I'm just thankful they didn't make you an airman. My little brother, JJ, is an airman. I just hope he's still alive."

I eagerly listened as Solomon pointed out the controls for the jeep, including the gas, brake and clutch pedals, along with the manual stick shift and how to put it in gear.

With only a few months until I turned fifteen, when I was technically old enough to have a driver's permit, the idea of learning to drive was exhilarating, especially since there was zero chance I would ever drive in the real world.

After Solomon finished his basic instructions, he had me repeat back what I had learned to make sure I understood everything.

"Okay, Private, start her up and let's get going. God willing, we'll make it there in one piece before the Colonel blows a top at us for taking so long."

I nodded, pressing the clutch pedal down with my left foot and the brake pedal with my right. I twisted the key in the ignition, bringing the dusty green jeep rumbling to life.

"Good, good. Now take your foot off the brake and give it a little gas while slowly releasing the clutch pedal," Solomon said, giving me a confident nod of his head.

I let go of the brake, gave it a little gas and let off the clutch. The jeep lurched forward and then died.

I started to swear and Solomon smacked me across the back of the head. "Watch your language, Private. Trust me, those words won't help you learn to drive and none of the ladies back home will appreciate a man who swears like a sailor."

I rubbed the back of my head. "Fine. I'll watch my language, but just lay off the head smacks, will ya." I returned my attention to the task at hand—namely learning how to drive—and shook my head with frustration as I repeated the process of starting the car and engaging the clutch. I nearly swore again, biting my tongue to avoid another smack, as the jeep lurched forward and died a second time.

I sighed. "Maybe you should just drive. I can't get this stupid jeep to work for me."

"Nonsense. If you'd got it to work right away, I would have been amazed. Try it again. Remember it's like life. You've got to keep the clutch balanced just right until you feel it catch as you give it fuel. That's the only way to move forward. If you're out of balance, you're dead in the water."

Solomon gave me another head nod and I started up the jeep. Giving it a little more gas this time, I revved up the engine louder than before and slowly let out the clutch. The jeep lurched forward again, like before, but this time it didn't die.

Solomon gave me a wink of approval. "Attaboy, Private. Now get ready to push in the clutch and switch to second gear."

We crept along the dirt road, still stuck in first gear, until the engine began to whine loudly. I pressed down on the clutch and attempted to pull the stick shift into second gear. The stick wouldn't lock into place so I yanked it again. There was a split-second grating noise until the stick locked in place and the whining of the engine calmed back to normal.

"Perfect. Now keep her steady in second gear, and if you can avoid running into giant potholes or trees, that would be a wonderful blessing from on high."

I tried to hide my satisfaction at actually getting the jeep to drive, but couldn't stop the smile that crept across my face.

After another mile of driving, I began to feel more comfortable at the wheel and decided to break the silence.

"So. What does the Colonel need? Are we going to fight in a battle somewhere?" I asked, remembering the horrible night in the foxhole.

Solomon shook his head. "Don't worry. I think our fighting days are over. The Nazis are on the run and it won't be long now until they all surrender. But the Colonel radioed for me to leave my patrol and hurry back to meet him at these coordinates. He said he was sending a Private from a different Company, namely you, to pick me up. Didn't they already tell you all this?"

I shook my head. "Sorry, I wasn't really paying attention. I've had a lot on my mind lately."

Solomon grunted. "Well pay attention this time, Private. Colonel Bracer said he needed all the German, French, and Hebrew speakers they could find. Called for full medical teams and all the food and water we could spare from camp as well. He didn't say anything more, except to hurry. My guess is the town of Landsberg got hit hard as the Germans vacated the area."

"So you speak German?" I asked.

"Nein," Solomon answered. "Well, only a little bit. But I do speak decent Hebrew. You're the one who speaks German, aren't you?"

Solomon gave me a wary look, like I was crazy, which was odd coming from him since he was the one with dementia.

"Me? Speak German?" I scoffed. "Yeah, I don't think so."

"Quit being so modest, Private. Colonel Bracer said you were just transferred here and that you were the best German speaker in the whole Division."

I was about to protest further when we rounded a bend and found ourselves approaching a large clearing. The open area was surrounded by high fences lined with barbed wire. Dozens of U.S. soldiers scurried about with transport trucks and jeeps parked outside the long fence line.

I pulled the jeep into an empty space next to a transport truck and killed the engine. Solomon and I sat frozen in our chairs, staring through the metal fence in disbelief.

"Oh…no," I whispered.

CHAPTER 22
CONCENTRATION CAMP

"They call it a concentration camp," I said to Solomon as I hurried to keep up with the man. He zig-zagged through the mess of soldiers unloading food and water, his eyes never leaving the haunting sight on the other side of the fence.

I lifted my hand to cover my nose as we approached the gate into the prison camp. The smell caused me to cough and gag. The only thing I could compare it to was when I was a little kid and my dad took me with him to the local dump to help unload a truck full of tree branches we cut down from our yard. But this didn't just smell like a landfill, it smelled like a burnt landfill as charred ashes and smoke filled the air with the pungent smells.

"What's a concentration camp? And how do you know about it?" Solomon asked between gritted teeth.

But before I could answer, a tall man with graying hair, sun-kissed skin, and dark eyes, whistled for our attention.

"Felsher. Greenburg. Over here with me!" the man shouted.

Solomon picked up the pace and jogged over to the stranger, with me close behind.

"Colonel Bracer," Solomon said with a sharp salute.

The Colonel returned the salute and I noticed how ragged and worn his face looked up close.

"Colonel?" Solomon asked. "What is this place and who are these people? It…it's like nothing I've ever seen before."

Colonel Bracer shook his head, his lips forming a dismal frown. We took a long look around the bleak scene playing out before our eyes with hundreds of men, and even some young boys, wandering around the prison camp like zombies. Their heads were shaven and their bodies so thin that they looked like walking skeletons with their skin pulled tight against their bones. Many were nearly naked while others wore faded black and white pinstripe shirts and pants that were nothing more than rags.

But that was not the worst of it. Strewn across the camp laid dozens of prisoners, unmoving. Their bodies and clothing were covered in blood and dust. The blood was fresh and the flies began to swarm around the bodies.

I gagged. Unable to control myself any longer, I turned to the side and heaved, throwing up the contents of my stomach into the weedy dirt at my feet.

Colonel Bracer looked at me sympathetically and released a deep, sorrowful, sigh. "This, Lieutenant, is hell on earth. Another patrol discovered the prison less than an hour ago. We're still trying to gather more details and that's why I called you and Private Greenburg in for assistance. A number of these prisoners appear to be Jewish. From what we've gathered so far, they can be identified by the gold stars sewn onto their shirts. We hoped your Hebrew would be useful, in addition to Greenburg's German, as we try to get more answers."

"Certainly, sir," Solomon answered.

Colonel Bracer nodded and motioned for us to follow him.

We walked a bit further into the camp, too stunned by the scene to care about the smell any longer. Death, pain and suffering surrounded us. Dozens of U.S. soldiers spread throughout the camp, passing out food, water and blankets, but it seemed like a drop in the bucket for what these ghostlike men needed. Looking at their hollow bodies, I wondered how many of them would even survive through the night.

Up ahead, smoke spiraled into the sky from rows of burnt-out huts that were buried halfway into the ground. We made our way to one of the huts where a young prisoner, maybe in his late teens, sat on a rock while talking to a soldier.

"Corporal Elwood. Any luck?" Colonel Bracer asked the soldier.

Corporal Elwood shook his head. "Sorry, sir. He's more talkative than most of the others, but I only know a few words in German. I didn't learn very much."

Colonel Bracer turned his gaze to me. "Private Greenburg. You're up."

I shook my head. "But Colonel, I can't speak—"

"Do you speak German?" the young man asked, cutting me off.

I turned my attention back to the young man and shook my head. "No, I don't speak German. Your English is perfect, though. Why didn't you tell us you spoke English?"

The young man narrowed his eyes. "Nein. I speak no English, but your German is flawless. Are you from Germany? Did you join the Americans to fight?"

"No. I'm from California back in the United States, but I—"

I stopped, realizing that the young man and I *had* been speaking in German the whole time. The German translation came effortlessly into my mind and the words came from my lips without a second thought.

"What did he say?" Colonel Bracer asked.

"Uhm, he wanted to know if I was German. I told him I'm from California."

Colonel Bracer frowned. "Ask him what happened here. I want to know why they were imprisoned. Are they criminals? And where did the Nazis go? They were gone when we arrived. Any details you can gather will be helpful, Private."

"Okay," I answered softly, causing Colonel Bracer to raise an eyebrow expectantly. "I mean, yes, sir."

I turned back to the young man, who was sipping water from a canteen Corporal Elwood had given him. I felt awkward towering over the shriveled teenager as he sat on the rock. Kneeling on the ground, I brought myself to his level and looked into his worn, gray eyes.

"What's your name?" I asked in a calm voice.

"Rubin Ullman," the young man replied.

"How old are you, Rubin?"

"Sixteen."

My heart ached, knowing this boy, this survivor, was only one year older than me. All of my problems, my sickness, being trapped in my body, my parents, everything—it all seemed so insignificant as I looked into this boy's eyes and sensed the horrors he had lived through.

"Rubin," I continued. "My name is Aaron Greenburg. We are Americans, as you already guessed. We want to know why you are all imprisoned here. Are you criminals?"

Rubin gave a quick shake of his head. "No! We are not criminals. I was a cobbler's apprentice. My father was a florist. My brother was a student. He was only seven years old.

"He says, they are not criminals," I said, translating the rest of the message back into English.

"All of us were regular people—teachers, shop owners, bankers, tailors…" Rubin continued.

"Ask him why they were put in prison?" Colonel Bracer asked.

Rubin was quiet for a moment after I relayed the Colonel's question. Tears filled his red, hollow eyes and his lip began to quiver. He pointed to the star patch sewn onto the chest of his ragged pinstripe shirt.

"We…we were the *unwanted*," he cried.

I sucked in a breath, and froze. I couldn't speak. Solomon knelt down beside me and rested a hand on my shoulder. "It's okay, Aaron. Tell us what he said."

I took a deep breath and looked up at Solomon and the Colonel. "He said... 'We were the 'unwanted.'"

Rubin nodded his head and continued. "The Jews, Gypsies, Muslims, Pols, the handicapped—we were all unwanted. Anyone the Nazis felt were inferior they collected like cattle and brought here to work and to die."

My shoulders slumped as I translated.

"How many camps are there like this?" Colonel Bracer asked in a whisper.

"Dozens," I responded, not needing to ask or translate for an answer.

Colonel Bracer reeled backward, dumbfounded. "Dozens of camps like this. There must be thousands of prisoners and thousands more dead."

I shook my head. "Not thousands, sir. Millions."

Rubin took another sip of water and spoke up again. "We worked all day doing useless things like moving rocks from one area of the camp to another, or we would dig trenches all day, only to fill them back up with dirt the next. If you slowed down to rest, they beat you, sometimes until you died."

Corporal Elwood shook his head in disgust as I translated.

Rubin's voice grew stiff as he continued. "They forced my father to stand at attention in the middle of camp, as a warning to our group, until he eventually fainted. Then they shot him."

Rubin paused, his sucking in deep breaths as he shook his head. "Luckily, my younger brother, Heinz, died early after one week. I am thankful he did not suffer long in this nightmare. But now, I am all that is left of my family."

Colonel Bracer took a deep breath and he let a moment pass before he spoke. "Ask him where the Nazis have gone."

I asked the question and Rubin pointed south. "The Nazis left quickly, right before you came. They began shooting at us as we worked in the field. We ran and dove to the ground, but they kept shooting until they ran out of bullets. Then, as they left, they burned our sleeping quarters with many men still inside."

Colonel Bracer closed his eyes and clenched his jaw.

"Corporal Elwood. Radio back to headquarters with this information. Tell them there are more camps like this and that we need more medics, food, water, and clothing. Give them the direction the Nazis headed and let's get patrols out there and find those monsters before they escape."

"Yes, sir," Corporal Elwood saluted, and ran off toward the trucks outside the gate.

"Greenburg, Felsher, I need you to go throughout the camp and talk to these poor souls. Try to get them organized into groups for us so we can get them the proper care faster. Find out who needs the most urgent care and get them up to the trucks now. Tell them we are here to help, and we won't stop until we get them back to their wives and children."

Solomon and I nodded and I relayed the message to Rubin.

But Rubin shook his head and stood up for the first time, pointing energetically to the north. "You mean you have not found the women yet? They are in their own camp further to the north. No! We must go there now! I will take you!"

"Oh, no," I whispered in English.

"What's wrong?" Colonel Bracer asked. "What is he saying?"

"Colonel, we have to hurry. He says there is a women's camp just north of here. He thought we had already found it. He said he will take us."

"A women's camp? Are you sure?" Colonel Bracer asked, shocked at the possibility of such a thing.

I asked Rubin if he was sure, causing the teenager to grip me by both shoulders. "Do you not understand? They didn't just take the men with them. They took all of us. They took the women. They

186

took the children. They took the babies. They took…all the *unwanted.*"

Rubin dropped his hands from my shoulders and slumped forward into my arms. I held him tight, my arms easily wrapping around his skeletal frame, and I wept with him. Colonel Bracer barked out orders to nearby soldiers to go search for the women's camp to the north.

Solomon came to my side as I held Rubin, and put his hand on my shoulder. I squeezed my eyes tight, thankful he was there with me, and the three of us stood there, weeping together.

"You're not supposed to be here," Solomon whispered as he leaned in close to my ear. "You're so young. I'm sorry you came here, my boy."

I felt Rubin's frail frame disappear from my embrace and I opened my eyes to find myself back in the white, clean hospital room. Solomon laid half-crumpled across the foot of my bed with his eyes closed and his hand outstretched toward my hand.

"I'm sorry," he mumbled, still half-conscious. "I'm sorry. I'm sorry," he repeated as he slid off the foot of the bed and hit the ground with a hard thump.

CHAPTER 23
PUSH THE BUTTON

SOLOMON! I called in my mind. Solomon, are you okay? Answer me. Wake up and answer me.

Solomon released a painful groan, but did not answer. He groaned a second time before whimpering like an injured dog.

Solomon, are you hurt? Can you get up?

No answer. Only groans and pained cries.

From the dim light of the moon, I saw it was now 5 a.m. The next nurse would not check on me for another hour. No help was coming and Solomon did not sound good.

"Ahhh...my hip," Solomon moaned between short breaths. "Oy vey...this...hurts...Ahhhhh!"

Solomon began hyperventilating.

Solomon, can you hear me? Can you move? I called with my mind.

I listened as Solomon took quick sips of breath, struggling to speak. "Aaron...I...I can't move...my hip."

I heard him trying to move from the floor when he shrieked in pain, "AHHHH!!"

I hoped a nurse would hear his cries, but we were at the end of the hall and no one came.

Hold on, Solomon. I'm going to get help, I called, trying to comfort my friend.

189

His breaths grew farther apart and deeper. Fear swept through my mind. Solomon had just travelled across the bay and walked up eight flights of stairs to see me. He was worn out, tired, probably hungry, and now he had a serious injury. But how serious? I didn't know. But his moaning and breathing shifted so rapidly. His breaths went from short and quick to long and spaced out. The way he sounded reminded me of my grandpa Greenburg right before...he died.

Adrenaline shot through me, pushing my determination into overdrive. I had to help him and I had to help him now. No one else was coming and by the time they did it might be too late.

How can I get help? HOW? I screamed in my head out of frustration.

From my peripheral vision in my right eye, I saw the red emergency button on the side of my hospital bed. My right hand was beside it with my pinky resting only half an inch away.

I pushed with my mind, willing my pinky to move.

Nothing.

MOVE I TELL YOU! I screamed at my hand. I felt my face redden with heat and a bead of sweat trickled down my forehead from the exertion.

Nothing.

Solomon took two more long breaths. Then all went silent.

NOOOOOOO!!! I shouted. My head felt like it would explode as I forced everything I could into one mental push. I visualized sending my thoughts down my neck, through my shoulder, along the length of my skinny arm, to my hand and into my pinky. My head felt like it was swelling and spinning with dizziness.

With a final shout, I felt my pinky move and touch the cold plastic button. From the corner of my eye, I saw the red button depress into the side of the bed railing as I pushed my pinky against it. There was a buzzing sound and I heard a nurse's voice echo over the small speaker in the side of my bed by.

"Nurse Meyers, how can I help you? Are you okay?"

I didn't respond. How could I?

"Wait. Is this Aaron Greenburg's room?" she stated more than asked. The two-way speaker went silent. Twenty seconds later I heard the pattering of footsteps running toward my door.

***

Dr. Idiot paced the room, pulling at the end of his mustache, before coming back to my bedside. "And you say the boy pushed the emergency button, with his pinky, by his own power?"

I caught a glimpse of Nurse Meyers rolling her eyes behind Dr. Idiot's back. "Yes, Doctor. As I told you before, when the old man—Solomon Felsher I believe is his name—fell down, I received an emergency call from this room. We rushed here immediately, found Mr. Felsher unconscious, without a pulse, lying on the floor. We immediately administered CPR, and luckily, he responded right away and we were able to resuscitate him. He's recovering nicely, though he does have a fractured hip and a bad case of pneumonia."

"Yes, yes, the old man is okay, though what that fool was doing here is beyond me," Dr. Idiot responded with a hint of annoyance.

This caused me to produce a guttural growl. Since Solomon's traumatic fall, my ability to produce noise had come back in full force. I could groan, I could grunt, and apparently I could growl.

Dr. Idiot froze at the sound of my intense, dog-like growl. "Remarkable," he whispered. "His ability to produce vocal sounds has returned since the old man snuck into his room."

I growled again, causing Nurse Meyers to snicker. "I don't think he likes you talking about his friend that way, Doctor."

Dr. Idiot shot a stink-eye glare toward the nurse before turning his attention back to me. "Tell me again, exactly what you witnessed from Aaron when you entered the room," he asked, gently twisting the corner of his mustache.

With Dr. Idiot's back to her, Nurse Meyers rolled her eyes, again, and shook her head, causing the blonde bangs of her hair to swish back and forth. "As I told you the first two times, Aaron was groaning when we entered the room. We thought he was hurt, but he was fine. He didn't stop groaning for fifteen minutes, until after I told him Mr. Felsher was alive and recovering. After we moved Mr. Felsher to the emergency room, I checked on Aaron a little closer and discovered that his pinky was still resting on the red emergency call button. He had moved his finger to push the button. He saved his friend's life."

I grunted my approval of her story.

Dr. Idiot took a step closer to the foot of my bed, still twisting the corner of his mustache. "Aaron. If you can hear me, answer me this. Is Solomon Felsher your friend? See if you can give me two grunts for 'yes' and three grunts for 'no.'"

I pushed against my mind and immediately produced two grunts. They came easily and naturally, and I could feel my body connecting to my mind as if it were awakening for the first time.

"Remarkable!" Dr. Idiot replied. "To make sure, I will ask you another question. Aaron, should Solomon Felsher be arrested for sneaking into the hospital and into your room?"

What? I thought. *You want to arrest him?* This caused an immediate growl of disapproval.

"I believe that's a no," Nurse Meyers commented.

Dr. Idiot nodded in agreement. He stared at me intently and I could see the wheels turning in his head.

"Aaron?" Dr. Idiot asked again. "Would you like to be moved to the same room as Solomon once he's released from the ICU?"

Of course I would, I thought, quickly grunting twice.

"And would you like to move back to your room at Restwood Suites after Solomon is well enough to return?"

Are you kidding me? I thought with surprise. *Yes! Now you're talking.* I gave two enthusiastic grunts that caused my chest to heave up and down. After months of being stuck in this hospital, going back to Restwood, with Solomon, was a dream come true.

Dr. Idiot's stern look of concentration seemed to melt away as his face pulled into a smile. He snorted and gave a slight shake of his head. "Here the answer was in front of me the whole time, and I took you away from your means of recovery. I'm sorry for that," Dr. Idiot said with a remorseful smile.

"Nurse, please contact Aaron's parents and inform them of my strong belief that he should be moved back into Restwood Suites with Mr. Solomon Felsher. I will contact the retirement home and make the proper arrangements for both of them to be moved back to their room once Mr. Felsher is well enough to be discharged. Aaron, we will continue your therapy and run future tests from there. Your parents will need to agree to the move first, of course, but I believe this will provide the best environment for your recovery. Is this agreeable with you?"

I grunted twice, hardly able to believe what I was hearing.

Dr. Idiot nodded and patted my leg. "Very good. I have a strong feeling you are about to make big strides toward recovery."

I sure hope so, I thought, giving two more grunts.

Dr. Idiot gave me a final nod and exited the room. Nurse Meyers stayed to change my fluid bags and I heard another pair of footsteps approach the room door. The door opened and the smell of oranges and baked bread filled the room.

"Aaron!" squealed Sarah, as she rushed to the foot of my bed.

Sarah, you're back from space camp, I thought, my mind relishing her scent and her voice.

Nurse Meyers stopped her work to greet the new guests. "Hello. Are you Aaron's family?"

"No," Talia replied, coming into my view. "I'm Solomon Felsher's daughter—the man who snuck into Aaron's room and fell. This is my daughter, Sarah."

"Grandpa and Aaron were friends and roommates in a retirement home together," Sarah added. "When we came to visit

Grandpa, I had to stop and see Aaron. I've been gone all summer at Space Camp and I haven't been able to visit."

Nurse Meyers walked closer to the foot of my bed and all three women were in my view.

"I see," said Nurse Meyers with a smile. "I'm glad to hear your grandfather is doing much better, though that broken hip will take a while to heal."

Talia nodded. "I still can't believe that crazy old man made his way all the way to the hospital, climbed the stairs up to this room, and then broke his hip. I'm not sure what we are going to do with him."

"Mom, Grandpa will be fine. He just wanted to visit Aaron. Maybe we can bring him back to visit more often so he won't sneak out."

So they don't know yet, I thought. *Soon we'll be roommates again. There will be no need to visit.* I gave a growl of disapproval at this idea, trying to let them know the visits were not needed.

"Whoa," Sarah said, backing up a step. "Aaron, what was that?"

Nurse Meyers chuckled. "I think he's trying to tell you that bringing your grandfather to visit Aaron will be unnecessary. You'll also find that Aaron has made some big strides toward communicating. Isn't that right, Aaron."

I gave two solid grunts in response, causing Sarah's eyes to light up and her smile, full of pink braces, to beam at me from across my bed.

I wanted to smile back and shout for joy. Instead I settled for two more grunts.

Finally, I thought to Sarah. *We can talk to each other, well sorta talk. I may not be able to speak words yet, but I'm getting there. You better be ready to join the choir.*

CHAPTER 24
SARAH'S BIRTHDAY PRESENT

"And that, my friend, is 'The End'," Solomon said with a satisfied smile. From his chair at the foot of my bed, Solomon set down a paperback copy of *The Chosen,* by Chaim Potok, on his lap. He had given me the copy of the book as a Hanukkah gift only a few weeks ago. He said I needed an English class, like in a real school, so every day he would read a chapter to me from the book and we would discuss it.

"So what did you think of my favorite book?" Solomon asked me.

It was good, I responded in my head. *I really like Daniel and Reuven.*

Solomon shook his head, causing his curls to bounce, and he held up a hand.

"No, no, no. I don't want to hear your thoughts. Use your words, like a big boy. Part of this 'English' class is to help your speech. We need to keep practicing before Sarah gets here."

I released a sigh, followed by a low growl of annoyance.

"Oy, enough with the growling already. It's no wonder Sarah calls you Tigger."

Solomon rose from his chair and used his walker to shuffle to the side of my bed. He moved slowly, a flicker of pain causing him to wince, but he quickly recovered, attempting to hide his pain while he rubbed the side of his hip.

Although it had been over six months, and many hours of rehab, since Solomon fell and broke his hip, the pain still plagued him night and day.

I turned my head ever so slightly toward Solomon and slowly rolled my eyes at him.

"B...b...b...ooooo...k. G..gg...gg...gg...oooooo....dd..dd," I stuttered.

Solomon nodded his head and winked at me. "Well done, Aaron, my boy. You're 'B' and 'G' sounds are coming along nicely. Dr. Idiot, I mean Dr. McPhearson, will be pleased."

"Aaaann...nn...nnk...sssss" I replied.

I growled in disappointment. *I meant to say thanks,* I said to him in my mind. *I'm still having a hard time getting the 'th' sound to come out.*

Solomon chuckled. "Attaboy, Aaron. Considering a year ago you couldn't make a sound or move a muscle, I think 'Aanks' is just fine. But seeing as it does take you forever to speak out loud, and I'm not getting any younger, go ahead and use your mind to keep telling me what you thought about the book."

You're ridiculous, you know that, I thought to Solomon.

Solomon snorted in response.

Well, I liked Daniel and Reuven. They were different in a lot of ways, but I think that's what made them such good friends. And besides being a super genius, I feel like I can relate to Daniel. I know what it's like to be an outsider and alone.

Solomon nodded in agreement and patted me on the arm. "In a way, we all have a little bit of Daniel and Reuven in us. Though, I must say, you are quite a genius in your own right. You have an amazing mind and will, Aaron. To be able to recover like you're doing is quite the feat."

This caused me to blush, and I slowly rolled my eyes again. Small muscle movement to my eyes, fingers, toes and neck had been returning to my body. Finally, I could look around a room again and even move my head to talk to people. It was amazing how much those small movements changed my everyday life.

You know, I continued my thoughts about the book, *the parts about Hasidic Jews were really interesting, too. Their beliefs and traditions and how Daniel studied the Torah with his dad. Do you know many Hasidic Jews?*

Solomon nodded, and gave a quick chuckle, as if remembering a funny memory.

"That I did. In fact, I played baseball with some as a kid, just like Danny and Reuven. I think that's one of the reasons I like *The Chosen* so much. It brings back memories of growing up in New York as a Jew. Oy, if I could go back and be a kid again, running around and playing baseball, just for a day, that would be something."

Tell me about it, I thought, remembering the days before my illness took over. *To be able to run and ride a bike, or just to walk, even for a day, would be a dream come true.*

"Someday, Aaron. Someday. Mark my words, you'll walk again."

"Ye...ye...yeee...ssss," I said out loud and then changed back to thoughts. *I hope so.*

"I know so," Solomon encouraged.

I heard footsteps outside our door and the smell of oranges entered the room.

"Sarah, my darling. Happy sweet sixteen!" Solomon proclaimed, embracing Sarah as she came into view.

"Thanks Grandpa," she said, pulling back a wisp of her light-brown hair from her face.

Immediately, I noticed that her hair was different. Instead of her normal frizz, it was long and wavy. Plus, there was something else. *Is she wearing pink lipstick?* I thought, surprised to see Sarah wearing makeup.

"Hey, Tigger," Sarah called to me with a wave of her hand. Normally I would have found a nickname like Tigger annoying, but not when Sarah said it.

"Dad sent me this new jacket for my birthday and mom took me to get my hair done and a makeover. Do you like?" she asked, twirling around in a circle for us.

Uhm, yeah. I like, I said in my mind and grunted twice.

"Thanks, Aaron," she replied with a wink. "I'm glad you approve."

This caused Solomon to give me the stink eye, but I ignored him, turning all my attention to Sarah.

"And guess who drove here all by herself!" she exclaimed, holding up a pair of car keys.

Solomon reeled back in mock surprise. "I can't believe your mother let you out on the road by yourself. Oy, I hope you're a better driver than she was as a teenager. Talia gave me at least three heart attacks when I taught her how to drive. It's amazing both of us are still alive."

Sarah giggled and flashed a bright white smile. "To tell you the truth, Grandpa," she whispered, "she's still not a very good driver."

Solomon and Sarah laughed out loud together. Seeing Sarah so happy caused the corners of my mouth to twitch in an attempted, but utterly failed, smile. She looked so mature in her new jacket, with the makeover and the car keys. She looked…like a woman. But there was something else different.

Sarah came to my bedside and smiled again, the pink lipstick accentuated her bright white smile.

That's it, I thought to Solomon.

"What's it?" Solomon asked out loud.

Her braces are gone, I told him. *I just noticed. I forgot they were coming off this week.*

Solomon relayed my observation and she smiled again, blushing this time.

Tell her she looks wonderful and I'm happy for her, I thought to Solomon.

Solomon snorted. "You ought to tell her yourself," he mumbled under his breath so only I could hear him. Then he relayed my message to Sarah.

"Thanks, Aaron," Sarah said with a grin, dimples forming on her freckled cheeks. "It's definitely been an exciting birthday."

Solomon smiled. "Well, the excitement is not over yet. Aaron has one last special gift for you. Don't you, Aaron?"

"Oh, really?" Sarah asked, arching an eyebrow. "And what might that be? You know you didn't have to get me anything."

I know, I thought. *But I've been working on this for a long time.*

"Ss..ss..ar..ah, y...y..y..yoou sh...sh..sh..shooul...d jo..jo..join choi..choi..rrrrr."

Sarah's jaw dropped and tears trickled down her face as she covered her mouth in surprise. It had been hard to keep the secret of my speech development from Sarah over the last month, but the look on her face made it worth it.

Bending over in front of me, Sarah grabbed both my hands in hers and kissed me on the cheek.

"That, Tigger," she said, choking back tears, "was the best birthday gift I could have ever asked for."

CHAPTER 24
MARY POPPINS

"How d..d..ooo I..l..ooo..k?" I slowly stuttered to Solomon.

We sat across from each other in our matching wheelchairs and Solomon wrinkled his nose at the question.

"You look okay, kid…but are you sure you don't want to wear the suit I lent you before? It was an expensive suit back in the day. I had it custom made when I opened for Bobby Darin in Miami. You should have seen that concert. We really swung the place, and Bobby took me and Dolores out for dinner afterward. We—"

Solomon, you've told me this story like ten times now, I said to him in my mind. Lately, he had been repeating the same stories over and over, often mixing two or three of them together in a jumbled mess.

Don't get me wrong, I continued. *I like your suit, although it still smells like mothballs and needs a good dry cleaning, but my parents just bought me this new suit, and they're coming with us tonight. I think they would feel bad if I didn't wear it.*

"Oy, they should have saved the money. I told them you could keep my lucky suit," he harrumphed. "You know I wore that to play with Bobby Darrin."

I narrowed my eyes in concern, preparing for Solomon to repeat the story again. This caused Solomon to release a whole-hearted belly laugh.

201

"I'm kidding!" Solomon said between laughs. "I know I'm losing my mind, but I couldn't resist. You should have seen your face."

I growled at Solomon. *You know, sometimes you're such a dork.*

This only made Solomon laugh harder before he took some deep breaths to calm down. "In all seriousness, your parents should have saved the money. It really is a lucky suit."

I rolled my eyes at him. *It was nice of you to offer, but when my mom agreed to let me go to Sarah's choir concert at the city performance hall, she insisted on buying me something nice to wear, since I've outgrown nearly all of my clothes.*

"Well, if you would stop growing like a weed, that wouldn't be a problem," Solomon pointed out. "If you get any taller you'll have a guaranteed career in the NBA, just like that Manute Bol fella. He's not a very good player, but he's taller than a tree."

I sighed out loud. *Manute Bol is like 7 foot 7 inches tall. Nurse Penny says I'm barely 6 feet. Plus, I've got to learn to stand and walk again. I don't foresee a career in the NBA.*

Solomon waved off my comment with his hand. "Details, details. You never know, kid. Life is a funny thing. At the rate you're going, I bet you're walking by the end of the year."

My lips twitched into a weak smile. "I ho...pe s..s..sooo."

Solomon wheeled his wheelchair next to my side and grabbed my forearm. "I know so, Aaron. I know it."

Solomon let go of my arm and I heard a cacophony of footsteps walking toward our room. The sounds were soon accompanied by a melee of smells. There was peppermint, baked bread, grass, lavender and chlorine. With my wheelchair already facing the door, I watched the crowd enter our room.

"Grandpa!" Jesse screamed, nearly tackling Solomon in a hug as he ran into Solomon in his wheelchair.

"Well don't you two look fancy! And that new suit looks very handsome on you, Aaron," my mom said as she came to give me a hug and a kiss on the cheek.

Nurse Penny smiled and nodded in agreement. "They're a couple of regular gentlemen, dontcha know."

This caused a friendly chuckle to ripple through the group. My dad gave me a wink as he walked behind my wheelchair to push me. He bent down close to my ear and whispered, "You look good, son."

"Th..thhhhh..thhh..ank..s," I stuttered back, the 'th' sound still giving me issues.

"I just have to say," Talia spoke as she walked behind Solomon to push his wheelchair, "Sarah is so excited to have you come. It means a lot to me, too. And I want to give a special thanks to Aaron for convincing my daughter to join the choir. She loves to sing, and it makes me so happy to watch her using her gifts. So, thank you, Aaron."

Talia kindly patted me on the shoulder and I felt my face turn rosy red as heat rushed up my cheeks.

"M..m..my plea...s..s..uuure." I stammered out.

This caused another round of friendly laughter.

"Well," Nurse Penny said with another big smile. "I think it's time we be on our way. I convinced Mr. Wilson to let us borrow one of the passenger transport vans. It has one of those fancy wheelchair lifts. Then we can all ride together. Oh, won't that be nice."

We carefully piled into the large white van, with the Restwood Suite name and phone number stenciled across the side, and drove to the city's performance hall.

It was June, and this was Sarah's end of the year choir concert. Through some serious finagling on Sarah and Talia's part, they had convinced the school to switch her out of her music appreciation elective so she could join the choir for the last half of the school year. Apparently, the choir director had Sarah try out in a private session before agreeing to the transfer. When she heard Sarah's voice, she signed the transfer paper immediately and admitted Sarah to the upper level choir, giving her a slot as a soloist on the spot.

Sarah had been stunned. She was so excited that she came to practice every afternoon in our room at Restwood, with Solomon giving her musicality pointers and tips.

"I may not have the best voice in the world," he had told her, "but I've still got a great ear. Plus, I've played with some of the best vocalists to ever walk this beautiful earth—Ella Fitzgerald, Bobby Darrin, Frank Sinatra, Billie Holiday, and don't forget your grandmother, Dolores Felsher. And let me tell you something— Sarah, my little sweetie pie—when you play with the best, you tend to learn a thing or two."

Over the last few months, Solomon taught and shared with Sarah, and by default, me, more musical wisdom than I ever thought I could possibly learn. I felt like I knew a lot about music from my former days as a trombone player and from listening to Solomon play and talk about jazz. But as Solomon taught Sarah, I realized how little I knew. I could feel the presence of good music, and appreciate it, but Solomon opened up a new world of understanding on what it took to *make* music, not just good, but great music—the kind of music that moved one's soul.

And the best part was Solomon seemed to love every minute of it. Since his fall and broken hip, his energy had diminished. Over the last few weeks, walking had become so difficult he had finally relented to Nurse Penny's pleas to use a wheelchair, but only after I became strong enough to sit up in a wheelchair of my own.

But when he dove into the music, teaching Sarah, it sparked a light in his eyes that I hadn't seen in a long time.

We pulled into the parking lot where the concert was taking place, and our group unloaded from the Restwood van. I was surprised by how many cars and people were in attendance, as my dad pushed me through the front doors and into the lobby. It had been a long time since I had been out in a large public gathering, and the immediate influx of scents and noises took me a few minutes to adjust to. Talia pulled out a handful of tickets and handed them out to the members of our group.

"Hey! Penny, Aaron, Solomon," called a familiar voice from the side.

I slowly turned my head to find Barry and his wife Whitney approaching us.

"Barry, my friend, how are you?" Solomon replied. "And who is this lovely young woman at your side? She's much too young to be your wife. A daughter perhaps?"

This caused Whitney to smile ear-to-ear as Solomon took her hand and kissed it.

"Hey, now. You better watch yourself, Solomon, my man. You do remember that I know where you live, right?" Barry joked.

"Hello, Barry," Nurse Penny said. "I believe you know Aaron's parents and Solomon's daughter."

"Of course," Barry said, grasping each of their hands in a friendly handshake.

"And it's so good to see you again," Whitney said to me, patting my hand in my forearm "Barry's always telling me about how much you're improving each day. What a miracle and a blessing to you, and your parents. The Lord must be watching out for all y'all," she said.

"Thh..thhhhaan..ks," I replied and worked my face muscles to into a smile.

"Aaron, my man," Barry said with a nod, "I should be thanking you. You inspire me each and every day I come to work. When things are tough I just think, 'Look at Aaron. Look at what that kid has gone through and look at him working to be better.' You make me want to be better myself."

Barry grasped my hand and gave it a solid squeeze. "And I'm so glad Sarah invited us to the concert. It's not every day the missus and I get to dress up nice and go out for a date."

Whitney raised an eyebrow. "And whose fault is that?" she chided through pursed lips.

Barry looked like he was about to argue back, but closed his eyes and took a quick breath, changing his face into a playful smile.

"It's my fault, baby," he said, pulling her close to give her a peck on the cheek. "But I'll make it up to you, starting with our date tonight."

This caused Whitney to relax her face and roll her eyes. She returned Barry's playful smile and kissed him back.

"Now, there's a lesson I wished I had learned earlier in my marriage," my dad said.

"No kidding," my mom snorted. "But you're making up for it nicely."

I heard a soft kiss from behind me where my parents stood. I smiled, thankful my parents were back together and doing so well.

"Oy, if I can interrupt the newlywed lovefest," Solomon said with a shake of his head. "How about we get to our seats before this show starts. I want to be front and center to listen to my granddaughter sing her solo."

Everyone agreed, and we turned in our tickets to go find seats. Solomon used his charm to convince a young teenage couple to move to a different row so we could all sit together.

There was no place in the theater for us to sit and stay parked in our wheelchairs—which seemed like a real oversight for the handicapped. So my dad and Barry helped move Solomon and me from our wheelchairs and into the red velvet, padded chairs at the end of the row.

After a few more minutes, the lights dimmed in the performance hall, and from behind the curtain, the choir began humming the tune to *Chim Chim Cheree* from *Mary Poppins*. The giant red curtains swished open, revealing the choir in their costumes. The girls all wore white dresses and large brimmed hats, just like Mary Poppins wore in the movie, and the boys were dressed like the character Bert, with red and white pinstriped suit coats, white pants, and short straw hats with a red ribbon around them.

They continued to hum the tune as their director, a slight female with wavy dark hair, came to the microphone at the front of the stage.

"We welcome you all to our end-of-the-year performance tonight. Tonight's theme is from the Disney classic, and one of my favorite movies, *Mary Poppins*. The Mount Diablo High School choir has worked tirelessly to prepare this concert for you, and we hope you enjoy the magic, and the music, of *Mary Poppins*."

The audience gave a round of applause and the director took her place in front of the choir, leading them into their first song.

The choir sang beautifully, performing *Chim Chim Cheree, Sister Suffragette, The Life I Lead,* and *A Spoonful of Sugar.* I turned my head slightly toward Solomon and caught him mouthing the words as the choir sang. He energetically tapped his hand against his thigh as they sang the upbeat songs of *Step In' Time* and *Supercalifragilisticexpialidocious.*

"I remember when we recorded these songs," Solomon whispered in my ear, still tapping to the beat.

No way. You played on Mary Poppins? I asked incredulously. This was a new story and I worried Solomon was mixing things up again. Or worse—making things up.

"Oy, are you calling me a liar?" he whispered back.

Well, no, I thought back, *but you've never mentioned this before. I'm just wondering if you're having a senior moment and getting things mixed up.*

Solomon snorted. "Senior moment, my rear end," he whispered as he continued to tap his hand against his leg. "I'll have you know, kid, that I've done a lot of things in life that I've never told you about—or that you've never seen in my dreams. I'm seventy-three years old and I've lived a full life, but that doesn't make me an old man."

Well, according to the sign at the Denny's we passed on the drive here, age fifty-five gets you the Senior Discount, so yeah, you're an old man.

"Alright, smart alec," Solomon whispered as he turned to give me a sly look. He stopped tapping his hand and instead grabbed my hand and lifted it up to my face, only to begin using my own hand to tap my face to the beat of *Supercalifragilisticexpialidocious*. "I may be old, but at least I'm not hitting myself. Stop hitting yourself, Aaron. Quit it," he taunted.

Very mature, I thought, as my hand kept tapping me awkwardly on the side of the face. *You're lucky my arm isn't stronger or I would totally sock you right now.*

"I can't believe you'd hit an old man," Solomon feigned protest, and softly chuckled to himself— enjoying the music and his new human metronome. Luckily, the song was near the end and Solomon rested my hand back on the armrest after the last note.

There was a pause for the next song and Talia whispered down our row, "I think Sarah is up next."

Solomon and I perked up as we watched Sarah take her place at the front-right of the stage for her solo. She looked like an 18th century angel floating in the darkness as the spotlights illuminated her white dress and white hat against the black stage and darkened room.

The choir hummed softly in the background for four measures before Sarah's sweet voice cut through the air, carrying with it the mournful, yet hopeful, melody of *Feed the Birds*.

The room filled with energy as she sang her solo. I had heard Sarah practice this song for hours on end, but she had never sung like this before. It truly was…magical.

I turned my head as far as I could to catch another glimpse of Solomon. The man was no longer tapping his hand or bobbing his head. Instead, his hands wrung together tightly.

"Feed the birds," he mumbled along with Sarah's voice. He spoke so softly now that only my super-hearing picked it up. "We're moving to…California. Find a job. Feed…our…family."

The large performance hall went black, and I thought there was a power outage. But when I blinked, I found myself standing in small stone room, high in my mind palace. There was a large window to the side with nothing but blue sky and clouds in my view. I stepped closer to the window and looked down. I was hundreds of feet in the air.

"Really!" I complained. "It's the middle of Sarah's solo and I'm getting pulled into my mind palace now?"

My frustration grew as I thought about the inconvenient timing of this mind palace trip, and I hoped I wouldn't be trapped in a prison cell again or pulled into another dream in the holocaust. I wasn't sure I could handle either of those again.

As I looked out the window a second time, I realized I had been placed in the south tower of the castle—the second tallest behind the massive north clock tower.

WHISH, WHISH, WHISH, came a soft sound from outside the window. I poked my head out again and found a full-grown elephant flying through the air, flapping ginormous ears like a pair of wings.

The elephant held a feather in its trunk and winked at me as it flew by. From on top of its back, the little gray mouse I had met in the castle dungeon rode the elephant and waved at me.

I blinked my eyes. "This place is getting weirder and weirder," I said out loud, not sure what to make of that since it was all in my mind.

Music and laughter echoed in the room and I turned to see a wooden door materialize in the stone wall. I took one last look at the massive elephant flying through the sky, shrugged my shoulders, and pulled open the door.

CHAPTER 26
WALT DISNEY

"Daddy, Daddy, it's Mickey Mouse and Pluto!" squealed a little girl as she dashed toward me at full speed. Her yellow sundress flapped in the wind and her black Mickey Mouse ear hat nearly fell off as she sprinted away from her parents. "Daddy, Daddy, can we take a picture?"

Struggling to keep up with her daughter, her dad, a heavy set man wearing bell bottom corduroy pants and a much too tight Disneyland T-shirt with the castle logo plastered across the chest, hurried to her side.

"Hold on, sweetie," the father said between heavy breaths. "We'll see Mickey, but you can't keep running off like that!"

A pregnant lady, wearing a long brown sun dress, walked up to the pair, pushing a stroller with a small toddler inside.

"Cherish," the lady said to the girl, "you have to stay with Mommy and Daddy so you don't get lost. Do you understand?"

Cherish nodded vigorously and giggled as a large white hand, the size of a trash can lid, extended into my view and waved the little girl over toward us.

"What in the world?" I said out loud.

This caused the girl to pause and look directly at me, her eyes going wide with excitement.

"Did Pluto just talk?" she asked excitedly.

"Pluto?" I whispered to myself. I tried to move and realized I was surrounded by a thick, fur-like shell. I could turn my head inside the shell, but I could only see through a circle of black mesh right in front of my face.

The black mesh made my vision a little dark and blurry, but I could still make out the little girl, Cherish, smiling at me and full of delight.

"Oh, Pluto!" she squealed. "I always knew you could talk. Wait until I tell Ginger and Sally."

I felt something hit me across the head repeatedly—well across the shell of a head I was stuck in. Since the only way to see out the mesh viewport was straight ahead, I turned my whole body to look at who was assailing me.

"No way!" I exclaimed.

Right in front of me stood Mickey Mouse. He was petting me, no, more like whacking me, across the head. I turned a little further and saw the massive Matterhorn Mountain directly behind us.

Okay, I thought to myself as all the puzzle pieces clicked together. *I'm dressed as Pluto, at Disneyland. Now the flying elephant from my mind palace makes sense.*

"Cherish. You just stand there next to Mickey and Pluto and I'll snap your picture," the little girl's dad said.

I was still staring at the giant Mickey Mouse character in front of me when Mickey gently laid a hand on Cherish's shoulder and roughly pushed my head forward to face the camera.

"Say cheese!"

"Cheese," I said without thinking as the camera went *CLICK. CLICK. CLICK.*

This brought another swift whack, or pat, to the back of my head from Mickey Mouse.

"Okay, Cherish. Say goodbye to Mickey and Pluto," her mother called. "It's time to go get some lunch before we do more rides."

"Weeee. More rides. Bye, Mickey!" she exclaimed, rushing to give the giant mouse a hug.

Then she turned to me and gave me a hug, pulling my shelled head down toward her. "And bye, Pluto. I know you're shy, but don't be afraid to talk. We all love you, too," she whispered.

Cherish and her family waved goodbye and walked away.

"Well, this is new," I chuckled, turning back toward Mickey.

"Oy vey, kid!" Mickey exclaimed. "You've only been on the job for an hour and already you've broken the cardinal rule: No talking to the patrons! You must be brain dead or something. Good thing that little girl was too sweet to notice."

"Solomon! Is that you in there?" I asked.

Mickey Mouse shook his massive head and whacked me— or was it a pat?— across the side of the head again. "Of course it's me, kid. I'm your trainer, and you're making me look bad. Do me a favor and zip those lips of yours for the rest of this shift. We've only got another hour until bandstand duty. So just be quiet and shake a leg every once in a while. You're a dog, remember."

"Uhmmm, yeah, sure. But what's-"

Solomon cut me off with another whack from his massive Mickey Mouse hand. "Shhhhh," he hissed. "Family of four at 2 o'clock. Keep those lips zipped until break time."

"Fine," I mumbled to myself. "I'll just sit here silently, shaking my leg, because I'm Pluto the dog."

The comparison made me think of the two years I had spent alone before Solomon arrived. I'd been silent then, too, and people always patted my head like a puppy dog when they visited. So in a way, I guess Pluto was a fitting character for me to play.

As the family of four approached to take a picture, I continued to lift my back leg up and down, shaking it in the air like I was doing the hokey-pokey. But as I went to put my foot back down to ground, my leg got caught on the inside fabric of the Pluto suit. I started to fall off balance with my leg caught and dangling in the air.

To keep from falling, I leaned against Solomon for support while I tried to unsnag my pants.

"Look!" a young teenage boy called, pointing in our direction as he walked by with a group of other boys. "Pluto's marking his territory on Mickey."

The teenage boys laughed hysterically as I realized how this must have looked, with my leg raised up against Mickey, to everyone passing by. The family of four frowned and turned around instead of approaching us for a picture.

After a few more seconds, I finally unsnagged my leg and was able to lower it, but the young teenagers continued to laugh and point at us.

Maybe it was the fact that I was hidden behind the Pluto costume. Maybe it was because this was a dementia dream and not supposed to be real. But I rushed right at the group of punks barking like a deranged pit bull.

Their eyes went white as I closed in on them, causing one of them to drop their ice cream cone as they stumbled backwards over one another and took off running away. I continued to chase them on all fours for another twenty yards until they ran out of sight.

I stopped to catch my breath and felt a pat, definitely a pat this time, across the top of my shelled head.

"Kid, you got moxie, I'll give you that. But I don't think you have a future as Pluto. Hopefully you're a better trombone player. What do you say we call it quits and take an early break before heading to the bandstand for warm-ups?"

"Sounds good," I said, smiling from inside my Pluto head. Apparently, I was going to get the chance to play the trombone again.

I followed Solomon to a less trafficked area at the base of the Matterhorn. There was a small alcove surrounded by bushes and a tall brown fence with a gate. On the gate a large red sign with bright white lettering read, "CAST MEMBERS ONLY."

Solomon pushed the gate open and I followed him to a metal door that stood next to a large roll-up garage door in the side of the Matterhorn Mountain. A man in a security guard uniform opened the door and gave us a friendly smile.

"Hey, Sol, that's you, right?"

"Yeah, it's me, George. How you doing, buddy?"

"I'm good. But, hey, Sol, you don't need to worry about me. How are you and Dolores doing? Peg and I feel awful for you guys. The funeral service was beautiful and touching. I'm sorry about your boy. Just let us know if you need anything."

Solomon peeled off the massive Mickey Head and gave George a solemn look, which, even though he was still wearing the rest of the Mickey Mouse tuxedo outfit, sent a chill of sorrow up my spine as I saw the sadness in his eyes.

"Thanks, George. I appreciate it," Solomon replied. His eyes drooped low and his shoulders sagged as he walked past George, leading me into the large room behind the walls of Matterhorn Mountain. Various props, exterior lighting, and even a few costumes lined the shelves and walls of the giant storage area.

Solomon led me toward a lit stairwell that seemed to go down a level, underground.

"Oh, and Sol," George called back to us before we reached the stairs. "I almost forgot. The boss wants to see you. Said he would stop by the bandstand before your performance."

Solomon waved a hand in the air without turning around. "Tell Harold I'll be there in another hour."

"Not Harold," George replied, causing Solomon to stop and turn around.

George gave Solomon a grin. "It ain't Harold coming to see you, Sol. It's the *big boss*. I heard it on the walkie just an hour ago," George said holding up his walkie set. "Just thought I would give you a heads up."

Solomon raised his eyebrows in surprise. "Thank you, George. I appreciate it."

We left George behind and walked down the stairs toward another doorway. Solomon looked so down-hearted that I was afraid to ask who died and decided to change the subject.

"Are we going into the underground tunnels?" I asked. "I heard there are giant underground tunnels throughout the park and that they were big enough for trucks to drive through and cast members to get around. Oh, and is it true there's a giant cafeteria underground for employees?"

Solomon turned and looked at me as if I were the craziest person he had ever met. "I don't know where you heard stories about underground tunnels and what not, but this is about as close as you get to anything like that."

Solomon twisted the doorknob and pushed it open, revealing a medium sized room with a handful of brown couches against the wall, a few tables and chairs in the middle, separate doorways for men's and women's locker rooms, and a tiny green fridge in the corner.

"Welcome to the glorious cast room. Hope you packed a lunch. There's no cafeteria down here."

A few other theme park workers, including a Snow White and three of her dwarves, sat at a card table playing poker and drinking sodas. Cinderella stretched out on one of the couches, gently snoring while she took a nap, and a man dressed as Prince Charming was eating a green apple from a fruit bowl on a side table, while reading an issue of TIME magazine.

As soon as we walked in the room, everyone stopped what they were doing and turned their full attention to Solomon—including Cinderella, who seemed to wake up as soon as we entered.

"How are you holding up, Sol?" the dwarves questioned.

"We all feel for you," Snow White spoke up. "We're here for you."

"Yeah, and I'm happy to cover your shifts. You don't need to come back to work so soon," Prince Charming offered.

Cinderella, who, upon closer inspection looked like a teenager, rose from the couch and gave Solomon a hug. "We're so sorry for your loss, Sol. Do you and Dolores need anything? Anything at all?"

Solomon nodded politely. "No thanks, Jill. We appreciate your concern, all of you, but we—"

Solomon paused, his thought trailing off into awkward silence. "I need to go get changed for the bandstand. I'll see you kids later."

Solomon marched toward the men's locker room and pushed his way through the door. The rest of the cast members dipped their heads and Cinderella, or rather, Jill, started to cry.

"Oh, Sol," I whispered to myself and weaved past Cinderella to go into the locker room.

"It was your son, Michael, wasn't it?" I asked Solomon as I sat across from him with my Pluto head under one arm.

Solomon pulled himself out of his Mickey suit and exchanged it for a white dress shirt with red slacks and a red bow tie.

He took a deep breath and nodded. "He died in Vietnam. Just had the funeral service last Friday."

My mind flashed back to the dementia dream when Solomon first learned he was a father. There he stood, clear as day, dressed in his army uniform as he, Big Tom, and the rest of us celebrated the birth of his son.

Through grief, violence, and death, Solomon had survived fighting in a war. But Michael had not been so lucky. It was no wonder Solomon never told stories about his son.

"Solomon, I'm sorry for you and your sweet wife. A wise man once told me that war is cruel and ugly, but we have to fight for our freedoms, because if we don't, who will? Your son was very courageous to do his duty to his country."

Solomon shot me a glare and his lip curled with bottled rage.

"Feh! How dare you talk about him! You don't know bupkis, kid. And you don't know my son from Adam!" Solomon shouted. He abruptly stood up from the locker room bench and began pacing up and down the row, muttering a string of Yiddish words I could only imagine were expletives.

"Yes, my boy had courage!" Solomon continued abruptly, though he stared at the floor, seeming to talk more to himself than to me. "My son had more courage than ninety-nine percent of the kids his age. He signed up to go to war right out of high school. He had a scholarship to the music program at UCLA. The kid could play piano and compose music like no one I had ever seen before. He could have skipped the war altogether, made beautiful music and become more famous and successful than I could ever dream of becoming. He had a life ahead of him. He had so much. But no! He felt it was his *duty* to fight for his country—to protect his friends. The idea of his friends being drafted while he stayed here, safe at college, drove him nuts. So yes, he had courage! But, Vietnam is different than my war. We were fighting for freedom back then. This, this war now, I don't know what we are fighting for. I don't know what we are sending our kids to die for."

Solomon leaned his back against the locker and wept like a child, his body slowly sliding to the cold tile floor.

"And now," he sobbed uncontrollably. "My boy, my sweet, handsome Michael, is gone. He's gone."

I hurried over to Solomon's side and wrapped my arm around the shoulders of this middle-aged version of himself. I sat next to my friend and held him like a brother, just letting him cry until his tears began to dry.

"You know," I said quietly. "This same wise man also told me that though we can never forget the pain, we should not dwell on it. Why dwell on the pain when there is so much good to remember. Remember your son and cherish him and his life. Let the good memories overpower the pain. Trust me. There was a time in my life when I was all alone and all I had were good memories to fall back on. It was the only thing that kept the pain from overtaking me."

Even though the words came from my own mouth, I felt like an outsider listening to them as the truth of the words touched me. Self-realization dawned on my mind and heart as I spoke to Solomon—realization that the good memories had sustained me in my dark times and that I was truly lucky to have those good memories to fall back on.

Solomon pulled out a handkerchief, wiped his nose, and we sat side-by-side in silence for another ten minutes.

"Thanks, kid" Solomon said, patting me on the leg. "Oy, sorry for the waterworks, and for barking at you like that. I guess I've been more bottled up than a shaken Coke this past week. I just needed a release."

"No problem. That's what friends are for."

"You know, kid. You remind me a lot of my boy—always looking for the positive. Thanks for the talk, and tell your wise friend thanks for the good words."

I chuckled. "I'll be sure to tell him, though I suspect he already knows."

I stood up and offered my hand to Solomon who was still sitting on the floor. "You know what else will help you with the pain?" I asked, grabbing Solomon's hand to help lift him up.

Solomon shook his head.

"Music," I answered. "It's good for the soul. We better get changed and over to the bandstand."

It took another twenty minutes for us to get changed and hustle over to the other side of the park, weaving in and out of the crowds and lines. With instruments in hand, we climbed into our seats on the bandstand next to a dozen other musicians. But this was no normal bandstand. This was a flatbed delivery truck with stadium seats and a large white canopy overhead.

I looked over at Solomon as he wet the reed on his saxophone, Betty. He seemed more calm and collected as we prepared to play. I rifled through the stack of sheet music the director had given me, realizing quickly that the music was above my skill level and I could only play half the stuff on the page. But I didn't care. I was getting another chance to play the trombone, and my experience in Chicago taught me that I could fake through the hard parts with the best of them.

"Okay, John," the director yelled to the driver after thumping the outside of the truck cab. "Fire her up."

The bandstand truck sputtered to life, but I was amazed by how quiet it was. Solomon had told me they put a special muffler on it to keep the truck quiet while they played, but I could hardly believe the big truck sounded so soft.

The truck pulled out from a blocked off area of garages behind an outdoor food court. As we drove through the opened gate, the director struck up the band with the tune *It's a Small World After All.*

We played song after song as the truck crawled at a snail's pace around the theme park. People cheered and danced to the music as we passed. It wasn't the same as playing in the Chicago nightclub, but it was just as satisfying as we played for the smiling faces of children and adults alike.

As we ever-so-slowly drove in front of the iconic Disneyland Castle, the truck came to a complete stop. The director kept leading the music, but turned his head to look toward the driver and see why we had stopped. Then suddenly, he dropped his hands and quit conducting in the middle of a tune from *Dumbo.*

This caused the band to awkwardly stop playing, blasting out random notes until it was quiet.

"I beg your pardon for the intrusion," said a kind-looking, older gentleman. He was standing to the side of a golf cart with a driver at the wheel. The man had a confident smile, slicked-back gray hair with a part on the side, and a neatly trimmed gray mustache. He wore a blue suit with a thin black tie, which he adjusted as he approached the director.

"Mr. Disney, sir," said the director, taken back in awe.

"Walt, please. Call me Walt. I wish to speak for a moment with your lead Saxophonist, Solomon Felsher. I meant to see him before you left, but my schedule held me up and now is the only time I have to see him. It will only take a minute, I promise."

The director nodded rapidly. "Yes sir, take however long you need."

Solomon unstrapped Betty from his neck and turned around to hand it to me. "Take care of this for a minute, will you, kid?"

"Sure thing," I said, taking Betty carefully into my arms.

Crowds of people began to gather as word spread that Walt Disney was standing in front of the Disneyland castle.

Solomon made his way down the steps of the bandstand, hopped off the truck, and walked directly to Mr. Disney.

"Oy vey, a bit dramatic of a stop, don't you think, Walt?" Solomon whispered as the two gave each other a firm handshake.

Luckily, thanks to my super-hearing, I caught every word between the two.

"Sorry about that, Sol, but it really was the only time I could see you this week," Walt whispered back. "I want to apologize for missing the funeral. I wish I could have been there. And I want to let you know you can take all the paid time off you need. No need to dress up as Mickey or play in the bandstand or the movie orchestra for now. Go home, spend time with your sweet wife and daughter."

Solomon smiled. "Thanks for the offer, Walt, but being back at work is the best thing for me right now. And dressing up as Mickey, seeing the smiles on those kids faces," Solomon said, choking on the words. "It's...it's good for me. I'd be a real schlump right now without this work."

Walt smiled back and slapped Solomon on the shoulder. "If anyone understands the joy of making a kid smile, it's me. But I tell you what, I arranged for you to get a substantial raise and you'll be spending a lot more time with the house orchestra on the next string of motion pictures we have coming out. There's this new film I've been working on like crazy to make a reality. It's called *Mary Poppins*. You're going to love it. And we have this idea for a film called *Jungle Book*, that I think will be right up your alley. Basically, we'll take care of you, Sol. You know you're the only musician to come through here I've ever asked for their autograph. Remember that time I heard you play back in New York? It still gives me goose bumps."

Solomon snorted. "Thanks for the compliment, but that autograph won't ever be worth a dime. I'm not famous and I'll never make it big. Dolores and I have been scraping by our whole lives while I tried to get my big break. Not that I'm not thankful for the work you've given me here," Solomon quickly injected. "It's been nice to have a steady paycheck, don't get me wrong."

"Well, now you can stop scraping along," Walt replied. "Not everyone is destined for fame and fortune, and quite honestly, I sometimes wish I didn't have it. I took a leap and got lucky. I'm turning into an old man now, and the more I look back, the more I realize it's not the success and the wealth that make my life fulfilling, it's the journey and the people, especially family. Now, that's easy to say for a guy in my position, but it's the honest truth, Sol. Enjoy the journey, and enjoy your loved ones. That's what it's all about."

Solomon gave Walt a nod and the two exchanged another firm handshake.

"My, look at this crowd of people," Walt said, eyeing the gathering tourists who stood in a circle gawking at him. "Not sure how I'm going to get out of here without accidentally running someone over."

"You know that big new Disney World you're getting ready to build," Solomon said. "Maybe you ought to build a giant tunnel system underneath it. You know, to get around without being seen. It would be great for the cast and employees to get around faster, and it would be safer to keep the supply trucks off the main roads and away from the crowds. Oh, and you could throw in an underground cafeteria for the cast as well—just some thoughts a friend of mine suggested," Solomon said, pointing up at me as I sat eavesdropping from the bandstand.

Walt Disney looked my direction, cocked an eyebrow, and slowly nodded his head. "Hm," he said, raising a finger to his chin. "You know what? I think we can make something like that work. It would be a lot safer and more efficient. We're about to submit the plans to the city, but I think it's doable—hidden tunnels under Disney World. What a great idea. Tell your friend I'm giving him a bonus and would love to hear any more ideas he has. Give his name to my secretary and she'll take care of it."

My eyes bulged in surprise and Solomon gave me a wink before turning back to Walt Disney.

"Will do—and thanks, Walt. Thanks for everything."

"It's my pleasure, Sol. Oh, and I want to hear what you think of the new score for the *Mary Poppins* film. Come over to the studio tomorrow, and the Sherman brothers can give you a look at what they've been cooking up."

With that, Walt Disney climbed back into the golf cart and was off—his driver deftly swerving around the gathered crowd.

"Oy, Mary Poppins," Solomon whispered and then shrugged. "I wonder if it will be any good."

I heard someone singing *Feed the Birds Tuppence a Bag* from behind me. No, it was in front of me now. Or was it above me? And it wasn't just anyone's voice—it was Sarah's. I turned around to look at the iconic Disneyland castle behind me and saw a girl dressed in white, singing from a window in the tallest tower. My body jolted forward, flying toward the castle window like a rocket. I blinked against the rush of wind blowing into my face, and when I opened my eyes I was sitting back in the city theater, next to Solomon, as Sarah finished her solo.

CHAPTER 26
SWEET SIXTEEN

...HAPPY BIRTHDAY TO YOU!

The boisterous singing ceased from the large group of friends and family gathered in my room. Their variety of smells created an interesting mix, much like the variety in their singing. My mom pushed my wheelchair a few inches closer to the double-decker lemon cake with raspberry icing sitting on the table in front of me. Someone turned off the lights and sixteen candles cast a soft glow across everyone's smiling faces.

"Happy sixteenth birthday, son," my mom said before embracing me in a hug. "Go on, make a wish."

"Tha..anks, mom," I answered back. I knew it was silly to wish for something, but I hesitated before blowing out the candles.

What do I wish for? I thought. *What do I really want?*

I looked at Sarah as she stood next to her mother. She had been gone all summer at another space camp, only returning last week. But while she was away, I had thrown myself into an intense regimen of speech and physical therapy, pushing my physical control forward with leaps and bounds. Words were coming easier, especially the "th" sounds, and although I was still bound to my wheelchair, movement with my head, fingers, and toes were steadily improving

225

each week. Sarah was amazed by my progress, and I finally felt like there was a chance I could be normal again.

But at the same time, Solomon was getting worse. He slept more often during the day and for longer periods of time. Frequently, I would catch him mumbling to himself, mixing old stories with things happening in the present. But even with his rapid deterioration, we continued to share our mental connection.

What do you think I should wish for? I asked Solomon in my mind.

"Listen to an old man," Solomon said out loud. "If wishes were fishes, we'd all swim in riches. Whatever you wish, only you can make it true. Now blow out the blazing candles so we don't have to eat melted wax with our cake. I'm starving."

This raised a round of laughter from everyone, including myself.

"Ok..kay. I ha..ave my wi..wi..wish."

My lips split into a wide smile and I slowly leaned over the cake, took a deep breath, and methodically blew out each candle.

The group cheered as the room plunged into darkness. Nurse Penny flicked the lights back on, causing my eyes to blink rapidly. After my dilated pupils adjusted to the brightened room, I looked around at the happy scene surrounding me.

My parents stood side-by-side, laughing as they teased one another while dishing out mammoth servings of cake and ice cream.

Nurse Penny was talking with Barry and his wife about the new *Indiana Jones and the Last Crusade* movie. "Oh, my. It was such a good movie. And that Harrison Ford is something else, dontcha know—a real looker." All the women agreed with Nurse Penny on that point.

JJ and Big Tom had shown up from Los Angeles, bringing their sweet wives with them this time. They were listening intently as Jesse rattled on non-stop, telling them all about how he was going to be a professional baseball player and a famous rock star drummer and an archeologist when he grew up.

Sarah and Talia were giggling and laughing as Sarah told her a funny story about how she almost threw up after they strapped her into some spinning contraption astronauts used for training.

And then there was Solomon. He sat directly across from me, staring at me from his own wheelchair. His gray curly hair seemed a touch whiter, and his bushy eyebrows furrowed as he leaned across the table.

"So," he mouthed in an inaudible whisper, knowing my super hearing would pick it up. "What did you wish for?"

I can't tell you, I thought to him, but even as I said it, the images of my wish flashed in my mind for Solomon to see.

Solomon's eyes crinkled with approval as he nodded. "Those are very good wishes indeed."

"Here you go, Aaron," my mom said, unknowingly interrupting my telepathic conversation with Solomon. "How about a bite of cake and ice cream?"

She held a spoon to my lips and I opened my mouth, letting the sweet taste of sugary goodness melt across my tongue. Though I had been eating solid foods for nearly 6 months, the simple pleasure of tasting and eating real food still made my mouth water with excitement.

And it showed with the twenty-three pounds I'd added to my previously frail frame. My body had begun to fill in to match my growing height. It still surprised me, whenever I looked in a mirror, at how much I had changed in so little time.

"How does it taste?" my mom asked. "This used to be your favorite cake as a child—lemon cake with raspberry frosting."

I nodded my approval and gave two thumbs up. "Ver..ery taaa..asty."

My mom squinted hard to hold back an emerging tear and quickly wiped her eyes with her thumbs.

"Oh, Aaron, my sweet baby boy. I love you."

"Mooom, I'mm no..ot aaa b..bb..bab..by any..mo..ore."

My mom snorted and rolled her eyes. "Aaron, you may be sixteen, but you will always be my baby."

The sounds of conversation and laughter continued to fill the room until JJ, Barry, and Big Tom called for everyone's attention.

"Since it's your birthday," JJ said with a sly smile. "We all decided to pitch in and get you something special. We figured at the rate you're going, you could join the Restwood Suites House Band in no time."

Big Tom grabbed something from behind Solomon's bed, revealing a long black case with a big circle at the end.

My eyes went wide with surprise.

"We know you haven't played in a while," Big Tom said in his deep voice, "and we heard you didn't have one of your own since you rented your instrument from the school before you got sick. So, here you go. Happy birthday from all of us."

My jaw dropped to the floor as JJ unlatched the black case and opened it. Inside, sitting in a red velvet formed frame, was a beautiful, brand new, rose colored brass, Bach trigger trombone.

"Oh…m..m..myyy," I stuttered.

"You just get those arms of yours strong enough to lift that beast, and you'll be playing in no time, Aaron, my man," Barry said with a grin.

"Yes, sir," JJ added. "Lord knows Big Boy Tom can use all the help he can get in the brass section."

Tom playfully slapped JJ across the back of the head. "I'd be happy to play side-by-side with Aaron any day. It's you I'm not so sure about."

"Tha..ank youuu!" I exclaimed, my eyes still locked on the beautiful new trombone lying before me. Bach brand instruments were not cheap, and I could hardly believe that they all pitched in to give me such a nice gift—especially when I had never really given any of them anything.

A flicker of movement across the table caught my attention as Solomon rubbed the gray stubble on his chin. He had been uncharacteristically quiet as the group presented me with the trombone. He simply smiled at me with his tired eyes.

Did you know about the trombone? I asked him in my mind.

Solomon remained silent, answering my question with a single nod.

Thank you, Sol. It means a lot.

Solomon gave me another nod, but said nothing.

My dad coughed into his hand, clearing his throat. "Uhm, I have one more gift for you, son. Actually, you have all been so kind and generous to our boy, it's a gift I'm willing to share with anyone in this room."

Dad held up a handful of long rectangular pieces of thick paper spread out in a fan.

"Work gave me a special prize for reaching my sales goals this summer. They gave me 6 season tickets to the Giants for the rest of this year and all of next year. We can go to any ballgame anytime we want."

"No way," a collective shout went up, mostly from the men in the room.

"They're playing great ball this year," Barry said excitedly. "Will Clark and Kevin Mitchell have hot bats right now. I wouldn't be surprised if they go deep into the playoffs."

"Yes, but what about the A's?" JJ spoke up. "Not that they are in the same conference, but the bash brothers, McGwire and Canseco, they're knocking so many balls out of the park that the league's going to have to extend the fences."

"The Giants are still way better than the Oakland A's, hands down," Sarah retorted, jumping into the conversation. Those that knew Sarah best, like I did, knew she loved the San Francisco Giants and the San Francisco 49ers almost as much as she loved singing and *Star Trek*.

"I don't know about that," my dad piped in. "The A's are looking pretty good."

My mom, Talia, Nurse Penny, JJ, Tom and Barry's wives all rolled their eyes and moved to the other side of the room to talk, letting the sports fans blabber away.

"Well, being from L.A. and a die-hard Dodgers fan," Big Tom continued, ignoring the fact his wife had left his side, "I hope they both miss the playoffs. But even I have to admit they are on a roll. Who knows, maybe we'll see them play each other in the World Series. Wouldn't that be something? A *Battle of the Bay!*"

"That would be something," my dad agreed. "And if they do, these special season tickets give us an automatic pass to any playoff game the Giants make, including the World Series."

Sarah let out a whistle. "Count me in if you need someone to take a few tickets off your hands during the playoffs. I'm always up for a Giants game at Candlestick Park. And maybe I can snag a few tickets for my dad to come with us as well. His tour is almost over in the Middle East, and he's coming home in September."

This brought a round of congratulatory remarks from the group, and I saw the other women all giving Talia a hug and patting her hand as they heard the news.

But my attention was brought back to Solomon, whose chin had dropped to his chest as he softly snored.

"Gu..uys," I said amidst the continuing conversations. "Sol is ti..ired. He nee..eeds slee..eep."

The room went silent as everyone turned to watch Solomon sleeping uncomfortably in his wheelchair.

"Oh, dear," Nurse Penny said. "I suppose it's getting late, and Solomon needs his rest. Perhaps we should quickly clean up and call it a night."

Looking at the clock I saw it was only 8 p.m., hardly late by most standards, but it was past Solomon's normal bedtime. The group helped clean up and straighten the room, one-by-one wishing me happy birthday and giving me a hug as they left.

Talia and my parents helped transfer Solomon back to his bed. The move caused Solomon to groggily open his eyes and mumble something about JFK and shark fishing in the Gulf of Mexico. But as soon as he was situated in bed, he fell right back to sleep.

While they moved Solomon, Sarah knelt down in front of me and grabbed both my hands. "Happy birthday, Tigger," she said smiling before she gave me a quick peck on the cheek. The kiss caused my face to flush red as I smiled back at her.

"I'm sorry I was gone all summer again. You sure have changed," she said, looking me up and down appraisingly.

"Tha..anks. I th..think," I replied, arching my eyebrow.

Did she just check me out? I thought, glad Solomon was asleep so he wasn't in my head.

Sarah laughed. "It's a good thing, I promise. I can't believe how much you've improved and how well you're moving and talking now. We can finally talk to one another like I always hoped. And you look," she paused for a moment as her freckled cheeks blushed back at me. "You look...older and quite," she paused, searching for the right word. "You look very handsome," she said matter-of-factly.

My eyes brightened at the compliment.

"I think she likes you," Solomon whispered under his breath so only I could hear him.

I thought you were sleeping, my mind spoke as I turned toward Solomon.

With his eyes still closed, Solomon gave me a sly smile before rolling over on his side.

Sarah gave my hands another squeeze. "Now that I'm back from Space Camp, I'll come over every day to see you and Grandpa. Plus, school starts in two weeks! I can't believe it. I'll be a junior this year. Promise you will help me with my homework again! I'm scared to death of Algebra II, and Algebra seemed really easy for you to figure out last year when I showed you my homework."

"I prom..mise," I answered back. It was true. Algebra did come easy to me. It all just made logical sense, unlike the rest of life.

"Time to go, kids," Talia called to Sarah and Jesse. Jesse hurriedly shoveled a few final bites of cake into his mouth before Talia pulled him away. "And happy birthday, Aaron." Talia continued. "We're so glad you're getting better. Keep an eye on Dad for me, okay?"

"Okay," I answered back without a stutter.

"See ya," Sarah said, stealing one more quick kiss on my cheek.

After they left, Nurse Penny pulled the curtain between Solomon and me and dimmed the lights on his side of the room. While she did a few more routine checks on Solomon, my mom and dad helped me change into pajamas and lifted me into my bed.

Nurse Penny popped her head around the sheet divider and smiled. "It's only 8:30, so you guys take your time," she said with a wink. "I know you have a lot to talk about."

What does that mean? I thought.

Standing at my bedside with arms wrapped around each other. My mom grabbed my hand. "Son, we want you to move back home with us. Dr. McPhearson says you're doing great, and we want to have you back home."

My eyes went wide with shock. I wasn't sure what I was expecting, but this definitely was not on my radar.

My dad patted his dark tanned hand on my leg and smiled. "It's time we brought you back home with us. It's time we became a family again."

At this final comment, my eyes narrowed in disbelief.

"No," I said firmly.

The smile on my parents faces faltered. But before they could respond, I continued.

"I ne..ever forg..got be..eing a fam..mily. You two did. Youu lef..eft me. Youu lef..ft each..other."

My words cut through my parents like an axe, leaving them looking like deer in the headlights.

"But son, we didn't know you were okay. We didn't mean," my mom pleaded, choking back her tears as she lowered her head in shame.

I held up my hand from my lap, as I finished speaking.

"I lo..ove youu both. You will al..always..b..be my fam..ly. B..b..but Sol neeeds me right now. He wa..was herrre whe..en I needed you. Sol is m..my fam..am..ily too. I c..ca..can't leeeave him. Not now."

My parents faces went pale and my mom's lip quivered at my words. I felt horrible for turning such a happy night upside down on them, but there was no way I was leaving Solomon. Yes, I was getting better and I could probably get by okay at home, but Solomon was not getting better—he was getting worse.

He had been there for me and I was not going to abandon my friend.

"But, we can bring you to visit Solomon during the week," Dad countered. "And, Restwood Suites isn't exactly cheap. We could take the money saved from Restwood and start putting it toward a college for you. Dr. McPhearson says there's no reason you won't be able to catch up in school and eventually go to college."

"Dad," I said without a stutter. "No. You owe me this much."

My jaw set as I stared at my parents like I was the adult reprimanding them.

Tears stung my mom's eyes and no one said a word for what seemed like eternity. My dad took a deep breath, breaking the silence. "You're right. I owe you. And I owe Solomon more than I can ever say for helping me and your mom get back together." He squeezed my mom around the shoulders in a side-hug. "But we want you home as well. Are you sure you don't want to come home? Will you at least think about it?"

I nodded. "I neeed t..t..to be here. At..le..ee..east forr now."

My dad released a sad sigh and nodded. "Okay, you can stay for now."

"And I'll be here to visit you every day," my mom hurriedly added as she tried to wipe away her tears and gave me a hug. "I'm so sorry I left you," she whispered in my ear. "It was the biggest mistake I've ever made. I won't ever leave you again. I promise."

Though her words were filled with love and remorse, part of me hoped she wasn't being too literal. Although I loved my parents and was grateful and happy we were becoming a family again, the years alone were hard to forget, and I had become used to my independence. Having my mom "helicopter parent" me, every day, just wasn't appealing. There's something to say for giving a teenager a little space.

But I tried to smile as best I could. "Thhaanks mom. Tha..at woul..d be ni..i..ice."

My parents each gave me another hug and wished me happy birthday before they left.

I lay in bed, thinking about the roller coaster of emotions from the evening—the party, the trombone, the kisses from Sarah, my parents—when a faint voice called from the other side of the curtain.

"Thanks, kid…for staying with me," Solomon whispered just loud enough for me to hear. "Oy, now if everyone is finally gone and done making a racket, I'd like to sleep until noon tomorrow."

CHAPTER 28
TAKE ME OUT TO THE BALL GAME

The smell of the salty sea blew through the air of Candlestick Park in San Francisco. Thousands of fans poured into their seats, creating an electric atmosphere as we waited for the game of all games to begin. "Ca..can you belieeeve it?" I asked Solomon. "We're at th..the World Ser..eries!"

Solomon and I sat side-by-side in our wheelchairs, perched in a handicap seating area about twenty rows up behind left field. Although Solomon looked ready to take a nap during the car ride to the stadium, his face was now more alive than I had seen in months. In fact, the only time he looked this happy anymore was when he played Betty, which was becoming a rare occurrence.

"This sure is something else, ain't it?" Solomon said. "The view is perfect from here."

It was true. We had a great view and we were a stone's throw away from the outfield. This was a prime location to catch a homerun ball—not that we could get one in our current condition. But my dad, Sarah, and Sarah's dad were sitting next to us, and they were sure to snag a ball if it came our way. In fact, Sarah had already picked up one homerun ball during batting practice. We had decided to come a few hours early to the game, so we could get a good parking spot and catch batting practice. Only a few minutes after we took our seats, Sarah snagged a homerun ball hit by the A's all-star, Mark McGwire. She almost threw it back since she's a diehard Giants fan, but being from the Bay Area, the A's *were* her second favorite team so she decided to keep it. And, c'mon, it was hit by Mark McGwire!

"You feel..eeling okay?" I asked Solomon, watching his tired eyes gaze over the field.

"Oy, kid, I'm fine. Quit fretting over me like a mother hen," he answered. "We're out of our prison, at game three of the 1989 World Series, between our two hometown teams. It doesn't get much better than this."

I know, I said in my mind. *You just look tired. If it's taking too much out of you to be here at the game, we can go back. I'm okay if we need to go back.*

Solomon rolled his eyes and muttered something in Yiddish. "Relax, Aaron and enjoy yourself. Enjoy the game. Enjoy the memories. Enjoy the company," he said, pointing across my shoulder as my dad, Sarah, and her father walked back to our seats with food and drinks in hand. They had foot-long hot dogs, sodas, nachos, shelled peanuts, and a giant, no pun intended, well maybe slightly, 'WE ARE #1' foam fingers with the Giants logo and one finger with the A's logo for my dad, who was the lone A's fan of our group.

Solomon and I were parked in the handicap section at the end of the row of bleacher seats, right next to the long column of steps leading down to the rows of bleachers below us. Sarah sat next to me while my dad and her dad, Richard, chatted away like they had been best friends forever.

"Here you go, guys," my dad said, passing down food for Solomon and myself.

The food smelled delicious as Sarah helped set it in my lap and passed Solomon his own foot-long hotdog, drink and a bag of peanuts.

"*Brrr,* it's getting cold," Sarah said before taking a bite of her hotdog.

Solomon nodded, pulling his blanket tighter around his legs before taking a bit of his hotdog. "That's why you always bring a good coat and a blanket to Candlestick Park. This place turns into an icebox once the sun goes down. That ocean breeze will get you every time."

"Are you warm enough?" Sarah asked me as she slipped on her coat.

"I'm war..arm, but..I..am..starv..vi..ving," I said, my stomach growling as I nodded toward the food in my lap. Though I could slowly lift my arms and bend my elbows again, I still wasn't coordinated enough to feed myself without dropping half my food in my lap.

"Oh my goodness, I'm so sorry Aaron. I spaced it. Here, take a bite."

She held my hotdog to my mouth and I took a large bit, moaning as I savored every flavor of the hotdog, mustard, ketchup, grilled onions and relish.

"Taste good?" Sarah teased, leaning in close.

"Mmmhmm," I moaned. "Very..good."

Her face was only a few inches away and I noticed a tiny blob of cheese stuck to the corner of her lip. Without a second thought, I awkwardly lifted my hand up to her face and softly held her chin, mostly out of necessity to balance my weak arm.

Sarah's face blushed crimson. "Aaron," she whispered, looking around to see if anyone was watching. "What are you doing? Not that I mind, but..."

Holding her face, I wanted to reach over and kiss her. She was the girl who had been by my side the last two years. She was the girl who had believed in me. She was my first date. My tutor. My friend.

We sat there, eyes locked for what seemed like eternity and I uttered the only words that came to my love-struck mind.

"Cheese," I said, moving my thumb to the corner of her lips to wipe away the blob.

Sarah saw the cheese on my thumb and blushed, wiping at her own face. "Oh my goodness, that's so embarrassing."

I shook my head. "Remem..member the fi..first time you met me?" I asked.

Sarah nodded.

"Remem..member how I had drooool drip..piping down my chin?

Sarah laughed. "Yes, I do. It was running down your chin and onto your shirt. You also had really long hair back then too. I actually thought you were a girl at first glance."

I rolled my eyes. "See. Now th..that's embara..ra..rassing."

Sarah and I laughed together and she reached down to hold my hand, giving it a squeeze. I squeezed her hand back and my pulse quickened when neither of us let go.

"What are you two laughing about?" Sarah's dad asked from the seat on the other side of Sarah.

"Nothing," Sarah replied, giving my hand another squeeze.

"Uh-huh," her father said, eyeing me as I held his daughter's hand.

Chief Warrant Officer Richard Clements, looked every bit a navy man with his short black hair, dark tan from being out months at sea, and a tattoo of an anchor with the letters USN across his muscular forearm. Luckily, my dad asked him a question and pulled Richard's attention, and overprotective gaze, away from us.

Sarah and I continued to hold hands, and she rested her head on my shoulder.

"This is nice," I whispered to her.

"Mhhm," Sarah responded, snuggling closer. "You're nice and warm and I'm freezing."

"Freezing," Solomon spoke up. "France is freezing. But letters from Dolores always warm me up. Sometimes the mail loses my letters. They disappear on the sixth Tuesday of each month. Jack Dempsey fights for them, but the Verve always wins."

I gave Solomon a sympathetic smile. Comments like these were becoming commonplace. It seemed he was only coherent half the time he spoke.

I'm glad Dolores writes you, I answered in my mind. *You're a lucky man.*

"Yes, I am. And here I get to go to the World Series and spend the day with my family and my second best friend. Life is good in America."

Curious, I asked Solomon in my mind, *Who's your best friend?*

"Why that's Dolores, of course. But she couldn't come today. She's making dinner for our party tomorrow."

I'm sorry to hear that. And who's your second best friend?

Solomon chuckled out loud, causing Sarah to whisper in my ear. "Are you talking to him in your head again?"

I nodded as Solomon placed a hand on my shoulder. "Oy kid, it's the same guy that's been there for me my whole life. A guy by the name of Aaron Greenburg. Great fella. Great fella. He's always there when I need him."

I froze, stunned by Solomon's response.

"What's he talking about?" Sarah whispered in my ear. But I couldn't answer her.

Always? He's always been there when you needed him? I thought. *You're talking about the dreams, right? I couldn't have been there in real life.*

Solomon furrowed his brow at the question and looked me in the eyes. "Kid. Quit being ridiculous. You were al—"

But his words were cutoff as the world shook apart.

CHAPTER 29
THE QUAKE

"Solomon. You need to stay awake," Sarah's dad yelled. "I need you to focus on my face and take deep breaths."

BEEEEEP! BEEP! BEEP! BEEEEEP!

My dad slammed on the horn, weaving our Dodge Caravan in and out of traffic. Solomon's eyes shot open as the horn blared in the background.

"Hold on Dolores," he spoke. His eyes were wide, showing more white than the brown of his pupils. "Just breathe sweetie. I'll get you to the hospital in a jiff."

"That's right," responded Richard. "We're going to go to the hospital. Just breathe."

An announcer's voice blasted over the radio as my dad swerved around a car.

> *Experts say a large earthquake, estimated at a 6.9 on the Richter scale, has struck the Bay Area, with severe damage in San Francisco and outlying suburbs.*

> *A long section of the double-decker Embarcadero freeway has collapsed on the lower level with commuters trapped under the rubble. We also have a report that the Bay Bridge is shut down*

due to a section collapse. There are reports of fires and damage coming in throughout the area, wreaking havoc for commuters stuck on the roads.

Listening to the radio, my mind replayed the horrific scene as the quake hit us at the stadium. The giant man-made structure shook like a rag doll, sending chunks of concrete crashing from the upper-deck into a nearby empty equipment area behind center field. The ground swelled with visible waves rolling across the baseball diamond like an ocean.

Amidst the shaking, I watched in shock, unable to move fast enough, as Solomon's wheelchair tipped over, sending him sprawling out of the handicap area and down the long concrete stairs to the side of our seats. He tumbled down a section of bone-crushing steps until crashing to a stop twenty feet below us.

Time slowed down and seconds felt like minutes as the earth rolled beneath our feet. When the quake finally ended, the stadium erupted in chaos. Sarah, Richard and my dad rushed down to Solomon as other fans rushed the opposite direction, up the stairway, to exit the stadium. Solomon's head and face were rapidly swelling with bruises, and a tiny gash above his right eyebrow was bleeding.

Solomon groaned, going in and out of consciousness, and my dad flagged down a security guard for help.

The young security guard blanched when he saw the blood covering Solomon's face. Richard helped Sarah press her coat against Solomon's head to stop the bleeding and soon her coat was covered in red. The guard called for help over his radio, trying to get a medical team over to us, but we soon found out help would not arrive anytime soon. Emergency responders were spread thin throughout the stadium, and the few ambulances that had been on site were already en route to the hospital with injured fans.

The quake had devastated parts of San Francisco, and though more ambulances were en route to the stadium, traffic was causing delays.

With no help in sight, Sarah's dad went into action. He asked—well, more like commanded—the young security guard to find us a stretcher. Eager to help, the young guard ran down through a locked gate in the outfield and toward the pitcher's bullpen down the third base line. A few minutes later he returned with a bright red stretcher.

The guard and a handful of kind bystanders helped us strap Solomon into the stretcher. They carried him up the stairs to where a wall of people pressed against one another, trying to get to the exits.

"We need to get out of here," I heard some woman shout.

"What if the stadium collapses?" I heard another man ask.

From up ahead I heard a child crying and the soft and loud murmurs of the crowd as they spoke to one another, trying to absorb what had just happened and worried about their family and friends back home.

We moved slowly through the packed crowd as fans trickled out of the newly opened emergency exit gates.

"Out of the way," a stranger called from in front of us as he helped clear a path for our convoy to get through. Soon a handful of strangers, seeing a bloodied Solomon unconscious on a stretcher, joined in, walking ahead of us and parting the sea of exiting fans so we could get through.

Sarah pushed me in my wheelchair, staying right on their tail as we rushed through the parking lot and back to our white minivan.

My dad removed the backseat of the minivan so we could keep Solomon on the stretcher as he was slid into the back of the van. With the backseat left sitting in the parking lot, my dad peeled out of his parking place, bullying his way past other drivers like a New York cabbie.

"Solomon! Open those eyes of yours!" Richard shouted. His plea pulled me out of my memory and back into the present.

Richard knelt at Solomon's side, checking the man's pulse. Solomon's eyes were closed, and his breathing was rough and uneven. Sarah and I sat in the middle chairs of the van, half turned to watch as her grandfather and my friend, slowly died.

Wake up Solomon! I shouted at him with my mind. *We're almost to the hospital. Open your eyes! WAKE UP!*

Solomon gave no response. I prepared to continue my mental shouts when an idea sprang into my adrenaline-packed mind. It was one of those thoughts that comes with instant clarity, and even though it seems odd and out of place, you just know it's the right thing to do.

"Da-ad," I called, turning toward my father as he ran a red light and half drove on the sidewalk to pass a brown Volkswagen Rabbit.

"What, Aaron? We're almost to the hospital. Maybe another ten minutes or so."

"Da-ad. Listen to me! P-put jazz on th-the radio."

My dad half turned to look at me, raising a gray eyebrow. "What?" he asked. His knuckles were white as he gripped the steering wheel and swerved through a set of cars, cutting one of them off.

"Dad. P-put on the jazz sta-sta-station, now!"

My dad shook his head, but did as I asked and turned the radio to the local jazz station, 91.1 FM. The voice of the news announcer disappeared and was replaced by the familiar, smooth melodic sound of Miles Davis and John Coltrane playing *Blue in Green.*

The slow, thoughtful blues melody played in sharp contrast to the chaos of the streets and my dad's wild driving.

I turned back to Solomon and spoke in my mind. *Solomon. Do you hear that? It's Blue in Green. Remember when you first played it for me? You asked how it made me feel. I told you sad, but that I understood the sadness and was okay with it. I knew the sadness would never fully go away, but I remembered that there had been good times before and that there would be good times to come. Do you remember?*

Solomon's breathing steadied a bit and his face flinched with pain.

Solomon. Listen to the music. Let it take your pain away. Remember the good times of life. Remember the Jack Dempsey fight. Remember meeting Dolores. Getting the news you were a father. Raising Michael and Talia. Playing the music you loved. All of the hundreds of friends and people you helped and inspired over the years. Remember your daughter Talia and your grandkids Jesse and Sarah. They are still here for you. And...and remember me. You're my best friend Solomon. You've helped me with so much. I still need you, Sol. Just listen to the music...and remember.

Solomon's eyes flickered open and he smiled amidst a groan of pain.

"Oy vey," he mumbled, taking a deep breath. "I remember, kid."

His eyelids flickered again and he looked at me for a moment before closing them. "I can stay...for a little longer...and listen. I remember."

CHAPTER 30
FREEDOM

I fidgeted in my wheelchair, slowly rolling the chair back and forth as I sat next to Solomon's bedside.

It had been three days since the quake, and I had not left Solomon's room since we arrived. All of Solomon's family and dozens of friends—many I didn't know—came to visit. JJ and Tom came. Nurse Penny and Barry stopped by. Even the manager, Mr. Wilson, and Dr. Idiot—I mean Dr. McPhearson—visited Solomon as he lay comatose.

They all spoke to Talia and lent comforting words, but when they spoke to Solomon, he didn't respond. His injuries had been so extensive that the doctors decided to place him in an induced coma.

X-rays showed he had multiple fractures to his arms, ribs, and a shattered hip. It was the same hip he had broken just months earlier, and the doctor did not know if Solomon would be able to handle a hip replacement in his current condition.

For the time being, Solomon lay fast asleep while his IV circulated meds into his body to keep him knocked out and to kill the pain. He had an oxygen mask attached to his face to help him breath, and I watched as his chest moved up and down with each new breath.

"It's 11:11. Make a wish," I whispered to Solomon after looking at the clock. Talia and Sarah were fast asleep on a neighboring couch and Richard had taken Jesse home a few hours ago to get some sleep. My mom and dad had tried to get me to leave as well, but I refused. Talia and Sarah appeased my parents by agreeing to stay with Solomon and me in the hospital for one more night.

Luckily, after years of not being able to move a muscle, sleeping in a wheelchair with a pillow and a blanket was a piece of cake.

I continued to wheel my chair back and forth a few inches, watching Solomon as he breathed. My emotions were all over the place. I didn't want my friend to stay in pain like he was, but I didn't want to lose him either.

Why did this have to happen? I thought. *Why did any of it have to happen? Why did I get sick and become paralyzed? That wasn't fair. And why does Solomon have to suffer like this? Why?*

I sat in silence, pondering these questions, when a new train of thought hit me, like a whisper from my mind. It was a moment of clarity that I wasn't prepared for.

If I had not been sick, I never would have met Solomon.

This thought struck me like a javelin to the heart. I mulled over what it meant. If given the option, would I trade the last two years with Solomon in exchange for a healthy, perfect body? That would mean I would never have known Solomon. I would never have shared the adventures in his dreams. I never would have met Nurse Penny, Barry, JJ, Tom, Talia, Jesse, and Richard. I would never have known Sarah.

As much as I wanted to have never been sick, would I trade all of these experiences and all of these people away from my life instead?

My body trembled and my voice shook as I whispered the answer, "No."

A wave of peace washed over me unlike anything I had ever felt before in my life. It was a warmth and a calm that enveloped me like an embrace from a loved one.

Just then, my eye caught a flicker of movement from Solomon's hand. First his pinky moved, then his ring finger, and then his whole hand flexed, squeezing shut and opening. I listened as his heart rate monitor continued to beep normal and steady, and watched as his eyes fluttered open to look at me.

Solomon, I said in my mind. *You're awake. But you should be sleeping. The meds they're giving you are supposed to help you sleep while you heal. What are—*

Solomon raised his hand to silence me. He winced with pain as he reached up and removed the oxygen mask from his face.

"Oy, kid," Solomon whispered. "Always with the questions."

I didn't know whether to laugh, cry or smile at the response. Solomon reached his hand toward me and I reached back, holding his hand in mine.

"Aaron, thank you for everything," Solomon spoke, his voice quiet, but strong and lucid. "You've been there for me through thick and thin. Thank you."

I smiled. "I'm the one who should be thanking you. You brought me back. You helped me get better. I owe everything to you."

Solomon shook his head slowly. "You owe me nothing, my boy. If we owe anyone anything, it is God. Remember that."

I nodded, unable to speak.

"It's time," Solomon continued, his eyes calm and his face relaxed.

I wanted to shout, *No!* I wanted to argue with Solomon that he couldn't leave yet, but the words wouldn't come.

"I want you...to take care of Sarah...do you hear?" Solomon asked, his breaths turning haggard.

I nodded again, choking back my tears.

"Good," Solomon continued. "Now it's time...for both of us to be free...you from your mind palace...and me from the pains of this mortal life."

Solomon smiled and closed his eyes. His chest rose once more with a final breath, but before I could cry out, my body reeled backward and I felt my mind fly into the darkness just as the heart-rate monitor flat-lined into a never-ending beep.

CHAPTER 31
THE NORTH TOWER

"No. Not now! How can this be happening now?" I shouted at the palace walls. "I need to be with Solomon! Not stuck here."

Solomon was taking his final breath in real life. How, or why, was I being pulled into my mind palace now? My heart raced. "I have to get out of here!" I said through gritted teeth. But no one responded. As usual, I was alone.

I spun in around, surveying the strange circular room, looking for a way out.

The high stone walls were lined with dozens of panels of ten-foot tall mirrors. Each mirror faced another mirror on the opposite side of the room. The stone walls extended twenty feet into the air above the mirrors with four large skylights nestled near the top of the domed ceiling. Sunlight poured through the skylights, shining onto a magnificent, golden chandelier hanging from the center of the dome. A dazzling display of bright light illuminated the room as the sunlight bounced off the thousands of crystals embedded in the chandelier.

I looked below my feet and found an intricate golden carpet, with amber lines extending from the center, where I stood, to each mirror panel on the wall.

There were no doors in sight and no windows I could reach. It appeared my mind palace had me trapped once again.

DONG-DONG-DONG-DONG, rang the palace clock bells twelve times in a row. The sound was deafening and I suddenly knew where I was—the north clock tower.

Back before Solomon, when I could pull myself into my mind palace at will, I had tried to find a way to reach the high clock tower at the top of the palace, but no matter which stairway or hallway I took, I could never find a way to the top. But now, here I was.

I shook my head in frustration and growled at the reflection of myself in the mirror. But then, I saw something behind me. The light in the room intensified as I stared at it.

In the mirror's reflection, I saw myself, and then behind me, I saw myself again, and again, and again, on and on for what seemed like eternity. I turned to look at the mirror behind me, seeing the same thing. Every direction I looked, I saw myself in bright, brilliant light, going on…forever.

Forever, I thought, letting the word sink in.

I walked closer to one of the mirrors and stared at it, looking into forever. I reached out my hand to touch the mirror, surprised when the cold, hard surface rippled at my touch.

"What in the world?" I asked, instinctively whipping my hand back away from the mirror. The mirror solidified and turned back to normal.

I touched it again, watching it ripple like a stone dropped in a pond, and I pressed harder. My hand slid through the mirror, disappearing from sight.

"Okay, then," I said. "I guess this is the way out."

Closing my eyes, I sunk the rest of my arm into the mirror and took a step forward. I felt the cool, liquid surface wash over me as I pulled myself through the mirror.

"Huh," I said when I opened my eyes. "This is so not what I was expecting."

I stood in the hallway of a hospital, looking through a glass window at a nursery full of newborn babies.

"Hello, Mr. Greenburg. Your daughter, Dolores, is just a darling," an elderly nurse spoke as she stood by my side, pointing to a tiny baby girl with red, curly locks of hair. She was wrapped in a thin white blanket with images of Sesame Street characters patterned across it.

"*My* daughter?" I croaked.

"Yes, you're a father now. And don't worry about Sarah. Your wife is doing splendid. She's just taking a nap in her room. But she told me all about how you chose the name Dolores. Such a beautiful name."

I looked at the nurse with wide eyes and then back to the red-haired babe, Dolores.

"But, I…uhhh…but…" I stuttered, causing the older nurse to chuckle. She smiled at me sympathetically, deep creases lining her grandmotherly face.

"Would you like to hold her?" she asked. Before I could respond, she disappeared behind a side door, and I watched as she picked up the babe and brought her outside to me.

"But I've never held a baby before," I said anxiously—a pang of fear rising inside me that I might accidentally drop the child.

The nurse smiled. "Just cradle your arms like this and be sure to support her head and neck with the crook of your elbow. There you go! Perfect!" she said as she handed the baby off into my arms.

I looked down at the child and felt a swelling of emotions. Although my mind was telling me this was not my child, my heart was telling me something different—that maybe, just maybe I could have a future like this and a beautiful little girl like this babe in my arms.

After a few minutes of holding baby Dolores, the child fell fast asleep.

"See that, you're a natural," the nurse whispered. She offered to take Dolores back into the nursery to sleep, and I carefully handed the precious little girl back to her.

"Take it from an old mother," the nurse continued in a whisper. "Becoming a parent is life-changing. There's no doubt about it. But when you give all of your love to your children and your spouse, that love only grows. It's life-changing, alright. And it will bring you more joy than you can imagine."

Before I could respond, and tell the nurse I was only sixteen, and definitely not married, the nurse turned and walked away without another word.

"Wait, nurse. I don't understand. What's going on?"

But the nurse ignored my calls and walked back into the nursery and laid Dolores in her crib, and then disappeared.

I stared down at Dolores and the infant smiled in her sleep. Or at least I think she smiled, because it caused me to smile back.

I leaned my head closer to the glass to get a better look and saw my dim reflection staring back at me. I looked...older. My sixteen-year-old self was replaced with a version of me that looked to be in my twenties and was sporting a reddish-brown mustache.

"Whoa," I said out loud, stroking the mustache resting on my upper lip. "Apparently the stache is back. This is so weird."

Someone tapped on my back, causing me to jump. I whipped around to find an oddly familiar young kid, maybe twelve or thirteen, staring up at me with big brown eyes. He wore a San Francisco Giants baseball cap, jeans, and a green camo T-shirt with the word PEACE spelled out in block letters.

"Sorry, mister. Didn't mean to scare you," called the young kid. "I was just seeing if you wanted to buy a paper. I sell papers here on the weekends to earn extra money for my family. Would you like a Sunday paper? It's got all the extras, like the Sunday comics and advertisements. The Archie strip is pretty funny this week."

The kid held the paper out to me with an outstretched arm.

"Uhm, no thanks," I answered, trying to figure out where I knew this kid from. He looked like someone I knew from somewhere, but I couldn't quite place it.

"Say, did you just have a baby?" the kid asked, taking a step toward the glass to peer in at the infants. "Well, I mean your wife *had* the baby. She's the one who did all the work. Let me guess, yours is the one with red, curly hair. Got your red hair, but must get the curls from her mom's side of the family."

"You're probably right," I replied, thinking of Sarah's frizzy curls.

"What's her name?" the kid asked, smiling at Dolores as he tapped the glass and cooed at her.

"Uhm, it's Dolores…I think."

The boy chuckled. "You think? Still not sure on the name? Well, I like Dolores. My best friend's name is Dolores. She's the cutest girl you've ever seen, and smart too."

Something about the way the kid talked seem to relax me. It was like I had known him before, but my mind just couldn't place it.

"Sounds like she's more than a friend. Is she your girlfriend?" I teased the kid.

This caused the kid's grin to widen and he gave me a wink.

"You know, hospitals are an interesting place," the kid continued. "Just down one floor I was selling papers and a family was huddled together, hugging each other with tears streaming down their face. Their mother had just died. Then up here you have all these new, beautiful, little babies being born. Up here parents are smiling and crying for joy over their new kids. All this life and death in one place. Someone dies and moves on, leaving a new child born to carry on. It's pretty amazing."

"I guess I've never thought about it like that before," I said. "Those are pretty deep words for a twelve-year-old kid."

The kid furrowed his brow. "Who said I was twelve?"

I shrugged my shoulders. "I was just guessing. How old are—"

"You nervous to be a dad?" the kid interrupted. "You shouldn't be."

Who is this kid giving me life advice? I thought. *I swear I know him from somewhere, but I can't remember.*

"I bet you'll make a great father," the kid continued, interrupting my thoughts.

"Oh yeah?" I asked. "What makes you so sure?"

The kid rolled his eyes and shook his head at me. For the first time I noticed little black curly locks of hair tug free from under his baseball cap.

"That's easy. I'll give you five reasons why you'll make a great father. One, you look strong and healthy like a professional baseball player or something. I bet you eat real healthy too, like a whole bowl of fruit every day, and you probably like to play sports and go hiking and camping and stuff. Kids like to play with their dads and go do things like that. Two, your polo shirt says Cal Berkeley Jazz Band on it. So you must be a musician or maybe a teacher or something. Kids like music and learning about instruments and how to play them. I play a few instruments myself. You'll be able to teach your kids about music and they will love it."

I looked down at the blue polo shirt I was wearing and sure enough, from upside down, I read the golden embroidered words of Cal Berkeley Jazz Band on the outside of my left shirt pocket.

"Three, you stand with a bit of a limp, leaning to your side like you had an injury in the past or you've been hurt real bad," the kid continued. "So you know what it's like to be hurt and go through something hard, and kids need moms and dads to help them when they get hurt and when they have to go through something hard. You'll know how they are feeling."

The kid paused for a moment, and I caught a glimmer of tear forming in his right eye.

"Four," he said, quickly blinking back the tear. "You've got kind, forgiving eyes. The world needs more kindness and forgiveness. A good parent will teach their kids to be kind and forgive others. If we had a little more of that in the world, it would be a much happier and safer place. And you look like a fella who knows a bit about kindness, forgiveness, and love."

His words struck me.

Do I really? I thought to myself. My mind rushed through the people in my life. There was Solomon and Sarah, and I definitely loved them. There was Nurse Penny, Barry, Big Tom and JJ who I cared about. Mr. Wilson and Dr. Idiot, I mean McPhearson, were not my favorite people, but lately they had been pretty nice. I didn't hate them anymore.

And then there were my parents. My parents, who struggled to care for me and left me. But now they were back and they were trying. Did I love them? Did I forgive them?

Yes, I do, came the answer in my mind.

As if he heard me thinking, the kid chuckled to himself. "Yeah, I can see it in your eyes. You're definitely the kind and forgiving type."

"I'm not so sure about that," I said, slightly abashed at the series of compliments. I ran a hand through my red hair, which I sadly found to be thinning on top.

The kid winked at me again, a knowing wink.

"Yup, indeed," the boy continued. "That's why you'll make a great dad and husband. I'm sure of it. And that's all that really matters in life. Your family and your friendships."

I nodded my head. "Thanks kid, for the pep talk. You're definitely wise beyond your years."

The kid raised his eyebrows and looked up to the sky. "I know," he said, full of confidence. "But, don't forget, I promised five reasons. Want to hear number five?"

"Sure," I answered, knowing he was probably going to tell me no matter what I said.

The kid winked again. "Good, because I think you'll like number five. The fifth reason why you'll make a great dad is that you're smart and smart people read newspapers."

The kid held out the Sunday paper in one hand and held out the empty palm of his other hand.

"That'll be $0.75," he said with a grin.

I couldn't help but laugh as I dug my hand into my pocket, miraculously pulling out a single one-dollar bill. "You know, you're something else, kid. I think you have a future as a therapist, or a con artist. I haven't decided yet."

"Thank you, sir, but I have another profession in mind." the kid replied, taking my dollar bill and fishing out a quarter from his pocket. "Here's your change."

I shook my head. "No, you keep it. You earned it."

"See, I knew you were a nice guy," the kid beamed. "And I can't wait until I meet with my Dolores again and tell her how your baby girl was named after her. She's going to love it!"

The kid reached out his hand again, but this time to offer me a firm handshake. "Congratulations," he said. "And good luck with the rest of your life."

I held the paper in one hand and watched as the kid walked down the hall toward the double-doors. But before he pushed through to the other side, he paused and looked back at me.

"And one more thing. You might find the sports headline on the front cover especially interesting."

I opened the rolled up newspaper and read the bold headline across the top.

DEMPSEY STILL THE CHAMP!

Below the headline was a large picture, taking up most of the cover page, showing Jack Dempsey giving a mean right hook to the The Wild Bull Firpo. In the background, seated just a few rows up from the boxing ring, were two kids circled in red pen.

I gasped, nearly dropping the paper as my hands began to shake. The two boys were standing next to a stout man with a face that looked like it had gone through a meat grinder, and behind them sat an elegantly dressed couple.

One of the boys was an eight-year-old Solomon who, upon closer inspection, I realized looked like a younger version of the newspaper boy that just left. The other boy, standing next to Solomon, was none other than myself.

My head flew up, looking for the kid who had sold me the paper—looking for Solomon. But instead of a kid, I saw a man with curly black hair walking away from me. He pressed his hand against the gray door at the end of the room and a sliver of bright light crept through the crack.

"Solomon!" I shouted. "Don't go."

Solomon stopped and turned his head, looking back at me. He looked ageless—young, old, and wise, all at the same time. But even more than that, he looked peaceful and happy. He held my gaze, gave me a broad smile, and winked. Then without a word, he turned and pushed through the large, gray doors, the outline of his body disappearing into the blinding light.

The doors slowly swung back toward me and closed. He was gone.

My vision started to blur, and I felt my mind being pulled backward. I glanced one more time at our picture in the newspaper, noticing for the first time a tiny message scrawled in red ink on the white backdrop of the boxing ring. I fought to keep myself conscious as the tugging on my mind increased tenfold. It took all of my concentration to keep from slipping away before reading the note.

Aaron, my dear friend.
Thank you.
You've always been there for me, at my side, when I needed
you most. I am truly in your debt. Tell Talia and Jesse I
love them, and take care of my little Sarah. Treat her right,
like I know you will. At long last, I'm off to be with my
sweet Dolores and my boy Michael.

Until we meet again.

Your friend,
Solomon the Great

INTO THE MIND OF JOHAN TWISS
FACT V. FICTION

The idea for *4 Years Trapped in My Mind Palace* came to me after watching a news story about a man who suffered a similar fate as Aaron. He contracted a rare form of meningitis as a boy that caused full paralysis. Though he was still alive, he was trapped in his mind for nearly fourteen years, aware of everything going on around him, but no one knew it. Eventually, he recovered limited mobility and speech, and was lucky enough to find love and be married.

This amazing story pulled my thoughts toward a few elderly men I knew, who in a sense were also trapped in their own minds, but their imprisonment was due to the suffering caused by dementia and Alzheimer's disease. These men were once strong, witty, vibrant, and full of life, with years of experiences and amazing stories to tell. But over time, their diseases took away those memories and/or jumbled them with others, leaving their family and friends to watch their slow and sad decline.

Merging these two experiences together, Aaron and Solomon's story developed— a coming-of-age story entwined with an end-of-age story written with a hint of nostalgia, a hint of the whimsical unknown, and a heart-warming hope for the beauty of life.

As the story unfolded, I soon realized I was very much writing a historical fiction that spanned sixty years between the 1920's to the 1980's. This led to more research than I had originally anticipated, but it also came with the added bonus of some cool discoveries and interesting facts—though not everything is fact. For the sake of the story, I took a few artistic liberties along the way. Below are some of my insights into scenes from the book, explaining where the ideas originated and separating historical fact from fiction.

JACK DEMPSEY FIGHT

Most of the Jack Dempsey fight is actual fact. I knew I wanted Solomon to have a boxing background, so I Googled "famous Heavy Weight Championship fights in the 1920's." Jack Dempsey's name popped up everywhere, along with an iconic painting of him being knocked out of the ring by Firpo.

I was surprised and excited to learn that the complete fight, from 1923 mind you, was available to watch in black and white on YouTube. Talk about source material. And the fight was as action packed as it sounded in the book, with the two men turning it into a real slugfest. Seriously, you should look it up on YouTube and watch it sometime.

Further research led to other discoveries about the amazing history taking place in New York in 1923. The Yankees had just built the iconic Yankee stadium and moved out of the Polo Grounds. This left the Polo Grounds solely to the Giants baseball team, and it all made for a great tie-in with the San Francisco Giants baseball game seen in Chapter One and the World Series at the end of the book.

The only artistic license I took here was adding the celebrity figures in attendance at the fight. I tried to find out if there was any record of celebrities at the fight and struck out. So, I did the next best thing and placed a few of my own celebrities from that time period in the story. There were mentions of Babe Ruth, J. Edgar Hoover, and most predominant were the scenes with the Fitzgeralds. The Fitzgeralds were New York socialites and seemed like the perfect couple to attend such an event and chat-it-up with Waxer, Solomon, and Aaron.

MACK THE KNIFE

Originally, I wanted this Chicago Club scene to take place with Al Capone, but the timeline wouldn't permit it. By the time Solomon was at the 226 Club in 1940, Al Capone had just been released from his imprisonment on Alcatraz, but he was deathly ill.

But Capone frequented the 226 Club back in the day when he controlled Chicago, and the club had notorious mob connections.

There was no real Mack the Knife mobster that I could find, so I created one for Solomon to fight and to loosely tie back to the history of the famous song.

By all accounts, the song really did originate from a German opera where the organ went out and the pit, composed of a jazz big band, improvised the accompaniment, leading to the song as we know it. Louis Armstrong helped make the song famous, and his encounters with the Chicago and New York mobs are fascinating to read about.

Bobby Darin and Ella Fitzgerald both received Grammies for their performances of *Mack the Knife*. Though I love all three of these takes on the song, Ella's is hilarious. They were recording a live concert and she couldn't remember the words to the song and started improvising and making up words as she went. You can look it up on YouTube and give it a listen. It's pretty funny.

All of the jazz history in the book brought back a lot of memories for me. I played the trombone from 5th grade through my freshman year at college. Like Aaron, I originally signed up to play the alto saxophone, but they were all taken. Instead, the director handed me a trombone and told me to play it instead. I made the jazz band at a younger age than most, while only in 6th grade. I would play cassette tapes on my Walkman (yes, I said Walkman) of Louis Armstrong, Bobby Darin, Count Basie, Miles Davis, Duke Ellington, JJ Johnson, Tommy Dorsey, and other legends. I would practice trying to copy their solos and play along with the music to help me improve my own improvisation.

The feelings Solomon and Aaron experience with the music are all first-hand accounts of the way jazz and music have moved me throughout my life.

IRAN-IRAQ WAR

The Iran-Iraq war of the 80's was a conflict with interesting implications for U.S. relations with both countries going forward. I wanted to put Sarah in a similar position to Aaron with her parents struggling in their marriage, but I also wanted to add more of the geo-political history of the 80's, and thus Sarah's father became Chief Warrant Officer Richard Clements, serving on the U.S.S. Carr. The U.S.S. Carr was a real navy ship that sailed to the Middle East during the conflict, though Richard Clements is a fictional character, and no one by that name, at least that I could find, was stationed on the ship.

Originally, I had wanted to add the fall of the Berlin Wall as another major event in the time period, but the wall fell down in November of 1989 about one month after the earthquake hit the Bay Area during the World Series. I tried to write it into the story, but that would have required postponing Solomon's rapid deterioration in health, and it just didn't fit the timeline.

BLUE IN GREEN

I enjoy a wide variety of musical genres—jazz, blues, classic rock, alternative, classical, hip-hop, and even a little bit of country and rap (but not mixed together).

With that said, *Blue in Green,* featuring Miles Davis and John Coltrane, is probably my favorite song of all-time.

But that declaration comes with a caveat. You can go to YouTube right now and look up the song with Davis on trumpet and Coltrane on sax, but you have to listen to it by yourself in a quiet place. That's the caveat. You need a place to listen in quiet, free from distraction, to fully appreciate this song. This isn't a listen-while-you-work song. It's not a bob-your-head-in-the-car-and-rock-out song. It's a close-your-eyes, clear-your-mind, sit-by-yourself, no-distractions, feel-the-emotion song. And at the end you whisper, "wow," as you sit in silence.

When Solomon and Aaron discuss how they felt after Solomon played *Blue in Green,* their words describe exactly how I felt the first time I listened to the song as a teenager. I had just received the CD *Kind of Blue* by Miles Davis. Sitting alone in my room, I put on my headphones and listened. When the track for *Blue in Green* came on, I sat mesmerized. The song literally took my breath away, and it still does today. This amazing piece of artistry encapsulates the sadness, the hope and the beauty of life. Life is *Blue in Green*.

FOXHOLES IN FRANCE

I never give an exact location for this World War II scene in the book, and that was on purpose. There are so many similar accounts of firefights like this and Allied soldiers practically living in foxholes as they pushed back against the German line, that I kept this scene generic in location.

The story Solomon and Big Tom tell the group of soldiers about playing at a dinner for Roosevelt, Churchill, and Stalin in Tehran, is mostly true. The Big Three leaders of the Allied nations met for the first time face-to-face in Tehran. I couldn't find any records of a band playing or not playing for a dinner party, so I inserted Solomon into this piece of history as a musician.

There are other accounts of U.S. soldiers being pulled from the warfront to play violin, piano and other instruments at similar gatherings with Eisenhower, Roosevelt, Churchill and Stalin later in the war, so it seemed an appropriate addition.

During this meeting, records indicate Stalin really did say he wanted to execute 50,000 German soldiers, to which Churchill blew a lid and left the meeting for a time. Roosevelt thought Stalin was joking and in turn joked back that 49,000 would probably do the trick. But many believed Stalin was not joking at all.

Later in the foxhole, when Big Tom's heart stops beating, Aaron performs CPR. The reason Solomon is bewildered by this medical tactic is that CPR would not be invented until 1960. In 1956, mouth-to-mouth resuscitation was invented by Peter Safar and James Elam. The United States military adopted mouth-to-mouth the following year in 1957, and in 1960 Cardiopulmonary Resuscitation (CPR) was developed and later brought to the mainstream.

As a young Boy Scout, I was first introduced to CPR training, practicing chest compressions on dummies, and every instructor I've had always says we should be pushing hard enough to break ribs if we want to keep their heart pumping the blood.

I've witnessed CPR save lives first-hand and hope everyone learns how to administer it.

RELIGION

I wanted to add some religious overtones and expression to the story, without being overbearing or preachy. From the beginning, Solomon's character was a Jewish jazz musician when it first came to life in my head. The other characters, such as JJ being Muslim, Big Tom as a Mormon, and Barry as a Baptist, just kind of came out as I wrote their characters, and I wanted to show the power of music and its abilities to cross some of those religious divides.

One of the biggest influences in this area came when I was listening to Muhammad Ali's funeral service on the radio. I was driving to Walmart when Billy Crystal began speaking at the service. His words were so touching, and the stories about his friendship with Ali were so compelling, that I didn't go into the store, at least not for a while. I sat in the Walmart parking lot and listened for fifteen minutes as he spoke about The Champ. Then I sat for another fifteen minutes thinking about what Billy Crystal said and I knew I needed to add this to the story.

If you want to spend fifteen minutes watching an inspirational, humorous, touching speech, then I suggest going to Youtube and searching for "Muhammad Ali Funeral Billy Crystal." I promise you won't regret it.

Their stories of friendship, between a Muslim and a Jewish man, are truly inspirational. I won't do the stories justice trying to recap or rehash them here. But I encourage you to go on Youtube and watch Billy Crystal's tribute to his friend, Muhammad Ali. You'll see what I mean.

CONCENTRATION CAMP

This chapter proved to be one of the most difficult things I have ever written, even harder than the stories I've been writing about human trafficking.

To prepare for it, I read dozens of first-hand accounts from concentration camp survivors and the Allied soldiers who first discovered the camps. On YouTube, I watched original black and white footage of the discovery of concentration camps as they were liberated. Many of these are silent films, adding a visceral realism to the horrors of these camps.

Part of my research led me to a YouTube clip from *Band of Brothers* (WARNING: if you look it up, it's a bit graphic in nature with some swearing). The clip is hauntingly accurate when compared to the black and white footage and first-hand accounts I read.

I tried to keep this scene as true to history as my research found, while walking a fine line between not writing too much brutal detail, yet not detracting from the reality of what happened.

The concentration camp near Landsberg was a sub-camp of the infamous Dachau concentration camp. Approximately 14,500 prisoners died in these sub-camps, and when the U.S. 12th Armored Division first found this camp, there were hundreds of bodies unburied. The German soldiers had slaughtered them as they retreated from the camp, burning many of the prisoner huts as they left.

There was a separate female prison camp a few miles to the north where similar atrocities took place. Colonel Edward F. Sellers, commander of the 12th Armored Division, took control of the camp when it was liberated. Colonel Sellers was so anguished and infuriated by what they found, that he had hundreds of local German citizens, from the nearby city of Landsberg, forced at gunpoint to bury the dead prisoners by hand.

WALT DISNEY

Writing the Disneyland flashback was one of those things that just came together perfectly. The only problem I had with this scene was I originally wrote about an extensive tunnel system under Disneyland, and I had Aaron following Solomon through these massive tunnels, eating together with cast members in the cafeteria, etc...

Then my aunt, who used to work at Disneyland, beta read the story and kindly pointed out that there was no underground tunnel system in Disneyland. Disney World was the place with the tunnels, and Disneyland only had rooms, hidden at different attractions, where cast members could retreat to take a break.

Thankful she caught this error, but super annoyed with myself because I would have to rewrite these chapters, I came up with the solution in the book.

Why not have Aaron be the one who suggests the tunnel system for Disneyworld? I thought.

The timeline worked perfectly for the suggestion, as this was just prior to construction starting on Disney World.

The meeting with Walt Disney became a bit of a tricky matter after I read an article about actress Meryl Streep calling Walt Disney an anti-Semite. You can see how this might present a problem with him being friends with Solomon, who is very much Jewish.

Streep made the comments surrounding the release of the movie, *Saving Mr. Banks*, which is about Walt Disney pursuing the movie rights for *Mary Poppins* from the author P.L Travers.

But I could find no evidence of him being an anti-Semite. Possible racist and sexist, yes, as this was an unfortunate standard practice in many of the film studios of the time. But it seemed the opposite with Jews. According to numerous online Jewish Journals, Disney actually hired more Jewish actors, animators, and employees at his studio than studios owned by Jewish film moguls. His merchandising chief was a Jewish man by the name of Herman

"Kay" Kamen, who once said that Disney's New York office "had more Jews than the Book of Leviticus."

He donated to Jewish orphanages and received the 1955 Man of the Year award by the Beverly Hills Lodge of the B'nai B'rith. The Sherman brothers, who were Jewish and also the composers for *Mary Poppins* and *Jungle Book,* called these claims of anti-Semitism "preposterous" and said they were treated more like sons by Disney.

The only evidence of Disney being an anti-Semite was when he joined the anti-communist Motion Picture Alliance for the Preservation of American Ideals. This MPA had anti-Semitic ties to it, but it appears Disney joined it in an attempt to show his support against communism, which was important for studios during the McCarthy trials of 1954 and the fear of communism.

BATTLE OF THE BAY WORLD SERIES EARTHQUAKE

The 1989 earthquake that hit the Bay Area brings back a lot of memories for me. We were living in Concord, California at the time and I remember lounging on the couch with my dad, brother, and baby sister, watching the World Series pre-game show. I was so excited for the game, since it was my two favorite teams going head-to-head in the World Series—the Oakland A's vs. the San Francisco Giants.

I grew up going to Candlestick Park and the Oakland Coliseum to watch these teams. Once, we went to a Giants game for my birthday and shared birthday cake with all of the fans sitting around us. It was in the upper-deck near one of the cameras, and the camera man panned on us, or rather I stood up in my chair since we were only a dozen rows below the cameraman, and I made it on the jumbo screen.

So here we are sitting on our brown corduroy couch, getting ready to watch this epic World Series game, and our apartment started shaking like a maraca. The floor in our apartment really did roll like the waves of an ocean. Pictures on the walls shook, the TV shook, we shook. After the initial 5 seconds of shock dissipated, my dad pulled us together, and we struggled to walk toward the hall bathroom, where we huddled under the doorframe, gripping the frame to keep from falling over, and my dad shielded us with his body.

To my young mind, it felt like the quake lasted forever, but after a minute or so it ended. My dad called my Mom right away to make sure she was okay, and luckily she was. Her office in Walnut Creek had minimal damage from items falling off the wall, but everyone was okay.

For the remainder of the night, we sat glued to the TV. But instead of watching our beloved baseball teams play each other, we watched with horror, and sadness, as the news coverage unfolded about the damage—the upper-level section of the Bay Bridge, the collapsed Embarcadero freeway, the fires, the injuries, and the deaths.

This was one of those moments in life, even at the young age of seven, that taught and humbled me. I watched the pain and struggles people were facing and the heroic efforts of others to help. I counted my blessings that day, and I grew up a little bit faster after that earthquake.

DISCUSSION QUESTIONS
(From the author, Johan Twiss)

1. What was your initial reaction to the book?

2. Did the book change your opinions or perspectives about coma patients and those suffering from dementia and Alzheimer's? Do you feel different now than you did before you read it?

3. Which character did you relate to the most, and what was it about them that you connected with?

4. Discuss the main characters—personality traits, motivations, and dynamics with one another.
- Aaron and Solomon
- Solomon and Talia
- Solomon and Sarah
- Aaron and Sarah
- Aaron and Nurse Penny
- Solomon, JJ, and Big Tom

5. What character growth did you see over the course of the story?

6. Can you pick out a passage that really struck a chord with you?

7. What themes and symbolism did you find in the depictions of Aaron's Mind Palace?

8. What did you think of the historical elements in the story? Did you have a favorite dementia dream episode?

9. If the book were being adapted into a movie, who would you want to see play what parts?

10. How did you feel about the ending?

11. Have you read any other books that I've written? (if not, feel free to grab them on Amazon.com :) Can you discern a similarity—in

theme, writing style—between them? Or are they completely different?

12. If you were to talk with me (the author), what would you want to know? (see below)

CONTACT ME:
Feel free to contact me and ask your questions. Seriously, I'd love to talk with your book club, or school class, via video chat. Just shoot me an message at www. johantwiss.com/book-club-visits.html.

> 66
>
> *The ladies absolutely loved it.*
> *The energy and excitement in*
> *the room was palpable.*
> *Thank you so much.*
>
> **- HELEN G.**
> **TIP TOP THURSDAY BOOK CLUB**
> COLUMBUS, GEORGIA

Thanks again for reading and I'd love to hear from you and/or participate with your book club. And if you enjoyed the story, leaving an honest review (and it can be a short 1-2 sentence review) on Amazon.com and Goodreads would mean the world to me.

All the best,
Johan

JOIN THE CLUB!

Join my Reader Club and get a free review copy of
I Am Sleepless: Sim 299
delivered right to your inbox.

You'll also gain insider access to giveaways, funny stories, upcoming events, and new releases!

Go to www.johantwiss.com to join the club today!

HOW TO BE AN AUTHOR'S BEST FRIEND

(In 2 Easy Steps)

STEP 1

Leave a short review for this story on Amazon.com.

STEP 2

Tell a friend about this book.

ACKNOWLEDGEMENTS

Aaron and Solomon's story was a true joy to write, often making me laugh out loud and cry as I typed at a desk in the local public library. But it would not be what it is today without the help of many willing, kind, and supportive individuals.

First, I must thank my wife, Adrienne, for her willingness to be my sounding board while brainstorming and for acting as my Alpha Reader. She spent hours reading this story, marking the manuscript to pieces with a red pen, and it's a much stronger story because of it.

Thank you to my editor, Heather Monson, for her diligent work and feedback, especially on such a short timetable, and for Kent Meyers for his additional proofreading and input as a Beta Reader.

Special thanks to all of the other Beta Readers and their invaluable feedback, including—Devora Burger, Renee Hirsch, Ken Meyers, Steve Meyers, Sarah Parent, Jen Johnson, Samuel Pereiro, Wendy Nitta, Jeri Lin Brown, Miriam Callison, Patricia Callison, Darrel Callison, Susan Semadeni, and bonus points to Sarah Peterson for keeping me in-line about Disneyworld having underground tunnels, not Disneyland (see the Fact v. Fiction section).

ABOUT THE AUTHOR

Dear Brilliant Reader,

Thank you for your interest in my books, and I hope you enjoyed reading *4 Years Trapped in My Mind Palace*.

I am passionate about writing clean science fiction and fantasy stories that are exciting and suitable for tweens, teens and adults alike.

Have a question? Complaint? Want to send me suitcases full of money in small denominations or a gift card to the Cheesecake Factory? Simply reach out to me at my website, Facebook, or Twitter pages.

www.johantwiss.com
www.facebook.com/JohanTwiss
www.twitter.com/JohanTwiss

Lastly, I want to ask you for a favor. If you enjoyed reading this book, **please leave a review for it on Amazon.com**. Your reviews help new readers discover my books, for which I am thankful.

All the best,
Johan

OTHER BOOKS BY JOHAN TWISS

I Am Sleepless: Sim 299 (book 1)

I Am Sleepless: The Huntress (book 2)

I Am Sleepless: Traitors (book 3)

4 Years Trapped in My Mind Palace

The Fourth Law of Kanaloa

30 Red Dresses